THE POWER OF A YOUNG NATION GR...
LIKE A STORM ON THE HORIZON,
SPREADING TURMOIL INTO THE HEART AND
HOMELAND OF A PROUD PEOPLE

Renno—The legendary Seneca warrior has proved his loyalty to the American cause with fortitude and valor. But as old wounds bring new pain, he stands on the threshold of his final and greatest struggle, one that will determine the fate and future of his family.

Ta-na—Renno's younger son, he's been chosen to become the new sachem of the Seneca. But in one explosive moment, he is tragically blinded. Now, although his eyes are clouded, he must find the vision to lead his people to their destiny.

Mist-on-the-Water—Only eighteen, she is already a mother and a widow. Her pain and desperation have led her down a path toward self-destruction, and the only question is how far down that path she will go.

Victor Coughtry—A shrewd and unscrupulous newspaperman, he is determined to take the Seneca's last remaining lands . . . no matter how treacherous or violent the scheme. Only one man stands in his way: Renno, the white Indian.

Cornplanter—A medicine man who has traveled from the mysterious, distant West, he offers a message of hope to the young Seneca Ta-na. But to realize Cornplanter's vision, Ta-na must be willing to make the ultimate sacrifice.

The White Indian Series
Book XXVIII

MEDICINE SHIELD

Donald Clayton Porter

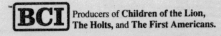

BCI Producers of **Children of the Lion,**
The Holts, and **The First Americans.**

Book Creations Inc., Canaan, NY • Lyle Kenyon Engel, Founder

BANTAM BOOKS
NEW YORK • TORONTO • LONDON • SYDNEY • AUCKLAND

MEDICINE SHIELD

A Bantam Book / published by arrangement with
Book Creations Inc.

Bantam edition / August 1996

ISBN 0-553-56144-8

Published simultaneously in the United States and Canada

Bantam Books are published by Bantam Books, a division of Bantam
Doubleday Dell Publishing Group, Inc. Its trademark, consisting of
the words "Bantam Books" and the portrayal of a rooster, is
Registered in U.S. Patent and Trademark Office and in other
countries. Marca Registrada. Bantam Books, 1540 Broadway, New
York, New York 10036.

PRINTED IN THE UNITED STATES OF AMERICA

OPM   10 9 8 7 6 5 4 3 2 1

WHITE INDIAN FAMILY TREE

Ghonkaba (1) = Toshabe = (2) Ha-ace
                          (3) Roy Johnson

Renno = (1) Emily Johnson
      = (2, 4) Beth Huntington
      = (3) An-da

Ta-na-wun-da

Rusog = Ena   El-i-chi = (1) Holani
                        = (2) Ah-wa-o

Mist-on-the-Water = Gao   Ah-wen-ga   Ha-ace

Renna = (1) Philip Woods, Jr.
      = (2) Comte de Beaujolais

Emily Beth   Louis Philippe Joseph

Rusog Ho-ya

We-yo   White Blanket   Little Gao

O-no-ga-nose   Jani (adopted)   Naomi Burns = Little Hawk

Summer Moon   Joseph Standing Bear

Michael Soaring Hawk

One

Hear my song, Birds of War,
As I follow your flight!
I see you cross the enemy line;
Like you I shall fly.
Give me the swiftness of your wings.
Give me the vengeance of your claws.
I shall prepare a feast for you,
A feast of carrion and blood.

From the south come their canoes.
Ho! Hear their approaching scream!
Happy I shall be to lie in that ground,
That battleground beyond the enemy line.

Hear my song, Birds of War,
As I follow your flight.
Mountains tremble at my yell!
I strike for life!*

---

* Adapted from an Ojibwa war song

Ta-na-wun-da sat low on his haunches, peering into the darkness as he loosened the drawstring of the beaded pouch hanging from his belt. After removing a generous pinch of tobacco, he stretched his arm out in front of him. He dared not risk being seen, so he opened his fingers and fed the leaves to the earth rather than to the flames. He began to hum softly as he envisioned a thin wisp of smoke curling to the heavens. The hum shifted into the faintest of chants . . . little more than a murmur on the breeze:

> "Oh, Great Spirit, Master of Life,
> Thank you for the silence of darkness.
> Now I offer you tobacco, Great Spirit.
> It lifts my voice through the darkness,
> So you will hear my song,
> So you will love my people with all power.
> You, the Master of Life!
> You, the breath of our people!
> I ask you to help us!
> I implore your favor!"

Rising, Ta-na-wun-da whispered, "I have spoken," and started up the incline. The moon had not yet risen, and he had to move carefully in the darkness. He knew he had reached the crest of the hillock when he saw the flicker of torches in the distance below. They flitted left and right, forming a barrier line on a narrow strip of solid ground between the river and the swampland that made up most of the delta country.

Ta-na could not see the Father of Waters as it rushed the final miles to the sea, but he sensed its presence, just as he could sense the movements of the soldiers debarking from their flatboats. No more than two hundred yards away, he could hear voices and shouted commands. And while he could understand only a few of the words, he recognized the thick accent.

"Redcoats," he muttered, his lips drawn into a sneer.

Confident he was cloaked by the darkness, the young Seneca warrior tucked his rifle under his arm and padded down the hill toward the enemy line. Every few yards he paused and listened, straining to hear what was being said. Then he resumed his advance, crouching lower as he angled to the right so that he would approach along their western flank.

They're not celebrating tonight, he observed, shaking his head in disappointment.

Such was not the case with the Americans. When he had left their ranks an hour earlier, the regulars and the militia—officers and enlisted men alike—were deep in their mugs, laughing off as ridiculous any talk of imminent attack. The redcoats, after all, were still sardined on ships out in the Gulf. They would not venture forth on a night such as this—a night meant for whiskey and dancing and song.

"New Year's," Ta-na grunted, dropping to his knees and continuing at a crawl.

Ta-na had little use for white men's holidays, most of which commemorated men long dead or events long past, with little connection to the daily lives of the people. The Seneca and their brother nations, on the other hand, gave thanks to the spirits that guided their world every day, through each change of season. And on special days of celebration, rather than give gifts to one another they offered them to the Master of Life, who had blessed each of them with the breath of being.

It was not that Ta-na-wun-da did not understand the reason for this night's festivities. He had participated in many a boisterous New Year's Eve back home in Rusog's Town, the Cherokee village to which his grandfather, Ghonkaba, had led a band of their people many years before. There was a time when he had donned the clothing of the whites and adopted their ways, for in fact he was one-quarter white. But in recent years he had felt the stronger call of his Seneca blood. He would walk the white path no longer.

Ta-na's lips pulled upward into a half-smile. Here he was, scouting the British emplacements for General Andrew Jackson's Tennessee militia. Could any path be more white?

When the general had come to Rusog's Town seeking soldiers and scouts, he had spoken plainly but eloquently to the Seneca and Cherokee council: *"If you help us defeat the foreign invaders, the Great Father in Washington will look upon you with kindness. He will listen no longer to those who would drive you far beyond the Father of Waters. Surely he will let you live in peace upon your land."*

The words had made a powerful impression on the tribal council, which immediately agreed to send several dozen warriors to assist in the defense of New Orleans. Though Ta-na had not been convinced, he had accepted the decision of the council and had offered to serve one final time as Jackson's chief of scouts.

There was an even more compelling reason why Ta-na found himself crawling through the muck on this dark, humid night. His older half brother, Hawk Harper, was back among the Americans, wearing the uniform of an army captain and the insignia of a graduate of West Point. Like Ta-na, he had joined the campaign at Jackson's urging. Unlike Ta-na, he was three-quarters white and was probably enjoying the New Year's revelries with his compatriots.

Easing closer to the growing enemy line, the Seneca scout brought his thoughts back to the situation at hand. He had known that it was only a matter of time before the British left their ships and launched an attack. Apparently they had determined that the perfect moment would be at dawn on New Year's Day, when the Americans would likely be sleeping off the effects of their celebrations. There was always the chance, however, that the redcoats would simply take up positions and dig in, then wait to see how the Americans would respond. To determine what their course of action would be, Ta-na would have to get a lot closer.

Having circled the western flank, Ta-na was now behind the enemy line and well behind the nearest soldiers. When he had crawled to within twenty yards of their position, he still could not decipher what was being said. But he was almost within range of the torches, and he did not want to be seen skulking up from behind on all fours. Instead he decided that the best protection would be to walk boldly forward and, if discovered, hope he would be mistaken for one of the Creek scouts employed by the British.

Lifting himself off the ground, Ta-na shifted the rifle to his left hand and eased a knife from his belt. Holding it blade-upward behind his forearm, he lowered the rifle barrel and sauntered casually toward the nearest group of soldiers. As he drew near, he noted that most were digging a trench and planting a row of pointed stakes in front of the facing mound of dirt, while several were muscling a cannon into position behind the crude breastworks. It appeared to be a twenty-four-pounder—a cannon that fired a twenty-four-pound ball and weighed more than one and a half tons. It was much larger than Ta-na would have expected to see off the ships and could not be moved easily once the battle began. But when he looked farther down the breastwork, he noticed a string of smaller cannons—three- and six-pounders—which could be maneuvered as needed and even brought out onto the field for a direct assault on the American positions.

Though Ta-na was not schooled in military theory, he had learned much from his older brother, who had made a study of the recent war in Europe, which had ended with Napoleon's banishment to Elba earlier that year. Hawk Harper had spoken often about the famous "Battle of the Nations" at Leipzig and how Napoleon had been defeated largely because the British finally adopted his artillery tactics. In Napoleon's own words, *"When once the melee has begun, the man who is clever enough to bring up an unex-*

*pected force of artillery without the enemy knowing it, is
sure to carry the day.*" From the heavy deployment of
artillery here in the Louisiana delta, it looked as if the
British were planning a similar assault against the Americans.

Ta-na tried to keep to the shadows as he continued
down the line, intent on determining how many troops
and fieldpieces were being assembled. On a couple of
occasions he was spotted by some of the soldiers, but to
his relief they gave him only a passing glance and returned
to their business.

Ta-na's tenacity and courage were rewarded when he
drew near a pair of officers inspecting one of the smaller
cannons. Keeping to the shadows, he eased closer and
listened to their somewhat heated exchange.

" 'Twas a damn sorry day the Adm'ralty turned brass
to iron."

The speaker was older than his companion, with
graying hair and a white walrus mustache, but he held the
lower rank of lieutenant. He ran his hand inside the end of
the barrel, then held forth his palm.

"See how the salt's done its work?" he told the captain, shaking his head in dismay. "She'll never hold up to
repeat firing. I'd wager she'll burst before the third volley.
Might as well hand 'er over to the colonists and let 'em
turn 'er agin our lines. At least then, when she blows, she
won't be taking our boys with 'er."

The captain's frown deepened. "It's talk like that
which puts our boys at risk. Damn it, James, you know
these iron guns don't fail any more than brass."

"But to have 'em all those months at sea." He waggled a stubby finger. "Saving money is all the Adm'ralty
thinks about. That and how to send some more good boys
to their deaths in this god-awful country."

"No one's going to their deaths," the younger man
insisted.

Walking forward, he thrust his torch at the cannon
barrel and leaned forward to inspect the inside of the rim.

The torchlight made his long blond hair glow almost white and illuminated a saber scar across his left cheek.

"It'll be child's play tomorrow, mark my words." He straightened and turned back to the lieutenant. "And a little bit of rust isn't going to hurt anybody."

"It'll damn well kill 'em, is all."

"Enough!" the captain snapped, fixing the lower-ranking officer with a scowl. "When those damnable Yanks feel the press of our big guns at dawn, then face a line of threes and sixes sweeping up the field with a thousand infantry in formation behind, there won't be need of a second cannonade, let alone a third."

"I hope you're right, Captain Woolsey," the lieutenant muttered without conviction.

"You just keep the fieldpieces on the move and firing. Hold the gunners to their task and let the Admiralty worry about iron and rust."

He started to turn away when a soldier shouted, "Halt there!"

The voice came from directly behind Ta-na-wun-da, who spun around to find himself facing a foot soldier with a musket trained on his chest. Out of the corner of his eye, Ta-na saw the captain push past the lieutenant and stalk over.

"Caught him skulkin' around," the private declared, smirking as he took a step closer.

"Who are you?" Captain Woolsey demanded, planting himself in front of Ta-na but enough to one side to keep the Seneca under the musket of the soldier. "Your name!" he snapped, stabbing a finger at the intruder's chest.

Ta-na shrugged, pretending not to understand their language.

"Name!" Woolsey repeated, moving closer and poking Ta-na in the ribs.

"One of our scouts?" the private suggested.

Woolsey stepped back and examined Ta-na with a suspicious eye. His gaze took in the simple deerskin over-

shirt and breeches and the design of the moccasins, then
lingered on the intricately beaded belt and brace of pistols. His eyes narrowed slightly, as if he had noticed something amiss. Ta-na realized at once that the man had
spotted the empty sheath, and he tightened his grip on the
knife still turned upward in his hand.

The captain shifted slightly to his right in order to
better see Ta-na's hand. Simultaneously, the other soldier
shouted, "A knife, sir!"

Ta-na-wun-da dropped his rifle and was springing
through the air when hammer struck flashpan and the
musket fired. The lead ball whistled past his shoulder as
he barreled into the captain, and the two men went tumbling to the ground. The private yelled for help and scrambled to reload his weapon. But Ta-na was already on his
feet, jerking Woolsey upright by the hair and jabbing the
knife blade against his throat just hard enough to draw
some blood. As the lieutenant and several other soldiers
came at a run, Ta-na spun behind Woolsey and twisted the
man's long hair, keeping the knife blade pressed firmly
against his throat.

"Move!" he snapped, pushing the officer toward the
shallow trench alongside the cannons.

"S-s-stay b-back!" Woolsey sputtered at the others,
his eyes wide with panic. Under Ta-na's prodding, he hobbled forward, skirting the trench and halting beside the
cannon he and the lieutenant had been inspecting.

Ta-na used the officer as a shield against the growing
number of muskets and pistols trained on him. The torchlight danced across Ta-na's face as the darkness beckoned
behind him. He had seen and heard enough—too much
for the redcoats to let him get away alive. He would have
to leap into that darkness and pray that it would shroud
him from their musket balls.

He felt the captain shaking in his grip and realized
how deathly afraid the man was. It would be only a moment's work to draw the blade across his throat and put an
end to one more British soldier. But for now the man was

more useful alive, his body protecting Ta-na's retreat. Dragging him backward, the Seneca eased between the row of stakes and headed out across the field.

Captain Woolsey must have sensed he would be a dead man as soon as they were beyond musket range, for he abruptly twisted to the right and drove an elbow into his captor's midsection. The air went out of Ta-na in a rush, and he felt the blade slice across the side of the captain's neck. The wound wasn't deep enough to disable Woolsey, who drew back his leg and kicked viciously at the young warrior's groin. Doubling over and dropping to his knees, Ta-na saw the captain's boot coming at him again. He threw himself to the side, just missing the blow, then lunged upward at the shadow looming over him. He felt the blade smash against bone, then slip past the man's rib cage and into his heart.

The captain gasped and fell in front of Ta-na, his body jerking spasmodically. Pulling the knife free, Ta-na rose to his feet and stood clutching his lower belly as he stared down at the dead man. Then he glanced at the nearby breastwork and saw the lieutenant sweep his arm in front of him, signaling the soldiers to fire.

Diving at the ground, Ta-na heard the report of muskets and felt the breeze of bullets whizzing overhead. He rolled twice, then sprang up and sprinted across the field. A second volley chased him, some of the bullets thudding into the dirt, others passing within inches of his head. By the time the third volley rang out, Ta-na had disappeared into the darkness, racing swiftly across the barren landscape toward the American lines beyond.

Captain Hawk Harper stiffened at the sound of distant gunshots. He rose and circled the campfire, tilting his head slightly to better hear the sound. It was hard to discern anything above the shouts and laughter and singing, but he was certain he had heard something more than the occasional random shots fired into the air by some of the more boisterous revelers.

As he approached the breastwork, he heard it again: a volley of muskets that sounded less than a mile away. *Perhaps Ta-na was right,* he thought. *Perhaps tonight is when the redcoats will land.*

Hawk turned away and started toward the tent that served as field headquarters, but he found his way blocked by a burly sergeant holding a flaming brand in one hand and a jug in the other.

"Take a swig," the man insisted, his voice thick and slurred as he thrust the jug toward Hawk.

"Not now, Morgan," Hawk replied, pushing away the offered whiskey.

"But Cap'n, in an hour it'll be 1815. G'wan. . . ." He rammed the jug against Hawk's chest.

"Not now, Sergeant," Hawk repeated in a slow, deliberate tone. Then he pushed the jug aside and strode across the field.

"All right, Cap'n," Morgan called after him, tottering on unsteady legs. "But e'en an off'cer like you needs a bit of celebratin'."

Hawk moved through the crowd of celebrants. The militiamen were a rough but friendly lot, and they rarely stood on ceremony where rank was concerned. They took orders and carried them out professionally, but beyond that, little distinction was made between officers and enlisted men. In fact, with no standardized uniforms, it was often difficult to distinguish between the two. Hawk, however, wore the uniform of the regular army, even though he had left the service more than two years earlier. But General Jackson had insisted, saying that having a West Point officer attached to the militia would instill confidence among the men.

It also engendered a fair amount of good-natured taunting. But tonight Hawk paid little attention to the jests that followed him as he passed through the camp. His thoughts were focused on one thing alone: whether the musket fire somehow involved his younger brother, Ta-na-wun-da, who was scouting the delta just south of the American lines.

Hawk was not the only one who had heard the muskets, and as he reached the tent he was joined by another officer as well as a corporal who had been on lookout duty along the breastwork. Together the three men entered and made their report to General Jackson. The general was nursing a mug of rum as he prepared a letter for Washington. He had not heard the gunfire but did not doubt that the others had, even though each indicated hearing a different number of volleys.

"You are certain you heard three?" Jackson asked the corporal.

"Yes, sir. With some sporadic firing in between."

"Muskets alone?"

"Yes. Perhaps pistols, but no field guns."

"Thank you, Corporal. You may return to your post."

The soldier saluted and made a hasty exit.

Rising from his makeshift table, Jackson crossed the tent and pulled open the door flap. He stared outside a moment, then let the flap fall back in place. Turning, he asked Hawk, "Have we had any word from the scouts?"

Hawk masked his private concern. "None of which I'm aware."

Jackson shifted his glance to the other officer. "How about you, Lieutenant Andersen?"

The lieutenant shook his head. "I've heard nothing, sir."

Returning to his chair, Jackson raised the wick on the lantern and examined a map of the region. After a minute he tapped the map and proclaimed, "I want to send a detail down the river to find out if the Brits are still on board their ships. Captain Harper, I'd like you to—"

He paused and glanced up as the door flap was thrust aside and a sergeant leaned in and announced, "General Jackson, one of the scouts is here to—"

"Send him in," Jackson directed with an impatient wave. He stood as Ta-na-wun-da entered.

The brothers shared a private glance. Then Ta-na turned to the general and announced, "I come from the British encampment."

"Then they've finally come ashore?" Jackson asked with barely contained enthusiasm. "Where are they camped?"

"May I?" Ta-na asked, indicating the map, and Jackson gestured for him to approach. "They're right here, on this strip of land between the river and the swamp." He ran a finger along the map. "We're separated by these two hills—if they can be called that."

"And they're digging in?" Hawk asked.

Ta-na nodded. "They're building a trench with facing earthworks and an outer abatis of sharpened branches."

"Then they are expecting us to attack," the lieutenant concluded.

"I don't believe so. We should prepare for them to launch an attack at dawn."

Straightening to his full height, General Jackson looked down at his chief of scouts. "Are you certain of this?"

Ta-na-wun-da gazed back up at the general, the conviction written in his dark, unwavering eyes.

"We heard musket fire," Hawk said.

"There is one less British officer for us to face tomorrow," Ta-na replied, and his brother nodded.

"You're convinced the attack will come at dawn?" Jackson pressed.

"I was close enough to hear some of the officers. They will start by shelling our fortifications, and then—"

"From such a distance?"

"They have eighteen-pounders, General. And at least one twenty-four."

Jackson gave a low whistle and sat back down, his gaze focusing on the map as Ta-na continued.

"After the initial bombardment, they plan to advance with their field cannons, with at least a thousand infantry behind."

"We've got twice that number," Lieutenant Andersen said smugly.

"They'll only need a thousand if we let those field cannons anywhere near our line," Hawk countered. Jackson nodded in agreement. "And they probably assume we won't be able to muster an adequate defense after a long night of celebrating."

"Well, they'll discover they're facing something altogether different come dawn," Jackson declared, pounding fist into palm. "I appreciate a little revelry as much as the next man, but we'll have to postpone the rest of tonight's celebrations until the job is done. Andersen, I want you and the other lieutenants to confiscate all spirits and prepare the men for battle."

"Yes, sir," the young officer replied with a smart salute.

"Well, move along." He waved the man away. As the lieutenant started through the doorway, Jackson called, "Hold on, Lieutenant. It might do well to have a few of our boys keep up the festivities—but without any whiskey. Let any redcoat scouts think we're still well in our cups. They'll learn differently come dawn."

"Right, sir," Andersen replied, then disappeared into the night.

"Captain Harper," Jackson continued, "we'd better gather the commanders and prepare a plan." He called for the sergeant posted outside and directed him to summon the other commanding officers. Then he turned to Ta-na-wun-da. "I want you on hand. We'll need to know the layout of their camp and your best estimate of their troop and weapon strength."

"Are you considering attacking first?" Hawk asked.

"Something of the sort. That is, if we can figure out a weakness in their defenses. I sure as hell don't want to send our boys marching across those fields under the fire of a hundred British cannons." He shook his head as he studied the map. "We could abandon this position and let them bombard it to their heart's content while we circle this swamp and launch an attack from the rear." He paused a moment, running his hand through his hair. "If we move out before dawn, their scouts will surely report our doings. I suppose we could sit tight until dawn and make our move when the bombardment begins." He shook his head. "What we need is something to disrupt their initial bombardment—cause confusion in their ranks and buy us the time to set our own plan in motion."

"With three good men, I could provide such a diversion," Ta-na-wun-da declared.

"You could? How?"

Ta-na stabbed a finger against the map. "Right here they are both weakest and strongest. Four men could exploit that weakness and turn their own strength against them."

Jackson shrugged in confusion.

"At dawn they will find the biggest of their guns turned against them," Ta-na continued. "Just give me three men, and this will be done."

"Two men," Hawk corrected. "Two men . . . and me."

General Jackson looked back and forth between the brothers. Ta-na-wun-da's plan had not yet been detailed in full, but somehow he knew—all three of them knew—that it was the very plan they would be launching come dawn.

Two

The grandfather clock sounded the last of twelve chimes, and a great cheer went up from the guests gathered in the formal parlor. "A toast!" a voice thundered above the din. "Ladies and gentlemen, raise your glasses!"

The group slowly quieted, and those whose glasses needed refilling hurried to the decanters on side tables throughout the large room. There were four women among the sixteen gathered at Huntington Castle, and even they joined in toasting the new year.

The tall man with raised glass stood bathed in the light of a dozen oil lamps that haloed his graying blond hair and made him look younger than his fifty years—a half century of joy and heartache and adventure that had earned him the position of sachem of the Seneca and wide renown throughout Tennessee and the surrounding region. But the lamplight was kind to Renno Harper. In truth, he felt much older than his years. Almost a year and a half earlier he had taken a bullet in the back from the murderer of his brother, El-i-chi. The wound had healed, but some of the bullet fragments had not been removed. A long journey to the Seneca home of his youth had also taken its toll, dislodging the fragments and causing increased pressure to his spine. As a result, his left side was somewhat numb, forcing him to use a walking stick and confining him, for the most part, to his home.

Still, Renno had kept his spirits up, and as he turned in place, he fixed his guests with blue eyes that were both solemn and bright with merriment. Most of the visitors were longtime friends and prominent citizens of Nashville, and it was a testament to the respect and warm feelings afforded Renno and his family that they had made the long journey to his home in the Cherokee lands in order to celebrate the occasion. A few new acquaintances were present as well, such as newspaper publisher Victor Coughtry, who had come to Huntington Castle to meet the celebrated man known as the white Indian.

Tonight Renno did not look much like a sachem or a Seneca, not even one who was only half Indian. Gone were the buckskins he favored. Instead he was attired like most of the male guests, in formal black cutaway suit, square-cut white waistcoat, and ruffled white shirt. His collar had upturned points and was held in place by a white silk cravat, and he wore long trousers—the latest fashion, preferred by his younger guests. Most of his contemporaries favored the traditional stockings and pumps.

Renno waited until everyone's glass was full, then intoned, "We have good cause to celebrate tonight, for the new year carries with it new hope."

Leaning on a simple hickory stick, he took a step closer to a young Cherokee man whose hair and simple outfit were in the style of the whites. Raising the stick and wrapping his arm around the man's shoulder, he motioned for him to lift his glass as well.

"Thanks to Joseph Blacksnake, who rode so hard to bring us the news from New Orleans, we know that our negotiators in Europe are near an accord and our boys in the militia no longer expect an attack by the British Navy. Indeed, the war we have fought for more than two and a half years may soon be brought to a successful conclusion."

His words were met with a great cheer, and as he waited for it to subside, Renno thought of his sons, Hawk and Ta-na-wun-da, who were with the militia in New Orleans. He was not overly concerned about Ta-na, for the manitous had revealed that it was his younger and not his older son who would one day wear the sachem's robe. That revelation had left Hawk's destiny in doubt, and Renno could not help but worry about him—and about Hawk's seven-year-old son, Michael Soaring Hawk, who was under the care of Renno and his wife, Beth, while his father was away. But with tonight's good news from New Orleans, Renno was able at last to put aside his concerns.

Again he raised his glass, proclaiming, "Let us drink to the peace that this new year shall usher in."

"And to the Tennessee militia!" a voice shouted. The toast was met with thunderous approval.

The glasses were emptied and refilled, and another toast was offered, then a third and fourth. As the group fell to conversing in small groups, Renno caught the eye of Victor Coughtry and waved him over. As Coughtry approached, Renno took a quick measure of the man who had recently taken the reins as publisher of *The Nashville Sentinel*. He looked to be in his late forties and sported a bushy beard that was a shade lighter than his thinning brown hair. Compact and muscular, he seemed constrained by his crimson waistcoat and white cravat and looked as if he preferred the plain, sturdy clothes of a farmer. Yet there was an air about him that suggested he had worked hard to achieve his current prominence in the Nashville business community and would not willingly return to hardscrabble frontier living.

"Those were words well spoken, Mr. Harper," Victor Coughtry said.

"You must call me Renno," his host replied, repeating a request he had made when they were first introduced earlier that evening.

"You have an impressive home, Renno. It puts the Hermitage to shame." He was referring to General Andrew Jackson's six-hundred-forty-acre farm just outside Nashville.

"That's my wife's doing." Renno glanced over to where Beth and the other women were conversing. "My bachelor years were hardly so impressive," he added with a grin.

"Which must be why my own quarters are no more than a few rooms above the newspaper."

"That will all change when you get married."

Coughtry gave a mock frown. "That takes a willing woman, which I don't seem able to attract . . . certainly not one such as Mrs. Harper."

"Certainly there is no shortage of Nashville women interested in a successful businessman—especially a prominent journalist such as yourself."

Another man, overhearing the comment, interjected, "Are you talking about V. J. Coughtry? A well-known scoundrel, is more like it." He grinned broadly.

"You're just jealous, Ned." Coughtry playfully jabbed Ned Pritchard on the shoulder. "But don't worry—that little broadside of yours catches the eye of more than a few folk 'round here. Why, someday you might even be able to add a second sheet."

"If you haven't already bought up all the newsprint." Pritchard turned to Renno. "Don't believe a thing this rogue tells you, Renno. If you're not careful, he'll have your nice little community sold to the highest bidder."

"I take it you didn't approve of my editorial on Indian rights?" Coughtry asked.

"Rights?" Pritchard gave a loud harrumph. "Just another wrong, if you ask me. Like all the other wrongs we've done to the Indian in the name of progress."

"I'm afraid I didn't see your editorial," Renno put in, his eyes narrowing suspiciously.

"Don't you read the *Sentinel*?" Coughtry asked.

"Only when someone brings one from Nashville,"

Renno explained, then said to Pritchard, "I'm afraid I only get occasional copies of your publication, as well."

"Ned is referring to an editorial we ran last week. It was on the right of Indians to control their land."

"To sell it, you mean," Pritchard challenged.

"If that's what they want." Coughtry turned to Renno. "Surely you'd agree that a tribe should be able to sell their own land."

"If that's their true desire. If they're not being forced into it."

"Precisely!" Pritchard blurted. "But V. J. would make their removal an act of law."

Coughtry glowered at the other newsman. "I guess *you* didn't read my editorial, either. If you had, you'd know that I advocated nothing of the sort."

"Maybe not in so many words," Pritchard conceded.

"Not in *any* words." Coughtry raised a protesting hand to Renno. "Ned has misconstrued my meaning. I suppose I shouldn't expect any better treatment from a competitor."

"Then you don't support Indian removals?" Renno asked bluntly.

"I'm a newspaperman, Renno. A realist simply reporting what I see going on around me. Tennessee was once Indian land, but it's their land no longer. Except for these Cherokee lands, that is."

"And you'd have the Cherokee, as well, removed beyond the Mississippi," Pritchard pressed.

"That's not what I wrote, and you know it," Coughtry shot back. "All I was arguing, Renno, was that when the time comes, the Cherokee should receive fair value for their lands. Not herded at gunpoint and marched out to the frontier like all the rest were."

Pritchard snickered. "Fair value? Even if they're allowed to sell, they won't get a nickel on the dollar once the order of removal is announced."

"Which is precisely why they shouldn't wait," Coughtry replied with the hint of a smile. "We all know that one day soon these lands will go the way of all Indian lands east of the Mississippi. If the Cherokee are as smart as they seem, they'll sell before that day comes."

Renno shook his head. "How can you be so sure we'll be forced to leave? Andrew Jackson himself has given assurances that—"

"I'm a realist, Renno," Coughtry interrupted. "And Andy Jackson's even more of one than I am. We both understand that Indian removal is inevitable—as I'm sure, in your heart, you do also. I'm only suggesting that the Cherokee take advantage of the situation and launch a preemptive attack, so to speak."

"If the army sets foot on this land without permission, you can be sure that many Cherokee and Seneca alike will be willing to attack," Renno warned ominously.

Coughtry raised his hands. "Don't blame me. I'm only the messenger."

"The agitator," Pritchard muttered under his breath.

"Look, I never said they must sell. Or move, for that matter. I'm only suggesting they can do a lot better for themselves if they, rather than the American government, choose the time and conditions of their departure."

"We'll never willingly leave this land," Renno declared emphatically.

"But you're a Seneca, aren't you? This isn't even your land," Coughtry countered. "Not your ancestral land, at least."

"My father and his people were forced to move once before, and the Cherokee welcomed us and shared all that they had—even their land. We will not be moved again, nor will we stand by and let anyone do the same to our Cherokee brothers and sisters."

"Then there's no price whatsoever that might induce the Cherokee to sell?"

"None," Renno said adamantly.

Coughtry's dark eyes flashed, almost with amusement. "Are you so certain the Cherokee council would agree with you?"

"They will. If that day ever comes, they will."

Coughtry gave a flourish of his hand. "I defer to one who obviously knows these people better than a mere newsman."

A hand gripped Renno's arm, and he turned to find an attractive woman with flame-red hair smiling at him.

Beth Huntington Harper fixed each man with a disarming smile. "You gentlemen aren't discussing politics, are you?"

"Not really. We were just—"

"I should hope not, Renno. You promised that tonight would be for celebration. No more talk of Washington or wars." She looked at Victor Coughtry. "If I could borrow you a moment, Mr. Coughtry . . ." She nodded toward a middle-aged woman standing across the room. "Delia Adams insists that Nashville has grown enough to warrant its own society column. She has the most delightful ideas, and I was hoping you might speak with her."

"I am your servant, ma'am." He turned to Renno and Ned Pritchard and gave a slight bow. "Gentlemen, if you will excuse me." He offered Beth his arm and accompanied her across the room.

"Watch out for that one," Pritchard advised, keeping his voice low.

"You don't trust him at all, do you?"

"I don't know him well—but I know him well enough to be wary."

"I'd heard he was a farmer. How did he manage to get control of the *Sentinel*?"

Pritchard chuckled. "V. J. enjoys the pretense of having been a farmer. In truth his family owns a chunk of Massachusetts about the size of New Jersey. Don't believe any of that bull about his being a self-made man. It was family money that handed him the *Sentinel*."

"But why Nashville? Why Tennessee?"

Pritchard shrugged. "Damned if I know."

They were interrupted by several of the men, who came over to wish Renno well. Ned Pritchard excused himself, and as Renno turned to speak with the others, he caught a glimpse of Victor Coughtry watching from across the room as he conversed with the women. He wore a curious, almost conspiratorial smile, and Renno knew there was more to be said between the two of them.

"Walk slowly! Don't spill the whiskey . . . and for goodness' sake, smile!"

The words of the cook rang in Mist-on-the-Water's ears as she made her way out of Huntington Castle's spacious kitchen and down the hall toward the parlor, clutching a large crystal decanter of whiskey tightly in both hands.

Stop worrying about him, she told herself, blinking her eyes against the demon images. *Just pay attention to what you're doing. Ta-na will be all right.*

The situation at New Orleans was the talk of the evening, but little of it made sense to the young woman. There were optimistic reports from the militia and rumors of a pending treaty, all of which gave cause for hope. Yet Mist-on-the-Water could not shake the terrible feeling that something tragic was going to happen before the guns finally fell silent and Ta-na-wun-da, her cousin by marriage and her late husband's best friend, came home.

As she headed down the hall, she did her best not to trip on the hem of the dress she had been provided for the evening. It did not help that her feet had swollen to the point of bursting inside a borrowed pair of stiff, cumbrous shoes. But concentrating on her movements did not make things any better—in fact, it seemed to distract her, for her foot caught on the edge of the carpet and she stumbled, almost losing her grip on the decanter.

Some of the golden liquid spilled over the brim and soaked her right hand, and she instinctively put it to her lips and licked it clean. As the smooth, bracing whiskey filled her senses, she took a calming breath and stared longingly at the decanter. She yearned for a real taste, but she had already managed a few stolen sips from nearly empty glasses she had returned to the kitchen. She would not allow herself any more.

Not here, she told herself with a firm shake of the head, as if attempting to convince herself. *Not at Huntington Castle.*

Straightening her shoulders, Mist-on-the-Water swept into the parlor and searched for anyone in need of a refill. She smiled politely as she approached one person and then another, all the while telling herself that it was after midnight and would all be over soon.

Then I can get out of these awful clothes. Then, perhaps, I can have a real drink. . . .

One of the guests, a squat man with a bushy brown beard, gestured for her to come over, hardly giving her a passing glance as he thrust forth his glass. He was paying so little attention, in fact, that he withdrew his hand before she finished pouring, causing some of the whiskey to slosh onto the ruffled cuff of his shirt.

As he spun toward her, his jaw tightened, and he hissed, "Damn fool!"

She stammered an apology, but he already had his back to her and was grumbling beneath his breath—about her ineptitude, she did not doubt.

At eighteen, Mist-on-the-Water was used to being around whites, having grown up at the fort at Vincennes in the Indiana Territory after her French trapper father had sold her and her Potawatomi mother to an American sergeant. She even occasionally wore the clothing of the whites, though she far preferred moccasins and deerskin skirts. But tonight was unlike any she had spent at Vincennes. Huntington Castle was far more exquisite than the military meeting hall, and the flounced, white silk dress she was wearing was a far cry from the coarse muslin dresses from the fort trading post. Yet all the elegance and gaiety were wasted on Mist-on-the-Water, for she could not stop thinking about Ta-na-wun-da and worrying that he would not survive a British onslaught.

She held her breath—a simple task in the excruciatingly tight corset—and filled another glass, allowing herself a small sigh of relief when none of the whiskey spilled. As she circled the room, she tried to avoid the other women. It was bad enough having the men stare at her. The ladies would be much more critical; she could only imagine what was hidden behind the polite smiles they gave her.

The young woman tried to avoid Beth Harper, as well, even though she knew that Renno's wife did not harbor any such judgmental thoughts. In fact, Beth had wanted Mist-on-the-Water to attend the festivities as a guest, not a servant. After all, as the widow of Renno's nephew, Gao, she was part of the family. But she had refused, agreeing to attend only if allowed to assist the household help.

Mist-on-the-Water approached one of the men, who was discussing the military standoff in New Orleans. Though she was not trying to listen, she couldn't help overhearing him comment that the situation was not as promising as Renno had suggested. He concluded by saying, "Our militia is no match for the redcoats. Why, their navy'll cut a swath through our boys like a scythe to grain. They won't let themselves be held back by talk of a treaty. Mark my words, our boys are in for a battle, and many will be the numbers that don't march home to Tennessee."

Seeing the young woman standing there, the fellow gave a half-smile and held forth his glass. Mist-on-the-Water raised the decanter, but as she tipped it to the glass, her hands started trembling.

The man looked at her curiously and asked, "Is something wrong, miss?"

"N-no," she stammered, forcing calm into her hands as she tried not to think about her cousin serving with the militia in defense of New Orleans . . . as she tried not to envision her husband lying in a field outside Fort Niagara, his body riddled with bullets.

The man reached for her hand, as if to steady it, but she jerked her arms back, the decanter slipping through her fingers as she gasped, "Ta-na!" It shattered against the floor, soaking the hem of her dress.

There was a hush, and all eyes turned toward Mist-on-the-Water. She saw Beth approaching from across the room and suddenly felt very ashamed. She gazed at her palms, felt the flesh quivering as her vision clouded with tears. Then she hiked up her skirt and pushed past the stunned guests. She dashed out of the room and down the hall, toward the front door and the safety of the night.

Half an hour later, the party had concluded and the guests had either retired to their rooms in Huntington Castle or departed for nearby homes. Victor Coughtry was one of the last to leave, and Renno accompanied him out to the verandah to see him off.

"Are you certain you won't accept our hospitality for the night?" Renno asked, halting beside Coughtry at the top of the steps.

"Not this time, thank you." He walked down off the verandah and took the reins of his black gelding from the middle-aged Cherokee who served as Renno's stableman. "I've friends in the village who are putting me up," he explained, gesturing beyond the fields toward the lights of Rusog's Town, the main Cherokee-Seneca community. In the distance, the sounds of drums and chanting could be heard; the Indian celebration of the white man's holiday was apparently still going strong.

Renno's brow lifted slightly, but he did not press the matter. No doubt he would hear all about the newsman's stay in the village after Coughtry's return to Nashville.

Coughtry walked back to the verandah and held out his hand. Renno reached down and accepted it.

"I'm sorry Beth isn't here to see you off," he apologized. "She must still be seeing the others to their rooms."

"Please thank her for me. I had a delightful time." He hesitated, then added, "And I'm pleased we finally met. I can see that folks were correct who told me Renno Harper is a person worth knowing."

Renno nodded politely. He was about to voice some pleasantry in return, but he could not shake the feeling that there was something unfinished hanging in the air between them. He decided to face it directly. "If you don't mind my saying, I sensed earlier this evening that something's weighing on your mind—something you came here to discuss with me."

Coughtry gave a sheepish grin. "I'm a journalist, and we pride ourselves on being able to mask our thoughts and feelings. Am I really so transparent?" He paused, as if awaiting a reply, then quickly added, "Don't answer! I'd rather not know."

"Why exactly *did* you come here tonight?" Renno asked bluntly. "Surely an evening of good food and conversation would be insufficient to drag a man all the way out here—away from the comforts of Nashville."

Coughtry patted his ample midsection. "Don't underestimate the power of food and talk—especially to a newspaperman." He chuckled. "But you're right. There is something on my mind . . . though it can certainly wait until another time—"

"What is it?" Renno asked, coming down the steps.

Coughtry's left eye narrowed, and he stood looking Renno up and down, as if gauging how much he should divulge. Apparently he made up his mind that Renno was a man who could be trusted, for he said forthrightly, "The reason I am going to Rusog's Town is to make an offer for land."

"Cherokee land?" Renno said warily, and Coughtry nodded. "How much?" he asked, a trace of contempt in his tone as he added, "All of it?"

"Nothing of the sort. I'm only interested in a small parcel along the northern boundary, not far from Newby's Trading Post."

"Which is why you wrote that editorial?"

Coughtry's smile was circumspect. "I'm a man who speaks his mind. I believe the Indians have a right to their land—to keep it or, preferably, to sell it."

"Then you don't advocate forced removal?"

"Certainly not," Coughtry insisted. "But I told you I was a realist, and mark my words, such removals will come, whether we wish it or not."

"Especially if men with voices in their communities don't speak out against such a crime."

"You mean men like me?"

"Newspapers shape the opinions of the public. And it's those opinions that shape the actions of our government." Renno paused, fixing the other man with a critical gaze. "And a newspaper that urges the Cherokee to sell their land is a newspaper that is probably willing to sell the Cherokee into slavery on a reservation."

The two men stared at each other a long moment. Then Victor Coughtry lifted himself into the saddle. "I probably shouldn't have brought up the subject—at least not until we've had a chance to get better acquainted and to fully understand each other's views. I think you'll find that I'm not as unfeeling as you might think."

"I didn't mean to imply—"

"It's quite all right. I'm a newsman; skin doesn't come any thicker than that." He chuckled. "If you don't mind, Renno, I'd like to send you a copy of my editorial, along with some information about what I'll be proposing to the Cherokee council. Perhaps you'll discover we don't think all that differently, after all."

"Perhaps," Renno said, unconvinced.

"In fact, it's my hope that you'll ultimately lend your support to my effort."

"I wouldn't count on that. Not if it involves the Cherokee lands shrinking any further."

"What it involves is looking out for our mutual interests. Yours, mine, and the Cherokee's. All I ask is that you keep an open mind."

"I'll read whatever you send me," Renno told him. "That's all I can promise."

"That's all I ask." Coughtry pulled back on the reins, turning the horse toward the long tree-lined drive that led away from Huntington Castle. "Good night, Renno. I look forward to continuing our discussion at a later date." He kneed the horse forward and headed down the drive at a trot.

Renno watched as Victor Coughtry disappeared into the night, listening to the fading hoofbeats as he gazed out across his fields toward the gathering of log cabins and longhouses that comprised Rusog's Town. There was nothing overly impressive about the setting; it certainly did not possess the grandeur of the forested hills that surrounded his childhood home near the lake of the Seneca in western New York. But this had been home to him and his family—and to his father's generation before. It had been a good home.

Renno would not give up this home without a fight, be it waged with words or with guns. Here among the Cherokee, the Seneca had made a new life for themselves. And here he himself would remain, until the day he put down his weapons and his walking stick for the last time, when he would make that final journey to the land of the manitous, to the land of his brother and his father and his father's father.

And on that great day, fast approaching, he would offer his body to this red earth, to this Seneca home, here in the Cherokee lands.

Three

Ma-ton-ga lay under the blanket, drifting between reality and dream. The world shimmered with a curious, hazy glow, and she realized it was the light of flames and smoke. She was back in her Creek village, surrounded by the rumble of hooves and the thunder of cannons. She staggered across the scorched earth, past lodges that crackled with flames. In the distance bugles blared and rifles popped, and though she could see no one, she heard their cries as bullets tore into the flesh of her warrior brothers and sisters.

Suddenly she was on the ground, held fast by the ghostly bearded men who had overrun her village. She flailed at them, but they pinned her arms to the ground and forced her legs apart, tearing away her clothes, pawing at her body as they fought over who would have her first.

Hawk! she gasped. And then the soldiers disappeared, and Hawk Harper stood in their place, smiling down at her. He lifted her from the ground, protected her from the smoke and ashes. He held her close as he carried her north, away from the place of death, to a new home and a new life. She felt his arms around her, his lips at her breast. She reached for him, drew him to her, heard his cry of pleasure as she took him into her, as she gave him her heart. . . .

Ma-ton-ga's eyes snapped open, and she struggled to make out her surroundings in the dim light that filtered through the small window. She was not in the Creek stronghold of Talladega, her former home, but in the Cherokee village of Rusog's Town, in the bedroom of the cabin she shared with her friend Mist-on-the-Water. The sounds were not of battle but of celebration. And the lips at her breast belonged not to Hawk Harper but to Mist-on-the-Water's six-month-old boy, Little Gao, named after his father, who had been killed escaping from Fort Niagara after being captured by the Americans during Tecumseh's final battle.

Little Gao stirred uneasily, searching for the breast of his wet nurse. Mist-on-the-Water's own milk had proved insufficient, and one of the village women had nursed the boy until a few weeks ago, when they had begun the process of weaning him. Ma-ton-ga considered getting him some milk, but as she patted his back, he quieted and drifted back to sleep. She started to roll over and close her eyes when she heard a loud gasp from the main room of the cabin. She lay perfectly still, straining to hear the voice, considering what she would do if it was an intruder. The sound was repeated, followed by a string of oaths in what sounded like Potawatomi.

"Mist . . ." she muttered, shaking her head as she eased Little Gao's mouth from her nipple and sat up in bed. Pulling her robe around her, she padded across the cold floor and opened the door.

The main room was illuminated by a lamp and several candles, which cast a flickering glow on one of the strangest sights Ma-ton-ga had ever seen. Her friend was in the middle of the room, her back to the door, her arms twisted behind her back as she fought the ties of a whale-bone corset. She appeared to be standing upon a silken cloud, the voluminous folds of the borrowed white dress that lay crumpled around her ankles.

Frustrated in her efforts to free herself from the confines of the corset, Mist-on-the-Water stepped clear of the dress and kicked it across the room, then almost fell down attempting to bend over and pull off her shoes. She let out another string of colorful Potawatomi and English curses.

"Quiet," Ma-ton-ga whispered as she stepped into the main room and pulled the bedroom door closed behind her.

She was Creek and knew only a little Potawatomi, so the two women used the one language they shared between them: English. Ma-ton-ga was far less fluent, having learned much of it only in the past year. Mist-on-the-Water, on the other hand, had spoken English for many years, though with a distinct French accent.

"Little Gao just get to sleep," Ma-ton-ga said, coming across the room. "Do not wake him."

Mist-on-the-Water looked at her friend. "Nothing wakes up my son," she replied with the hint of a frown. "Come help me out of this . . . thing!"

She turned her back and gestured at the ties. It took Ma-ton-ga a few minutes to undo them, and then the corset fell away and dropped to the floor, eliciting a gasping sigh from the poor woman who had spent the evening caught in its grip. After removing her underclothes, Mist-on-the-Water snatched up one of her buckskin dresses and slipped it over her head.

"You not go to bed?" Ma-ton-ga asked as her friend donned moccasins.

"Not yet. I'm going out."

"Don't," Ma-ton-ga implored, afraid to say more.

"Just for a while." She glanced through the window at the lights of the fires that continued to burn around Rusog's Town. "I . . . I need to."

Ma-ton-ga took the younger woman's hand. Though

only in her midtwenties, she often felt more like a parent than a friend—as if Mist-on-the-Water and Little Gao were not mother and son but her children.

"Go to bed," she urged. "Nothing outside for you."

She felt Mist-on-the-Water tremble at her touch and knew that there would be no dissuading her. It was the demons again. First the demon of having lost her husband to the white soldiers. And now the fear that she might lose Gao's cousin, Ta-na-wun-da, the same way. Mist-on-the-Water was not Ta-na's woman. Not yet. At the moment she saw him as protector and friend. But already Ma-ton-ga sensed that the younger woman's feelings were stirring with a deeper passion, despite her efforts to feel nothing in her heart—to drown her feelings in the hot fire that flowed from the white man's whiskey jug.

"Please don't," Ma-ton-ga begged as tears welled up in her friend's eyes. "Stay here. Nothing outside—"

"I won't be . . . I won't be late," Mist-on-the-Water stammered, pulling away from Ma-ton-ga and crossing to the door. She jerked it open and hesitated, staring out at the dancing firelight beyond, then looking back across the cabin toward the doorway that led to the bedroom and her son. For a moment it appeared as if she might change her mind and make the short walk to where her child was waiting. But then she spun around and dashed into the night, taking the much easier journey to that increasingly familiar place that promised no sorrow, no fear.

"Nothing outside . . ." Ma-ton-ga whispered, her shoulders slumping.

Wiping away her own tears, she walked to the door and closed it. She heard the soft cries of a child, and she turned and headed to the bedroom and to Little Gao.

Victor Coughtry grinned, marveling at the spectacle as he stood in front of a longhouse in an open area encircled by smaller log cabins. More than two dozen Cherokee and Seneca men and women were gathered around a great bonfire that blazed in the center of the clearing, a few of them beating drums and chanting while the rest danced and passed around jugs of whiskey and rum. Whoever was handed a jug would halt and take one or two long pulls, then pass it along and resume the dance.

It was not the music or dancing or singing that made the scene so surreal but rather the outfits worn by the celebrants. About one quarter had donned their finest traditional clothing—colorfully embroidered blouses over deerskin skirts or leggings, with beaded moccasins and a variety of feathered headbands. Another quarter wore the best European-style outfits they could muster, the men in boots and ill-fitting black suits, the women in severe homespun dresses. The largest group, however, wore a mix of both styles, creating a patchwork of hats, head-dresses, suit jackets, and breechclouts.

"They like gift," a thickly accented voice said from behind Coughtry.

The newsman glanced over his shoulder and nodded to a slightly hunched Cherokee who looked to be in his fifties. The man wore buckskins and a beaver derby crowned with an osprey feather.

"Did you distribute all of it?" Coughtry asked.

"Everything in wagon."

"Good."

Coughtry reached into his vest pocket, removed a gold coin, and handed it to the man, who beamed and nodded in thanks as he stuffed it into a pouch at his waist.

"Tall Grass not drink any," the man promised, patting his own chest to indicate he was referring to himself.

"Even better," Coughtry said approvingly. He turned and again watched the dancing. He had brought Tall Grass a wagon loaded with almost fifty jugs of liquor before going to Huntington Castle, and apparently the gift was already earning him the goodwill of the people of Rusog's Town—a significant number of them, at least, for this was one of a half-dozen similar gatherings around the village that had benefited from Coughtry's gift. To express their thanks, one or another of the celebrants would periodically approach the Nashville businessman and offer the jug. Coughtry would always accept it and lift it to his lips, but he never actually drank. He did not approve of drinking—at least not when he was on the job. And this New Year's Eve, Victor Coughtry was definitely working.

"When will you take my offer to the council?" Coughtry asked over his shoulder.

Tall Grass came up beside him and raised a bony finger toward the people dancing around the fire. "Two council members there," he replied in halting English. "One with drum. Other lie on ground."

Coughtry squinted against the glare of the flames and noticed the shadowed image of someone who apparently had passed out on the far side of the fire.

"No worry," Tall Grass assured his benefactor. "He wake up tomorrow ready to make talk. He smile upon words of Etutu Ekwa."

"Etu . . . ?" Coughtry looked questioningly at the older man.

"Etutu Ekwa," Tall Grass repeated. "Cherokee call you the Great Grandfather."

Coughtry knew it was an expression of respect and did not point out that he wasn't even a father. He also knew that it was the whiskey that had brought him such instant popularity. Come sunrise, when the liquor was all gone, he could not count on being called Grandfather, great or otherwise.

"Can I speak to the council myself?" he asked the Cherokee.

The Indian's eyes widened with worry, and he raised his hands in protest. "Not speak. Not allowed."

"But I need to explain why they should sell me that parcel."

"I go council for you. I tell them."

Coughtry frowned, but he had not really expected to be allowed an audience with the council. At least not until they had heard his proposal and had thought upon it for a while. Even though he wasn't pleased at the prospect of

Tall Grass acting as his intermediary, he knew he would have to go along with it for the time being.

"You will tell them exactly what I say," he pressed.

"Tall Grass your voice and ears. Tall Grass speak your words."

"Good. Do you think they will agree?"

Tall Grass hesitated, a frown creeping across his face. "Job not easy. Chief Rusog not want sell Cherokee land. Not even small piece."

"But you told me you could convince them," Coughtry said impatiently.

"Many listen to Rusog." Tall Grass allowed himself a half smile. "But many more listen to Tall Grass. And to gifts of Etutu Ekwa."

"Then they *will* sell. And when they do, you will be given all that I promised."

Tall Grass looked at him curiously. "Why want such small land? Worthless land. No water. No tree. No game." He swept his hand up to his chest and then away from him, as if dismissing the whole idea.

"Yes, worthless. Which is why I'm willing to offer so much, if need be."

"This talk crazy. Tall Grass not understand."

Coughtry smirked as he turned to face the other man. "No, it isn't so crazy. Sometimes I buy something just to see if the other person is willing to sell—just to find out their price."

"Then you not want land?"

"I want the land, all right." He patted the Cherokee on the shoulder. "And I want Tall Grass to be my partner in obtaining it."

The older man nodded eagerly. "Tall Grass your partner. Tall Grass speak your words."

"Then let's go to your cabin, and I'll tell you the words I want you to speak to the council tomorrow."

He started to turn away but was interrupted by a young woman who staggered over and thrust a jug in front of him. She was not very attractive and quite drunk, and as he took the jug and lifted it to his lips, he looked beyond her to a pair of women standing nearby. They were whispering and giggling and apparently had challenged their friend to go up to him.

One of the women caught his eye. She appeared to be of mixed blood and probably was not yet out of her teens. Yet there was a womanliness—and a haughtiness—about her that he found quite appealing. And there was something else, a familiarity he couldn't quite place.

He lowered the jug and returned it to the woman who had brought it over, and she spun around and lurched back to her friends. The three of them shared the jug, all the while watching the white man who had brought the gift wagon to their village.

Coughtry was about to turn away when suddenly he recalled where he had seen the haughty young woman before.

"That one," he said to Tall Grass, nodding toward the three women. "The one in the middle. Who is she?"

"That one?" the Indian said with a derisive sneer. "She not Cherokee. Not even Seneca. She half-breed."

"Her name. What's her name?"

"Mist-on-the-Water. Her husband Seneca. He dead."

"I'm certain I saw her earlier, at Renno's home."

Tall Grass nodded. "She go many times there. Her husband's father was El-i-chi, sachem of Seneca and brother of Renno."

Coughtry nodded and smiled. "Yes, that was her." He reached up and stroked his beard; he could still smell the whiskey on his cuff. "She looked quite different."

"Forget Mist-on-the-Water. She not help you."

"Tell her I want to speak with her."

"Now?" the man said incredulously.

"Go. Tell her."

"She know English," Tall Grass replied, gesturing that the other man could speak to her himself if he wanted.

"You tell her for me."

Tall Grass shrugged, then shuffled over to where the women were gathered.

One of the women nudged Mist-on-the-Water, who turned to see Tall Grass approaching. She knew even before he spoke that he had come for her.

"Why does he send you here, old one?" she asked in the Cherokee tongue, trying not to let the liquor slur her words.

The woman beside her giggled and said, "He would have you be the mother of his children."

"Be quiet, foolish one!" Tall Grass snapped. He turned to Mist-on-the-Water and smiled. "He wants to speak to you," he explained, also in Cherokee.

"Why would he speak with me? I do not know him."

"He has brought us many gifts. He will bring us many more. It would be a little thing but a good one for you to speak with him and give him our thanks."

Mist-on-the-Water was holding one of the jugs, and she boldly raised it and took a long swallow, savoring the bracing liquid. Lowering it, she pressed it against Tall Grass's chest, forcing him to take it from her.

"He brings us only the disease that comes from the white man's bottle. Why should we give thanks?"

"You seem to like this gift he has brought," Tall Grass said pointedly. He held forth the jug, and when she did not accept it, he thrust it into the eager hands of one of the other women. "But that is not his only gift." Reaching into his pouch, he held up the gold coin. "He has many more."

It took Mist-on-the-Water a moment to focus on the object glimmering in the old man's hand. When she realized it was a coin, her expression darkened. "He would buy me with his gold?" she asked contemptuously.

"This gold is not for you." He stuffed the coin back into his pouch. "But such gold can help our people. He asks only to speak with you, nothing more."

Through a whiskey haze, Mist-on-the-Water looked past the Cherokee at the white man standing near the edge of the clearing. She remembered how he had snapped at her in Huntington Castle, and she wondered if he wanted to berate her again for spilling liquor on his sleeve. She had no great wish to face him again, but neither did she want him or the other women to think her afraid.

"I will talk to this man," she announced. Straightening, she moved forward, willing her numb legs to remain steady as she walked. She did not stop until she was directly in front of the Nashville businessman. She stood in silence, determined not to let him know that she recognized him from the incident in the parlor.

He was the first to speak, with a slight bow at the waist. "I am sorry if I spoke rudely earlier. I didn't mean to upset you."

She neither replied nor moved, her expression as impassive as before.

"I want to make up for my bad manners. I'd like to give you something."

One eyebrow arched slightly, but she remained silent.

"It's over there."

He gestured to the left, and she had to squint slightly to see what he was indicating. It was an empty wagon beside one of the cabins, and she recognized it as the vehicle that had carried the whiskey to Rusog's Town.

He offered his hand. "Will you come with me?"

She took a step back. "I do not need anything from you," she declared, painfully aware that her voice showed the effects of whiskey.

Coughtry chuckled. "You're probably right. You may not need it, but you might like it. Come with me . . . it's just over there."

Mist-on-the-Water looked back and forth between the man and the wagon, then glanced at her friends, who were watching the proceedings with great interest. She considered turning her back on the man and walking away. She knew that was what she ought to do. But then, almost as if in spite, she reached out and took his arm.

"I will see what you want to show me. But that is all I will do."

"That's all I'm asking," he said quite charmingly as he placed a hand upon hers and led her toward the edge of the clearing.

When they reached the wagon, Coughtry kept walking right past it, into the darkness. She pulled her arm free and halted, suddenly frightened.

"It's in my saddlebags," he explained, gesturing beyond the wagon.

In the thin, flickering light she could just make out a horse tied at the rear of the cabin. Nodding cautiously, she took Coughtry's arm again and let him lead her deeper into the shadows.

"Here we are," he said, halting beside the horse. He untied the saddlebags and reached inside. "I have two things to show you, in fact." He pulled out a length of material. "Go ahead, take it," he urged, holding it out to her.

It was hard to see the pattern, but from the feel she could tell that it was silk.

"A shawl from Paris," he explained. "Almost as lovely as you. I want you to have it."

"I cannot," she said and started to hand it back.

"No, I insist." He held up his hands, refusing to take it. "I acted horribly; this is but a small token of my apology."

She ran her hands over the material, then pulled the shawl around her. It felt lovely indeed, and she could only imagine how much more beautiful it would be in daylight.

"Here's the other gift." He pulled a bottle from the saddlebags. "Those jugs from the wagon are only local brew. This Scotch is the real thing, straight from Edinburgh."

Mist-on-the-Water felt the warmth of the shawl wrapped around her, imagined the heat of the liquor flowing down her throat—not the rough, biting kind in the jugs but real Scotch like she had been serving others at Huntington Castle.

She knew she should turn her back on the man and walk away. Just as surely she knew she could not.

There were no horses hitched to the wagon, and yet it seemed to be moving—swaying gently up and down and side to side on long, languorous waves. Mist-on-the-Water's legs dangled off the back of the wagonbed, and she gripped the side panel with her left hand to steady herself as she sought the bottle with her lips. Tipping it upward, she waited for the smooth heat to flow through her. But only a faint trickle moistened her tongue. She lifted it overhead and shook it, and a few last drops spattered on her face.

Lowering the bottle, she held it out to the darkened figure standing in front of her. She saw him reaching for it and felt it slipping through her fingers. She tried to tighten her grip, but her hands were thick and numb, and the bottle clattered to the hard-packed earth.

The man's hands closed around her wrists. She heard him speak but did not know what he was saying. Was it about Renno again? He had wanted to know so much about Renno and the Seneca and the Cherokee. She had not understood most of his questions and had answered whatever came into her mind. Anything to appease him. Anything to put him off so that she could enjoy another taste from the bottle.

He was asking something now, but the words seemed all twisted and confused. The only thing she could think to say to this strange, dark figure was, "Who are you? Why are you here?" But when she tried to speak, the sound that emerged was a garbled cry.

The man continued to hold on to her, pulling gently. She sensed him moving closer, then felt him press against her, as firm as the bottle, as warm as the whiskey they had shared. He released his grip on her wrists and took hold of her waist, sliding her back onto the spinning wagon, climbing up alongside her. And then he was on top of her, his breath hot and urgent, his rhythm matching the sway of the wagon.

"Gao . . ." she moaned, thrilling as her husband's strong arms wrapped around her, his lips nuzzling her breast, his hands caressing her hips and thighs. She thrilled at the touch of his fingers as they eased under her skirt, lifting it higher, touching, claiming her as his own.

The wagon rocked ever faster, ever harder. She heard percussive bursts of gunfire and saw the faint distant flashes of rockets. He was running toward her, reaching out, eager to take her in his arms. She froze as the line of soldiers raised their weapons . . . shuddered as the tip of the lieutenant's sword swept to the ground . . . gasped as a dozen musket balls thudded into her husband's body.

"Gao!" she shrieked, pushing herself upright.

"Whaa?" the man grunted as he was thrown off her and onto his side.

Mist-on-the-Water struggled to a sitting position on the wagonbed. She held on to the side panel, dizzy and nauseated, the world spinning riotously beneath her. The gunfire continued to ring out, and for a moment she thought she was at Fort Niagara, where she had sold her body in a desperate attempt to gain her husband's freedom, only to see him die in a hail of bullets. But then the truth flooded back, and she recognized the explosions as coming not from a battle but from pistols being fired into the air by some of the more inebriated New Year's celebrants of Rusog's Town. And she realized with a shock that she was not with Gao—not even with her dear Ta-na-wun-da. She was in the back of a whiskey wagon, her body and her spirit claimed for the price of a bottle.

A pair of hands took hold of her waist, pulling her down. She tried to slap them away, but they held her tight, forcing her onto her back as the whiskey man's dark, ghostlike figure loomed over her. He pressed down upon her, his lips growing ever more eager and frantic with

each squirming movement she made. She wanted to struggle, to fight back. But she felt herself weakening, her arms
and legs going numb again as he forced himself inside her,
as he plunged into her again and again.

She wanted to strike out, to tear open his flesh the
way those musket balls had torn away her heart. But she
could not find her power. She could not summon her
strength. She squeezed her eyes shut, trying to make him
disappear, to make the comforting tears flow. But she was
floating away, not upon an ocean but a desert. A landscape
stifling hot and dry. A world devoid of life.

Her lips parted, and she tried to call out her husband's name. But she could no longer find her voice.
Could no longer remember what or why she was calling.

She let go. And in that timeless instant, the pain
touched her no more.

Four

Ta-na-wun-da warbled the low coo of a mourning dove as he crawled across the marshy stretch of delta. At intervals he paused and repeated it, until he heard a faint return call. Moving in its direction, he soon came upon three men hunkered behind some scrub bushes. In the faint predawn light he discerned their ill-fitting red jackets with yellow facings and white leather bandoliers. Each man wore the cocked tricorne of a British light infantryman.

"I was beginning to think you wouldn't get here," he whispered as he came up beside them.

"It took a while to put all this together," Hawk Harper replied, looking dejected as he fingered the material of his uniform. "Were you able to get close to their line?"

His younger brother nodded.

"Is it as you described?"

"Exactly as last night," Ta-na replied. "A twenty-four-pounder holds down the western flank some forty yards from the nearest gun. Six cannoneers are manning it, with the nearest soldiers also forty yards away."

"Good."

"The cannoneers are artillery—dressed in blue," Ta-na pointed out, gesturing at Hawk's red jacket. "Not infantry."

Hawk shrugged. "This was the best we could do. I assume they've got infantry along the line."

"Plenty."

"Then this should allow us to approach without raising suspicion."

"I'm just glad it's not me dressed up like that," Ta-na said, suppressing a grin as he stared from one man to the other.

"Thanks to Captain Harper," one of the other men put in. "We were gonna bring you a uniform, but your brother said you'd be more convincing as a Creek scout."

"Ta-na, this is Sergeant Humphries," Hawk said. "We call him Nestor."

"An honor to meet you, Ta-na," Nestor said as the two men shook hands.

"And that skinny one swimming in his jacket is Corporal Roger Thomas."

The militiaman reached over to shake the scout's hand. "Just call me Thom."

"And for the duration of this mission, I'm Hawk, not Captain Harper," he told the two men, then turned back to his brother. "How do you suggest we proceed?"

"We've got no more than a half hour, I'd say. I've tracked a path around that way." He pointed off to their right. "It's a bit wet, I'm afraid. But it will bring us right behind their position. There'a a dry, sheltered hollow about a hundred yards to the rear. We can wait there until the cannonade begins."

Hawk nodded. "Shall we get started, then?"

They gathered up their rifles and followed Ta-na-wun-da into the swampland, keeping close to the ground, taking care to keep their powder dry.

*   *   *

As the first rays of the sun slanted across the eastern horizon, a single rifle fired into the air. A few seconds later, several booming explosions shattered the morning calm, followed almost immediately by a series of smaller bursts from the three- and six-pounders.

Hawk Harper stiffened as the ground shuddered beneath him. He nodded silently to the two militiamen, who checked their charges and set their bayonets. Then Hawk rose and started forward. He winced as the big eighteen- and twenty-four-pounders thundered again. Their projectiles would easily reach the American lines, and he prayed that General Jackson and the officers had already begun moving their men to safer positions. He also prayed that Ta-na-wun-da would have no difficulty closing in on their target from his lone position in the swamp.

Shouldering their rifles, Hawk and his fellow "redcoats" marched purposefully up out of the low hollow and across the relatively flat stretch of ground on which the British breastworks had been laid. Approaching from the rear, Hawk saw the line of infantry spread out all the way to the river. In front of the infantry, the cannoneers scurried around their guns, soaking down the barrels, setting their charges, and firing. It was a sea of red uniforms, peppered with the blue jackets of the artillery and navy. In such a chaos of activity, he was confident that three stray soldiers out of position would not raise suspicion.

For the first time, Hawk spied the big twenty-four-pounder that commanded the western flank, standing just to his left on a slight rise at the edge of the swamp. As Ta-na-wun-da had promised, there was a gap of perhaps forty yards between it and the next gun, a six-pounder to his right that marked the beginning of the infantry line.

The three men marched resolutely toward their objective. Out of the corner of his eye, Hawk glimpsed a shadow moving through the swamp, and he quickened his pace, not wanting his brother to face the enemy alone. When he and his men were within twenty yards, they broke into a run, lowering their rifle barrels and timing their charge to bring them to the cannon just before it was ready to fire.

Hawk saw a cannoneer lowering his brand to the vent hole and realized they would not make it in time. Halting, he drew up his rifle and was about to pull the trigger when a dark figure hurtled through the air. Ta-na-wun-da barreled into the cannoneer, knocking the flaming brand from his hand. The man struggled a moment, then lay still, Ta-na's long-bladed knife protruding from his chest.

With a furious cry, Hawk and his men entered the fray, each using his bayonet to make quick work of one of the artillerymen. Ta-na, meanwhile, handled the remaining two soldiers alone, slitting one man's throat and shooting the other as he tried to run for help.

Hawk knew it was only a matter of moments before someone among the nearby infantry realized what was happening and raised the alarm. Shouting orders, he directed his comrades as they raised the rear of the carriage and muscled the gun into position, turning the barrel ninety degrees until it was aiming down the British line.

"Stand clear!" Hawk shouted, snatching up the still-burning brand. He touched it to the charge in the vent hole, then leaped out of the way.

There was a whooshing sound, and then the charge went off with a ferocious boom, knocking the gun backward about six feet. Through the thick smoke, Hawk saw a small cannon halfway down the line explode, decimating the surrounding troops and scattering the survivors in all directions.

As Hawk lowered the angle of the barrel, Ta-na and the other men quickly reloaded. The second shot was even more effective, destroying one of the big eighteen-pounders.

An eerie silence settled over the field as the British guns ceased firing. Hawk and his men worked frantically to reload the cannon, aware that the full attention of the enemy had been drawn to their position. As Hawk prepared to fire a third round, he saw the nearest infantry

falling into ranks, some kneeling, others standing just behind as they awaited the order to fire upon what appeared
to be a renegade band of their own soldiers.

This would have to be the final shot, he realized, and
he ordered his men back toward the swamp. After setting
off the powder in the vent hole, he dropped the brand and
made a hasty retreat. The big gun fired, sending its missile
into the midst of the British line, echoed by a volley of
muskets.

Hawk clambered down a slight incline to the swamp,
where his men were stripping out of their red jackets to
avoid being shot when they rendezvoused with their own
troops. As Hawk pulled off his jacket, he realized that Ta-
na-wun-da was not among them. He looked around frantically, shouting, "Where is he?" above the din of musket
fire.

Nestor shrugged, but Thom grabbed Hawk's arm and
pointed his rifle barrel toward the cannon. Spinning
around, Hawk saw his brother scurrying around the big
gun, seemingly dodging musket balls as he doused sparks
in the breech with one of several pails of water lined up
along the ground. Tossing aside the pail, he hefted a gunpowder sack and stuffed it down the end of the barrel,
then grabbed a second charge and added it to the first.

"Get going!" Hawk ordered his men, motioning for
them to retreat through the swamp. They hesitated, but he
repeated the order more forcefully, and finally they started
back toward the rendezvous site.

Gripping his rifle, Hawk dashed back up the incline.
By the time he reached the gun, his brother had finished
stuffing the last of four charges down the barrel and was
following it with a cannonball and the contents of a shot
bucket of nails and scrap iron. Glancing past Ta-na, Hawk
saw the infantry approaching in ranks, occasionally pausing to let loose a volley. Raising his own rifle, he fired into
their midst, knocking one of the soldiers to his knees.

"What the hell are you doing?" he shouted above the

whine of bullets smacking into the dirt and whistling around them.

"Another!" Ta-na nodded toward the pile of cannonballs.

Hawk dropped his empty rifle and hefted a twenty-four-pound projectile. As he rammed it into the barrel, he noticed that Ta-na's arm was bleeding; apparently one of the musket balls had found its mark. It didn't seem to slow him down, however, as he raced around the side of the gun and started jamming a length of wadding into the vent hole. The cloth would serve as a fuse, giving them enough time to get clear of the cannon before the charge ignited.

Snatching up the brand, Ta-na yelled, "Get out of here!"

Hawk ran to where his brother stood, protected from the musket fire by the large cannon. He grabbed Ta-na's good right arm. "Are you crazy? There's enough powder in that barrel to blow it off the field!"

"That's the plan. One less to use against us." He jabbed the brand in the direction of the swamp. "Now, go on! I'll be right behind."

Hawk hesitated. But he saw the determination in his brother's eyes—and saw, as well, the line of infantry closing in on their position.

"Hurry!" he yelled over his shoulder as he snatched up his rifle and sprinted down the incline.

He had not gone far when something made him look back. His brother stood to one side of the gun, holding the brand to the end of the cloth and waiting for it to catch fire before making his own retreat. Suddenly it burst into flames, and he dropped the brand and turned to run.

A musket ball caught him in the leg, spinning him around and knocking him off his feet. He tried to lift himself off the ground, but his leg collapsed beneath him. A few feet away, the flames reached the top of the fuse and set off the priming powder in a shower of sparks.

"*No-o-o!*" Hawk shouted, dropping his gun and racing back up the hill. He managed only a few steps before he was thrown backward by the force of the blast. The breath was knocked out of him, and for a few moments everything went black. When he was able to focus again, the world was an inferno of swirling smoke and flames.

"Ta-na!" he screamed, struggling to his knees and finally to his feet.

He staggered forward and beat at the thick, choking smoke. It slowly dispersed, revealing what remained of the big gun. It had been lifted off the carriage and thrown to the ground, the end of the barrel now a mass of twisted iron. The carriage lay upside down and in flames, twenty feet behind where it had stood.

His eyes watering from the acrid smoke, Hawk stumbled to the site of the explosion and searched frantically for his brother. He called Ta-na's name again and again as he turned in circles and surveyed the devastation. A mere thirty yards away, the infantry was a shambles, for the cannon in its final gasp had spewed forth a deadly charge of missiles and molten iron. Farther down the line, the remaining British force was also in disarray. The British guns were trained on the American emplacements, and some of the smaller fieldpieces had already begun to move out across the battlefield. But during the diversion provided by Ta-na and the militiamen, the bulk of the American force apparently had completed a predawn sweep from their own fortifications to positions behind the British lines, for now they were launching a counterattack from the rear, shielded from enemy artillery.

Hawk watched as the opposing forces engaged each other. He could see the flaming muzzle blasts, the clouds of black smoke as one line of soldiers fired upon the next. But he realized with a start that he could hear neither guns nor shouting—only a dull, throbbing roar. Covering his ears, he shook his head to clear the fog that seemed to mask his hearing, but the muffled roar did not abate. And when he withdrew his hands, his palms were covered with blood.

In the near distance the infantry was regrouping, and

Hawk knew they would soon overrun his position. None of that mattered any longer. Dropping to his knees, he clutched the earth where he had last seen his brother. Sobbing and calling out Ta-na's name, he lifted his hands to the heavens, the dirt slipping through his fingers and raining down on him.

A musket ball slapped into the ground a foot away. Hawk gazed numbly at the furrow it left in the dirt. He felt a rush of wind as a second and then a third ball whizzed past, and he swatted at them as if they were bothersome insects. Slowly he rose and turned toward the infantry, offering his chest to their bullets. Most of the soldiers just stared up at him, uncertain if he was enemy or friend. A few raised their muskets and fired without hitting their mark.

Turning his back on them, Hawk stared across the swamp, awaiting the stinging bite of the bullet that would bring this nightmare to a close. He stood motionless, taking in the landscape, wishing for darkness to descend.

And then an object about twenty feet to the left caught his eye—a dark, indistinct mound that might have been a sack tossed aside and forgotten. Or perhaps something hurled there by the force of the blast.

"Ta-na . . ." he whispered, taking a cautious step forward. "Ta-na-wun-da . . ."

As he drew closer, the mound took the form of a person curled on the ground. He dropped beside it, rolling it over and wiping away the blood that streamed from his brother's ears and eyes.

Hawk lifted Ta-na's head into his lap and caressed him, speaking gently, willing him to life. There was no movement, no response, only an abiding stillness that blocked all sounds of muskets and cannons—that shrouded even the roaring in Hawk's head.

As Hawk gazed desperately at his brother, another image intruded on his consciousness, and he glanced up to see a force of perhaps a dozen British regulars break away from their ranks. Their bayonets were fixed, and they were charging directly at Hawk and Ta-na, intent on reclaiming this small patch of ground on which their big cannon had once stood sentry.

Instinct told Hawk that he had to get his brother away from this field of death. He lifted Ta-na into his arms and staggered down the incline toward the swamp. He did not expect to get far, but at least he would die at his brother's side.

Through the roaring din, he heard or perhaps only sensed a faint popping noise, like a volley of muskets, and his back stiffened in expectation of the impact. The sound repeated to his right, and he turned to see Corporal Thomas standing with rifle raised, puffs of smoke spiraling from breech and barrel. At his side, Nestor was furiously ramming home his charge. The sergeant threw the rifle to his shoulder and fired into the ranks of the infantry just starting down the incline behind Hawk. Seconds later, Thom got off yet another round.

Over his shoulder, Hawk saw that several British soldiers had fallen, the rest dropping to their knees to fire. Their smooth-bore army muskets were no match for Kentucky rifles, which provided effective cover as Hawk raced the remaining yards to where the two militiamen were waiting.

Nestor waved him past, motioning in the direction of the American forces. Hawk knew he should assist his comrades in their retreat, but at that moment he could think only of his brother, lying so limp in his arms.

"Don't give up, little brother," he whispered as he ran toward the safety of the American lines. "For God's sake, Ta-na, don't die."

Five

News swept through Rusog's Town that despite optimism about a pending treaty with the British, fighting had broken out in New Orleans. The first word came via an Indian runner, who had heard it from a military courier passing through the eastern edge of Cherokee land en route to Washington. Additional details were provided the following evening by a second courier, who arrived at Huntington Castle seeking to borrow a change of mount for the remainder of his journey to the fort at Nashville.

While Beth Harper gathered food and supplies for Sergeant Cosgrove, Renno accompanied him to the stables to choose a horse. As the stableman went about transferring saddle and bags from the exhausted army horse, Renno pressed the young soldier for any information he could offer about the battle.

"Sorry, sir," Cosgrove replied, "but the reports I'm carrying were sealed by General Andrew Jackson himself. I'd let you read 'em, but they're to be unsealed only at militia headquarters."

"Of course," Renno said with a sweep of the hand. "I

was hoping only for some firsthand news. All we've heard is that battle commenced on New Year's Day. What was the outcome?" He gripped his walking stick, trying not to betray his private fears about the fate of his sons. "Were casualties high?"

"Hell sure enough broke loose on the first," the sergeant acknowledged with a solemn nod. "From what I heard, some of our scouts discovered British batteries being set up near our own works the night before. The redcoats dug in and began their bombardment at dawn—figuring, I suppose, that we'd be softened up by a night of celebrating. But the general had us sober and ready, and we launched a counterattack. By nightfall we'd forced 'em back down the river to their ships. They withdrew so fast, they had to spike the vent holes and leave most of their guns behind."

"Casualties?" Renno repeated cautiously. "Were there many?"

"We fared pretty well. Just a minute . . ." Walking over to where the stableman was cinching the saddle, the sergeant rummaged through one of his bags. "The injury list was put together just as I was leaving. It isn't sealed."

He checked through the papers and returned all of them to the bag except one small packet. Opening it, he scanned the column of names.

"Eleven killed, twenty-three wounded," he announced. "At least, that's the count when I left. Should've been much worse, but we sure as hell got the best of 'em."

"What about Harper?" Renno asked as the sergeant started to stuff the packet back into the saddlebag. "Anyone with the surname of Harper?" He felt his stomach roil as the man again took out the papers and ran his finger down the list.

"Harper . . . Harper . . ." he muttered, shaking his head. "No one by that name. No, sir."

Light-headed with relief, Renno strode over to the young man and clapped him on the back. "Well, Sergeant

Cosgrove, you've certainly eased the worries of a foolish old father. I should've realized that Hawk and—"

"Captain Hawk Harper's your son?" the sergeant said, wide-eyed.

"Yes," Renno replied proudly. "He's my firstborn. Both boys are on General Jackson's staff."

"It's an honor to serve under him," Cosgrove commented, then added almost offhandedly, "Too bad about his Indian friend."

Renno felt as if he had been kicked in the stomach. "Indian?" he muttered.

"Yeah, that scout." Reopening the packet, he tapped a finger on an entry near the top of the first page. "Ta . . . na . . ." He struggled with the pronunciation, then managed an awkward "Ta-na-wun-da." He gave a bittersweet smile. "They say he took quite a few with him. A real hero—especially for an Indian."

Renno tried to speak, but the words caught in his throat. His left leg threatened to buckle as he struggled to remain on his feet.

Nearby, Cherokee stableman Ben White Eagle had been listening to the conversation. Coming up to the sergeant, he asked, "What happened to Ta-na-wun-da? Was he wounded?"

Sergeant Cosgrove glanced down at the document and shook his head. "Not wounded. He's listed with the dead." Again he tapped the entry as he read, " 'Ta-na-wun-da . . . Seneca . . . chief of scouts . . . killed destroying enemy cannon emplacement.' "

The hickory walking stick slipped from Renno's grasp, and he felt himself falling. He was unaware of ever hitting the ground.

Renno lay propped against the pillows, his grim visage illumined by a single candle flickering on the nightstand. He had hardly moved since reviving shortly after being carried to bed. He looke at his wife lying beside him, her red hair splayed on the sheets, her eyes dark and swollen from a long night's tears, her breath ragged and faint as she drifted in and out of an exhausted sleep. He knew how devastated she had been at the news of her younger stepson's death—knew, too, that she was afraid she might lose her husband, as well. Yet he was unable to take her in his arms and comfort her. It was not, as Beth feared, that he had suffered a stroke and was incapable of movement. Rather he had lost the will to do anything but lie there, staring hollowly into the distance.

Ta-na-wun-da. . . . Is he really gone?

For many years Renno had taken scant notice of the boy. They had been apart much of the time, Renno attending to his business, Ta-na growing up in the Seneca home of his uncle, El-i-chi. During those years, Renno had devoted most of his attention to his elder son—known in those days as Little Hawk—convinced that one day Hawk would assume the mantle of the white Indian. But during the past year, Renno and Ta-na-wun-da had grown close. A special bond had formed, made even more special by the vision and the promise the manitous had given Renno.

As he lay in bed, he recalled the night almost a year earlier when he had looked into Ta-na-wun-da's eyes and had discovered not the moon's reflection but the same light that as a child he had seen burning in the eyes of his father, Ghonkaba—the same light that had blazed forth from his grandfather Ja-gonh and his great-grandfather, the first Renno.

It all came flooding back. . . .

The night the manitous had shouted: *Hush! The sachem approaches! Look into his eyes!*

The night he had gripped Ta-na-wun-da's forearms and felt the rush of blood, the power surging through him, the spirit that came not only from sharing the lineage of the first white Indian but from being part of a line that stretched back to Ghonka and all the full-blooded Seneca shamans before him.

The night of the vision and the promise, when Renno had seen the spirit of the sachem descend upon his younger son and had realized: *He is the one! It has been Ta-na-wun-da all the time!*

And now, tonight, the promise had been broken. The vision was no more.

The empty place within Renno's heart filled slowly with anger. Never before had he felt such rage toward the manitous, toward the Great Spirit, toward God. *Why?* his heart cried out. *Why Ta-na-wun-da?*

The manitous had shown him the vision. They had promised that Renno would not die until he passed the mantle of the sachem to Ta-na-wun-da. But now his son had gone before him. And the manitous remained silent.

Speak! his mind railed. *Why do you not speak to me now?* And for an instant he recalled the words of Jesus alone on the cross: "My God, my God, why hast thou forsaken me?" His shattered heart replied, *It is finished.*

"No!" Renno cried out, bolting upright in bed. Beside him, Beth stirred but did not awaken.

I will make them tell me, he resolved. *They must explain why he is gone.*

With some effort Renno pulled his legs over the edge of the bed. He was not tired, but his entire left side felt even weaker than usual. Still, he managed to lift himself to a standing position. Leaning on the wall for support, he made his way across the room to his dressing bureau, where he painstakingly removed his nightshirt and got dressed. Soon he was moving through the doorway and down the hall, his right hand clutching his hickory walking stick, his left foot sliding along the floor. He no longer looked like the well-to-do master of Huntington Castle but instead had on a buckskin hunting outfit last worn the previous winter on the journey to his Seneca homeland.

Downstairs he gathered a brace of flintlock pistols and a sheathed knife and tucked them behind his belt, then slung a shot pouch and powder horn over his shoulder and shuffled outside to the stables. The sun was starting to rise, providing just enough light for him to find his way through the barn and to saddle his favorite mount.

With the help of a stepping stool, he hoisted himself onto the animal's back.

As he was about to ride out of the barn, Ben White Eagle appeared, lantern in hand.

"It's me, Ben," Renno assured the stableman.

Ben lowered the lantern slightly, looking perplexed as he approached his employer. Only the night before, he had carried Renno from the stables to his bed; he did not expect to see him up and about, let alone on horseback.

"Are you all right?" he asked cautiously.

"I feel much better."

"You're going for a ride?" Ben said incredulously. "So early?"

Renno nodded. "And I want you to give Beth a message—but not until after she awakens."

"Yes, sir."

"Tell her I've gone to find out what I can . . . about Ta-na-wun-da."

The man's jaw dropped. "All the way to New Orleans? But you shouldn't—"

"No, Ben, not New Orleans. I'm just going off by myself for a while."

He did not have to say any more. Ben White Eagle was well aware of the many times Renno had gone to speak with the manitous. After all, he was sachem of the Seneca, and wasn't that what a sachem did? Ben needn't understand it, only accept it as common behavior for the sachem who was also master of Huntington Castle.

"I'll tell Mrs. Harper that you've gone," he promised, holding open the barn door.

"Thank you, Ben."

Renno kneed the horse forward and rode out into the yard. With a glance back at his house, he set the horse at a trot across the fields that separated Huntington Castle from Rusog's Town. His left side was still quite weak, and at first he had difficulty staying in the saddle. But the animal had a smooth gait, and after a few minutes Renno was able to compensate and maintain his balance with little difficulty. In fact, he felt increasingly strong as he traveled west.

The sun rose bright in the sky, yet it was still chilly, so he wrapped a saddle blanket around his shoulders as he rode. He traveled for many hours, beyond Rusog's Town and the surrounding forests, beyond the small lake where he had hunted with his grandson, Michael Soaring Hawk. After stopping briefly to water the horse, he continued through the afternoon, coming at last to a grassy plateau overlooking the western branch of the Tennessee River, near the edge of Cherokee land.

Sliding from the saddle, Renno ground-tied the horse and walked across the plateau without the assistance of his hickory stick. He sought out a cluster of boulders that formed a small outcropping above the river curling through the valley below. He had come to this place many times before, and he took his favorite seat on the largest of the flat rocks.

For long hours Renno remained cross-legged on the boulder, his blanket draped over his shoulders, his weapons laid out on the stone before him. At first he simply sat, listening to the churning water, trying to still the anger that continued to churn within him. Then as the sun began to dip, he closed his eyes and chanted the Seneca rites for the dead:

> *"Onenti ton sargon ennya ehtha arguas*
> *hiyargatha tejogegrar.*
> *Onenti sargon argwar nentakten skennen*
> *ginkty then skar artayk. . . ."*

His chant began as a low, throaty moan that slowly rose on the wind, transforming into a piercing wail that poured from deep within him. He continued the chant in Seneca, then repeated it in English:

> "I will make the sky clear for you,
> so that you will not see a cloud.

I will give the sun to shine upon you,
so that you can look upon it peacefully
    when it goes down.
You shall see it when it is going.
Yeh! the sun shall seem to be hanging
    just over you,
and you shall look upon it peacefully as
    it goes down."

There was no body for him to place in the ground. Ta-na-wun-da would already be lying in unfamiliar soil far from the fields and forests that had been home to the Seneca. Renno tried to envision his younger son in a traditional burial outfit. Instead he conjured up an image of his nephew, Gao, buried in a casing of birch bark near the lake of the Seneca, where Renno and Mist-on-the-Water had taken him after his death at the hands of his captors. It had been near there, when Ta-na saved them from those same murdering soldiers, that Renno heard the words of the manitou and recognized his son's true destiny—a destiny that had proved an empty promise.

"Speak!" Renno shouted, throwing off his blanket as he ordered the manitous to appear. "Tell me why you took him too soon!"

The only sound was the brisk January breeze, the only memory an image already fading into the past.

"Damn you!" he cursed, tears streaming down his face. He collapsed forward and pounded fists against stone. "Damn you to hell!"

Through a veil of tears, Renno saw his pistols laid out before him. He lifted one in his good right hand and felt the heft of it, imagining the quick finality it would bring. Slowly, almost aimlessly, he unstopped his powder horn and poured a small amount of gunpowder onto the flashpan, then delivered a full charge down the barrel. Opening his shot bag, he removed wadding and ball and rammed them into place on top of the charge. He pulled the hammer to half-cock and raised the barrel until it was tucked under his chin. His hand shook—not in fear but anticipation—as he fully engaged the mechanism and slid his finger through the guard and around the trigger.

He thought of Beth and immediately forced the image from his mind. He was only fifty but felt like an old man, weak and crippled from the remnants of the bullet in his back. *No use to anyone,* he castigated himself. *No reason to go on. No more reason to live. . . .*

.Live! The word thundered within his head, and he shook it away. *Live!*

"Leave me be!" he shouted, but the word bellowed all the louder, an echo of some tenacious part of him that would not give up life without a fight.

He refused to listen, refused to allow anything to keep him from his destiny. Somehow Renno had proven unworthy and thus had lost something far more worthy than his own life: He had lost his son—his sachem. So now he would complete the journey begun more than a year before, when he had taken a soldier's bullet in the back. By all rights he should have died that day, but he had been given back the breath of life so that he could prepare the mantle of the sachem for his son. And now that dream—that promise—was dust, and Renno would finish the journey he had started. The journey home.

The wind swirled around him, singing in his ears: *Hush! The sachem approaches! Hush!*

Renno shut out the deceitful voice. He grabbed his wrist and steadied his shaking hand, holding his breath as he squeezed down on the trigger.

Look into his eyes! Look into his eyes!

The trigger jerked, releasing the hammer. As flint ignited priming powder, some force threw Renno's hands forward, knocking the gun out from under his chin. The charge ignited with a deafening blast, the bullet screaming skyward less than an inch in front of his face, the recoil slamming the pistol against his chest.

Renno sat in stunned silence, cloying gun smoke burning his nostrils.

Hush! Hush! the voice screamed in his head, in the wind, in the night. *The sachem approaches!*

Was it only the ringing in his ears from the retort of the gun? Perhaps a trick of the wind? A trick of the night?

Look into his eyes!

"But he's dead," Renno whispered, lowering the pistol onto the rock in front of him. "Ta-na-wun-da is dead."

His eyes!

He recognized the voice of the manitou but could not see him in the faint, fading light. He blinked his eyes against the darkness, struggling ·to see something, anything, but no image emerged. He half expected Ta-na to come walking out of the distance. Instead there was only the same tormenting chant.

Hush! The sachem approaches!
Hush! The sachem approaches!

The manitous were playing with him; he would abide their trickery no longer. With a furious oath, he snatched up his knife and jerked it from its sheath. He flailed at the air in front of him, cursing his ancestors, the manitous, the Master of Life. He lashed out at the dark, unseen forces, damning them for bestowing the vision and then wrenching it so brutally from his heart.

He could bear the pain no longer and would tear it away, lay it to a final rest right here on this ground.

Turning the blade toward himself, he drew it from left to right, ripping open his buckskin shirt and carving a long gash along his chest. He felt the sting of steel, the warm rush of blood. And he smiled.

The sachem approaches! Look into his eyes!

"Yes!" he shouted, slashing back and forth across his chest, laying open long ridges of flesh. Rivulets of blood oozed down his belly and pooled on the stone beneath him. He shouted and slashed and cursed until his arm grew weary and his vision clouded over. He held the knife in front of him, willing himself to drive it into his heart. But both hands had gone numb, and he heard metal clatter against stone. He could no longer feel the boulder beneath him, and he spread his arms and let himself fall, fly, finish the journey home.

Six

Ma-ton-ga sat on the bed in the glow of an oil lamp, holding Little Gao and trying not to look through the open doorway at the boy's mother. Mist-on-the-Water had been drinking almost continually since early that morning, when Beth had come to tell them of Ta-na-wun-da's death. Now she was hunched over the table in the main room of the cabin, her head resting on her left arm, her right hand clutching an overturned, empty bottle. Her breath was ragged and shallow, and Ma-ton-ga could not tell if she was awake or had passed out again. But then her hand shifted, knocking the bottle to the floor, and she did not stir when it shattered against the plank floor.

Little Gao jerked slightly at the crashing noise, then dozed off again. After gingerly tucking him under the covers, Ma-ton-ga padded out into the other room and gathered up the shards of glass. She disposed of them, then stood for a long moment looking down at her younger friend. She did not approve of Mist-on-the-Water's drinking, which had increased noticeably since Ta-na-wun-da had left with the militia. Now, with the news of his death,

Mist-on-the-Water was doing her best to bury herself in the bottle.

Ma-ton-ga could not really blame her this time, and in fact she had been tempted to share the whiskey. But she knew that someone had to care for Little Gao. While ideally that person should have been his mother, the responsibility had increasingly fallen to Ma-ton-ga. Furthermore, Ta-na's death affected Mist-on-the-Water much more deeply. It was true that Ta-na was a friend to them both, but Ma-ton-ga could see within Mist-on-the-Water's heart and understood what the younger woman would not admit to herself—that she had fallen desperately in love with Ta-na.

Ma-ton-ga understood such love, for her own heart ached for Ta-na's older brother. And while she and Hawk had not yet voiced their love, she knew that in time they would walk together as husband and wife. She also knew that if her own dream had been shattered as Mist-on-the-Water's had been, she would most likely be seeking solace in that same whiskey bottle.

Ma-ton-ga laid a gentle hand on her friend's back and felt the rise and fall of her breath. She appeared to be asleep, and Ma-ton-ga decided to risk moving her to the bed. Crossing to the side table, she lowered the wick of the lamp to soften the light, then lifted Mist-on-the-Water's head.

Mist-on-the-Water awoke with a start, flailing out with her arms. It took Ma-ton-ga a few moments to explain to her where she was and calm her down.

"You go sleep now," Ma-ton-ga soothed in halting English as she tried to help her from the chair.

"No-o-o!" Mist-on-the-Water blared, slapping away the other woman's hand. She rose from the chair on her own and stood on wobbly legs, staring around the cabin. It was obvious that she wanted something, and Ma-ton-ga knew exactly what it was.

"You drink all up. All gone. Now time to sleep."

Mist-on-the-Water shook her head violently. Pushing

away from the table, she staggered across the room, knocking into chairs, yanking open anything that was closed. "Where?" she bleated.

Ma-ton-ga came toward her, but the younger woman spun around, swinging her arms as if trying to strike her friend.

"No more!" Ma-ton-ga shouted, throwing hands up to defend herself. She caught the other woman's wrists and forced her to a halt. "You drink enough. Drink no more."

"I'll say when it's time to stop drinking!" Mist-on-the-Water shot back in a surprisingly firm and clear voice. "When Ta-na comes home . . . when Gao returns . . . then I'll stop drinking!"

She jerked her hands free and stormed back across the room. She searched a few moments longer, then strode to the bedroom door and kicked it open. Dropping to the floor, she felt underneath the bed, searching for one of several bottles she had stashed away for just such an emergency.

"All gone!" Ma-ton-ga insisted, following her into the room. "You drink all!"

Mist-on-the-Water turned her attention to a wooden chest at the foot of the bed, forcing it open and tossing the contents—blankets, clothing, and several books—on top of the bed. When a leather-bound volume nearly struck Little Gao in the face, Ma-ton-ga dashed over and gathered him into her arms. He immediately burst into tears.

"Go!" Ma-ton-ga shouted at the other woman. "Leave us alone!" Holding the boy close, she tried to soothe his cries.

"Gao . . ." Mist-on-the-Water muttered, a light of recognition sweeping across her face. She tottered over and reached a hand to her son.

"Go!" Ma-ton-ga repeated, turning away and clutching Little Gao to her chest.

"Give me my boy!" Mist-on-the-Water demanded, trying to snatch him away. "Give me Little Gao!"

Ma-ton-ga pulled free and backed across the room.

Her eyes aflame with fury, she bent down and reached behind a basket in the corner. Straightening up, she held forth a corked bottle of whiskey. "Here! Take! . . . And go away!"

Mist-on-the-Water stared at the nearly full bottle and then at the crying baby in the other woman's arms. She took a cautious step forward, her own arms outstretched to Little Gao, her eyes fixed on the bottle. Her hands trembled, flexing and balling into fists. Then with a pained sigh, she seized the bottle and clutched it to her. Turning her back on her child, she struggled with the cork and finally managed to pull it with her teeth. She spit it to the floor and started to raise the bottle to her lips, then seemed to realize what she was doing and stood shivering, looking trapped and confused.

Ma-ton-ga cautiously circled her until they were facing each other. "Give me," she whispered, gesturing at the bottle with her hand.

The younger woman's eyes welled with tears. She dropped to her knees, sobbing as she cradled the bottle in her arms and shook her head back and forth.

"Gao dead . . . Ta-na-wun-da dead." Ma-ton-ga's tone was soft but direct. "Little Gao must not lose mother, too."

"Mother? He doesn't have a mother," Mist-on-the-Water whimpered, pressing her cheek against the neck of the bottle. "His mother is dead already."

"No!" Ma-ton-ga knelt on the floor in front of her friend. Little Gao had begun to quiet down, and Ma-ton-ga held him so that his mother could see his face. "Little Gao need mother. Little Gao need you."

"Not me," Mist-on-the-Water mumbled, looking away. "He needs you. You're the one he cries for."

"Not so." Ma-ton-ga again offered the child. "Take him. Hold your son."

Mist-on-the-Water's eyes widened with a curious mixture of anger and fright. Her breath caught in her throat, and her face reddened, blue veins ridging her forehead and neck. Then she let out a sudden, mournful shriek. Lashing out with the bottle, she struck Ma-ton-ga across the shoulder, knocking her onto her backside and spraying Little Gao with whiskey.

"I don't want you!" she wailed, pulling herself up and retreating across the room. "Either of you!" She threw her head back and took a long, desperate drink.

Little Gao burst into tears again. Holding him close, Ma-ton-ga rose and stared incredulously at her friend. When Mist-on-the-Water kept guzzling the whiskey, Ma-ton-ga turned and walked from the room. Slipping into her moccasins and shawl, she eased open the front door and hurried out into the gathering darkness.

As her eyes adjusted to the thin moonlight, Ma-ton-ga moved cautiously through Rusog's Town, her thoughts on her friend back at the cabin. Her shoulder ached where the bottle had struck, and she could not help but wonder if Mist-on-the-Water might become even more violent when the whiskey ran out.

She continued to soothe the boy in her arms, humming a Creek song from her youth.

The boy, she thought, then said aloud in her native tongue, "I must protect the boy. I must protect my Little Gao."

As she neared the edge of the village, a plan took shape in her mind.

Beth Harper will know what to do, she told herself as she sought out one of the many footpaths that led across the fields to Huntington Castle. *Beth will help protect my little boy.*

As Ma-ton-ga returned from Huntington Castle an hour later, a bank of clouds swept in front of the moon, turning Rusog's Town into a land of dark, looming formations. Here and there lights winked in cabins and longhouses. Reading them like a hunter traveling by the stars, she veered to the right toward the flickering light of the cabin she shared with Mist-on-the-Water.

She approached cautiously, uncertain of the condition in which she would find her friend—or if Mist-on-the-Water was even there. Stepping up to the window, she peeked inside but did not see the younger woman. Drawing in a calming breath, she opened the door and entered. All was quiet; Mist-on-the-Water either had left or had passed out in the bedroom.

Removing her shawl and approaching the open doorway, she saw what appeared to be someone lying on the bed. She eased closer, whispering her friend's name, hoping for some movement, some sign that Mist-on-the-Water was all right. There was nothing, and as Ma-ton-ga walked up to the bed, she realized that the mound was not a woman's body but merely the rumpled blanket.

"Mist-on-the-Water!" she called aloud, looking beyond the bed to see if someone was lying on the floor.

Something touched her shoulder, and she jumped. Spinning around, she found herself facing Mist-on-the-Water. With a shock she noticed how red and swollen her eyes had become. She was teetering back and forth, as if it took a supreme effort to remain on her feet.

"Mist—"

"Wh-where?" the younger woman stammered, her breath reeking of whiskey, her hand variously pinching and pawing at Ma-ton-ga's shoulder. Her gaze fluttered between Ma-ton-ga, the bed, and the empty bottle gripped in her other hand.

Assuming she was again seeking more whiskey, Ma-ton-ga gestured at the bottle and said, "That last one. No more."

Mist-on-the-Water slapped her hand away, shaking her head in frustration. "Where? Where is he?"

The young woman's voice was so slurred from the effects of the alcohol that it took Ma-ton-ga a moment to realize she was asking about her son. Forcing a smile, Ma-ton-ga replied, "Little Gao fine. Boy sleeping."

Mist-on-the-Water pushed past her and yanked the

blanket off the bed. Finding it empty, she staggered around the room, looking everywhere.

"Little Gao not here," Ma-ton-ga explained, grabbing her friend to hold her still.

Mist-on-the-Water jerked her arm free, shoving so hard that Ma-ton-ga was thrown against the bed. Steadying herself, Ma-ton-ga raised her hands defensively in front of her.

"Little Gao fine. I bring back tomorrow."

"No! Now!" The rage steadied her voice. "I want my boy now!"

"You drink too much," Ma-ton-ga told her. "Boy safe. I bring him tomorrow."

"You can't have him!" Mist-on-the-Water raved. "I won't let you have him!"

She leaped forward and barreled into Ma-ton-ga, driving her backward onto the bed. Landing on top of her, Mist-on-the-Water grabbed a fistful of hair and twisted violently.

"Bring him back!" she screamed, slapping her friend's face.

Ma-ton-ga was too stunned to resist. Fortunately Mist-on-the-Water was so drunk that the few blows that connected were weak and ineffectual. When Ma-ton-ga had had enough, she threw Mist-on-the-Water to the side and sent her sprawling across the floor.

Getting off the bed on the opposite side, Ma-ton-ga moved toward the door. But as she came around the bed, she was confronted by Mist-on-the-Water, who had managed to scramble to her feet and stood blocking the doorway. Ma-ton-ga was about to push past when she spied something glinting in the younger woman's hand—the blade of a knife Mist-on-the-Water often wore strapped to her leg.

Ma-ton-ga froze in place, waiting for Mist-on-the-Water's next move. The knife began to quiver in her hand as her resolve weakened and the hatred in her eyes slowly turned inward. At last Mist-on-the-Water seemed to real-

ize what she was doing, and she looked down at the
weapon in revulsion. She threw it aside, and as it clattered
on the floor, Ma-ton-ga went to embrace her.

"Get away!" Mist-on-the-Water shouted, pushing
Ma-ton-ga from her. She backed into the main room, shaking her head and sobbing.

"Stop!" her friend called after her.

The troubled woman kept shuffling backward until
she bumped into the front door. She reached up behind
her, raised the latch, and pulled it open. Still sobbing, she
stumbled out into the village, her eyes fixed on Ma-ton-ga
as she backed away from the cabin.

Ma-ton-ga ran across the room and out into the yard.
She called Mist-on-the-Water's name and tried to make
out her form in the darkness. But the clouds had fully
enveloped the moon and stars, making it all but impossible
to see anything but a smattering of lanterns in the surrounding cabins and longhouses.

She stood there for what seemed an eternity. Then in
resignation she stepped back into the cabin, closed the
door, and leaned against it, tears running from her eyes as
she prayed for her friend—as she prayed no harm would
befall Mist-on-the-Water or Little Gao.

Beth Huntington Harper paced from room to room
on the spacious second floor of Huntington Castle, her
anxiety increasing as the evening lengthened. She had
been alarmed upon awakening that morning to discover
Renno gone from their bed. But Ben White Eagle had
informed her of Renno's departure, and while that hadn't
entirely eased her concern, at least she knew he was all
right and in fact had not suffered a stroke as she had
feared. She was not surprised that he would go off on his
own to consult the manitous, but it troubled her that he
would do so in such poor health—especially after the
shock of last night's news.

In some ways her worry for her husband allowed her
to suppress or at least postpone her grief over the death of

her younger stepson. The idea that Ta-na-wun-da was gone had not yet registered and probably would not until Hawk came home alone. Whenever an image of Ta-na arose in her mind, she forced it away, focusing instead on the immediate tasks at hand. The most difficult of those had been her visit to Rusog's Town early that morning to bring the news to her sister-in-law Ah-wa-o, who had raised Ta-na and had lost her own husband and son within the past two years. Beth's visit with Mist-on-the-Water and Ma-ton-ga had been equally difficult, for she knew they looked upon Ta-na as a brother.

Now as evening turned to night and Renno had not returned, Beth felt terribly alone and afraid. Often his vision quests took him many miles from home for days upon end, but in his current condition she did not expect him to go far. And she could not shake an indefinable, desperate certainty that something had gone wrong. But it was too late to send anyone in search of him; she would have to spend the long night alone in the large, suddenly cold manor.

Not entirely alone, she reminded herself, walking down the hall to her grandson's room. The door was open, the lamp still burning within. She had allowed the seven-year-old boy to stay up later than usual and was even tempted to invite him to spend the night in her room. But she changed her mind when she reached the doorway and saw how lovingly he was rocking his old cradle at the foot of his bed.

The cradle held Michael's six-month-old cousin, Little Gao, who had not awakened since being delivered by Ma-ton-ga an hour earlier. Beth hoped he would sleep at least until Ma-ton-ga returned in the morning. If not, Beth would give him warm milk in one of Michael's old bottles.

"I'm helping him sleep," Michael announced, sitting up straighter to indicate how seriously he took his job.

Beth smiled as she crossed the room and sat beside him on the bed. "He looks just like his father," she commented. "Do you remember your uncle Gao?" She used

the term "uncle" even though Gao actually had been
Hawk's first cousin and therefore Michael's cousin once
removed.

"I guess so," the boy said with a shrug. "I think Little
Gao looks like Uncle Ta-na."

Beth choked back her emotions and simply muttered,
"Yes." She hoped to wait until Hawk returned before telling Michael about his uncle's fate.

"Is Little Gao going to live here?" Michael asked,
looking up at her.

"Just tonight, I think. His mother will come for him
tomorrow." She prayed this was the truth. Mist-on-the-
Water had taken Ta-na's death especially hard, and Ma-
ton-ga's description of her drinking did not bode well for
her son.

"Can I play with him when he wakes up?"

"Of course you can. But I don't want you to wake
him, all right?"

"I won't," he promised, turning back to the cradle.
Suddenly he popped up from the bed and walked to a low
table that had been built just the right height for him.
"Will you read to me?" he asked, picking up a book with a
pasteboard cover. Carrying it back to the bed, he dropped
it on his grandmother's lap.

"It's really quite late," she told him.

"Please. Only one."

He opened the book, which was filled with poems
illustrated with woodcuts of children and animals. Flip-
ping through the pages, he jabbed his forefinger at the
picture of large black dog marching resolutely down a
street lined with merchant shops, a pair of metal milk
canisters strapped to its back.

"This one about the milkman's dog. Please?"

"All right," she agreed, stroking his hair. "Come over
by the light." She moved to the end of the bed and turned
up the wick of the lamp on the dresser.

Michael hopped onto the bed beside her, fidgeting

with anticipation as she held the book to the light. He settled down as she began the recitation:

"When Bob does an errand he never delays,
And to play or to talk never stops
In the streets or the squares, and he never once stares
In the windows of pastry-cooks' shops.

"He never complains of the distance he's sent,
Nor sulks at a few drops of rain,
But his cheerful 'bow-wow,' says 'Good-bye! I'm off
     now,
I will hurry home quickly again!'

"If you saw trusty Bob when his errands are done,
How he capers and gambols in glee!
On his broad curly back, carries Nelly or Jack—
None so fond of amusement as he."

As Beth began the final verse, Michael joined in, reciting from memory:

"Some children I know might take lessons from Bob,
If they followed his good, honest way . . ."

Reaching the final two lines, Beth stopped reading and let him finish alone:

"No tasks would they shirk, but work hard when they
     work,
And be merry and glad when they play."

As he concluded, Michael clapped his hands, careful to muffle the sound so as not to wake up Little Gao.

"Will you read one more?" he asked.

"It really is time for bed now." She started to rise, but her grandson pulled at her sleeve.

"Can *I* read one? For Little Gao?"

Beth eyed him uncertainly. His expression was so earnest that she could not help but smile. "You can read just one. But a short one."

Michael snatched up the book and searched through the pages until he found what he was looking for. The picture showed a group of children playing tag, with one boy wearing a blindfold over his eyes.

Michael read the title: "Baby Going to Sleep." He drew in a deep breath and began, pronouncing each word slowly and carefully as he kept place with his finger:

"Hush! baby is going to sleep, girls and boys,
So just now I can't have you making a noise,
But if, till he wakes, you'll be quiet and still,
By-and-by you shall play, dears, and shout if you will."

This time it was Beth who applauded, then hugged the boy to her. "And so you shall play soon enough. But now let's get you to bed. Little Gao will be waking you up before you know it."

Michael reluctantly returned the book to its place on the table, then climbed into bed.

Rising, Beth pulled back the blankets and helped him slide underneath. She started to tuck him in, then halted and cocked her head. "What's that?" she muttered as the knocking sound repeated and grew louder.

"Someone's at the door, Grandma."

"It appears so. Anna will attend to it," she said, referring to Ben White Eagle's Seneca wife, who served as their housekeeper.

The banging grew more insistent, and Beth straightened, her muscles tensing as she stared into the hallway.

"Perhaps I'd better see what they want," she told Michael, smiling down at him. "I'll just be a moment." She started from the room, then glanced back at the boy. "I'll turn down the lamp when I return."

The banging finally stopped as Beth descended the stairs to the first floor. She entered the foyer and saw the shadowed figure of Anna White Eagle in the open front doorway. Someone outside appeared to be seeking entry.

"What is it?" Beth asked, hurrying over.

The housekeeper was engaged in a heated exchange in the Seneca tongue with someone outside. As Beth approached, she recognized Mist-on-the-Water. The young Potawatomi woman saw her, as well, and tried to push past Anna, all the while babbling something indecipherable.

"She's drunk," Anna said, stating the obvious as she pushed Mist-on-the-Water back across the verandah. Mist-on-the-Water swung her arms, her feeble blows glancing off Anna's sturdy frame. Anna managed to grab her and spin her around, pinning her arms at her sides and holding her in place from behind.

"Let her be," Beth said, stepping outside and closing the door. When Anna did not seem eager to comply, Beth came around in front of Mist-on-the-Water, who was squirming and trying to break free. "It's all right," she assured her, holding out a hand. "No one's going to hurt you." She glanced over the young woman's shoulder to Anna. "You can let her go now. She'll be all right. Won't you?" she added, smiling at her inebriated niece.

Mist-on-the-Water's head lowered, the fight going out of her. Slowly Anna eased her grip, finally letting go of her altogether.

"There." Beth reached forward and touched the young woman's cheek.

Mist-on-the-Water looked up at her with eyes rheumy from whiskey and muttered something, her words as incoherent as before. When Beth shrugged to indicate she did not understand, Mist-on-the-Water repeated it again and again. Finally Beth understood what she was saying: "My son! My son! I want my son!"

"Little Gao is all right," Beth reassured her, nodding toward the house. "He's sleeping."

"Give me my son!" Mist-on-the-Water demanded, her jaw tightening with anger. She shook a fist at the two women.

Anna started to come forward, but Beth raised an arm to hold her back.

"Little Gao is asleep. You can take him home in the morning."

"No!" Mist-on-the-Water raged, pushing Beth aside. She started toward the door, but the housekeeper blocked her way. She screamed even more furiously, then lowered her head and charged, taking Anna by surprise as she barreled into her and knocked her down. Dashing past the stunned woman, she jerked open the front door and ran inside.

Anna jumped up, but her ankle gave way and she fell back down. Grimacing, she rubbed where it had been sprained when Mist-on-the-Water knocked her down.

With some effort, Beth got Anna up into one of the verandah chairs. She bent down to examine the sprain, but Anna waved her away, insisting she would be all right. Nodding, Beth ran down the verandah steps to the side of the house. Cupping her hands around her mouth, she shouted toward the stables for Ben White Eagle, then raced back up onto the verandah and into the house.

Beth paused at the bottom of the stairs, listening. She had expected to hear doors banging and Mist-on-the-Water stomping from room to room in search of her son. But all was strangely quiet. Then she heard Little Gao, a soft whimper at first that built rapidly into a full-throated cry. She hurried up the stairs, slowing as she reached the second-floor landing. Down the hall, the light still flickered in her grandson's room, and she approached with trepidation.

Beth stepped into the doorway and halted. Across the room, Michael sat up in bed, tears running down his cheeks, his body trembling as he stared beyond the empty cradle at a dark form on the floor that looked like a crumpled blanket. Moving closer, Beth saw Mist-on-the-Water lying there motionless, her son wailing as he lay sprawled at her side.

A moment later Ben White Eagle rushed in. Beth was

already at Mist-on-the-Water's side, lifting Little Gao and rocking him in her arms. All the while she soothed Michael with calming words, assuring him that Little Gao and his mother were all right.

Ben examined Mist-on-the-Water and announced that she was breathing steadily and had probably passed out from the exertion and the whiskey.

"Take her down the hall," Beth directed. "We'll let her sleep it off in the corner room."

As Ben carried the unconscious woman from the room, Beth brought Little Gao to the bed and placed him under the covers beside Michael, who wrapped a comforting arm around the small boy. Little Gao quickly calmed down and drifted back to sleep.

Kneeling, Beth caressed the sleeping boy's cheek, then her grandson's. She saw the fear in Michael's expression, and again she told him that everything was all right. He seemed to accept her explanation, and soon his eyelids began to flutter. He forced them open, fighting sleep.

Beth's voice was as gentle as a wisp of breeze as she sang the lullaby:

"Hush! baby is going to sleep, girls and boys,
So just now I can't have you making a noise,
But if, till he wakes, you'll be quiet and still,
By-and-by you shall play, dears, and shout if you will."

Michael's eyelids drooped and finally closed. Beth watched the two boys a moment, making certain they were asleep. Then she lowered the wick of the lamp and tiptoed down the hall.

Seven

From deep within a world gone dark and silent, a small point of light grew and took form. Renno was not so much aware of its approach as of the darkness receding, melting into a thin, shimmering haze that embraced a glowing figure. Uncertain if he was awake or dreaming, Renno blinked and tried to speak, to ask where he was and who was this manitou who had appeared.

A voice responded to his thoughts—a recognizable voice, yet unlike any he recalled.

"Rise, for the sachem approaches. . . ."

"Is it you?" Renno asked, his own voice weak and hollow.

"You have seen the sachem. You have looked into his eyes. He awaits you in a land of shadows."

Renno could see the manitou's features clearly now: long black hair, strong aquiline nose, and dark eyes. There was something so familiar about him, and for an instant Renno thought it was his brother, El-i-chi, looking the way he had as a young man.

With a sudden burst of awareness, Renno whispered the name of El-i-chi's son: "Gao . . ."

"You must return." The manitou's lips did not part, for the words flowed not from his mouth but from within. "You must wear the sachem's robe one final time before you pass it on."

"To whom? Who will be the next sachem?"

"You will find the sachem in the land of shadows. When the sun again pierces that darkness, then shall he put on the robe. Then shall your father and your brother come to you. Then shall you hunt at their side."

"But Ta-na is dead. How can I find him in this land of shadows? This land of the dead?"

"A young woman will show you the way. Her heart has been broken twice; she stands now at the edge of the light. Find her before she leaps into the darkness, and then your son shall return."

"A woman?" Renno said uncertainly.

The manitou started to recede, the light swirling and folding around him.

"No!" Renno snapped, lifting himself up, realizing for the first time that he had been lying on his back on the ground. "Don't leave yet, Gao!"

"Make her a daughter to you," came the reply. "She is lost on a path that claimed her mother . . . that has brought death to so many of our people. Only by leading her to the light may your own son's darkness be lifted. Such is the challenge and destiny of the sachem."

Renno reached toward him, but the manitou was fading into the distance.

"Arise! The sachem approaches!"

And then he was gone. Hovering in his place, the moon dipped toward the horizon. Renno looked around, trying to identify his surroundings. This was not the land of shadows, he realized; it was the plateau above the Tennessee River where he had come to seek the voice of the manitous. He was lying on the hard earth, raised up on one elbow, and in front of him was the cluster of boulders on which he had sought his vision. When was that? he wondered. Last night? How many days had passed before the manitou's appearance?

It did not matter, he told himself. He had seen and heard the manitou, but it had not brought back his son—or alleviated the pain. Instead it had left him yet another mystery. Something about a young woman standing at the edge of death.

"Mist-on-the-Water!" Renno blurted. That was why the manitou had come. Gao's wife was in trouble, and he wanted Renno to intercede. That talk of a land of shadows must have referred to a place between the worlds of the living and the dead, and the promise of finding Ta-na-wun-da probably meant that father and son would be reunited in the next world—the land of the good hunt—after Renno had completed this final service.

Renno slowly lifted himself from the ground and stood on numb, weakened legs. His chest burned, and he winced as he ran a finger across the raw, encrusted wounds he had made with his knife. Lowering his arms to his sides, he balled his hands into fists. He saw the world clearly in the thin moonlight, and he desired no more part of it. He yearned to stand once more upon those boulders and rail against the manitous who had taken Ta-na from him. He wanted to open his arms and leap into the abyss toward the dark, churning river below.

But something even greater churned within him: a conviction that Ta-na and Mist-on-the-Water were calling. He did not know how or why, but he sensed their voices reverberating within him, and he could not turn his back on them. He could not complete his journey until he discovered what they were saying and what he must do.

His left leg dragging on the ground, he hobbled to the boulders and recovered his knife and pistols. Taking up his blanket and wrapping it around himself, he made his way back across the plateau to where his bay gelding was nibbling at the grass. He stuffed his weapons into the saddlebags, then took up the reins and struggled to lift his left foot into the stirrup. Finally succeeding, he reached for the horn to hoist himself into the saddle. But the horse shifted and moved forward a few steps, causing Renno to lose his balance and fall backward onto the ground, his foot stuck in the stirrup. The noise made the animal spook, and he trotted forward, dragging Renno several feet before his foot worked free.

Renno was bruised but not otherwise hurt. Muttering an oath, he managed to lift himself off the ground. He turned in place, searching for his horse, but the moon had set and the sun had not yet risen. As he listened, he thought he heard a horse moving off to his right and called gently to it, but the rustling sound grew fainter, as if the animal were walking away.

"Damn you," he muttered, shaking his head in dismay. "Damn all of you!"

Dragging his bad left leg along the ground, he stumbled across the plateau, swearing that when he caught up to the beast he would throttle him—and throttle the manitous, as well.

Renno was not the only one the manitou of Gao visited that night. When Mist-on-the-Water jerked open her eyes, she saw him standing at the foot of her bed. She gasped with recognition and fright, catching her breath as he raised his arms to her.

"Gao!" she whispered, sitting up on the bed.

The sudden movement sent a wave of nausea through her. Her vision blurred, and when she could focus again, the vision had passed.

A dream, she told herself, her eyes welling with tears. *Only a dream.*

Lying back down, she rolled onto her side and looked toward where her son would be sleeping on the padded mat beside her bed. When she saw neither him nor the mat, she raised herself on one elbow and peered blearily at her surroundings in the faint light of a lamp that had been left burning beside the bed. Everything looked unfamiliar, and she struggled to remember where she was and how she had gotten there. Slowly it came back to her—the drinking, the fight with Ma-ton-ga, and how she had run off in search of her child. She recalled nothing more, but as she looked around her, she began to recognize where she was.

Huntington Castle, she told herself with a nod. Apparently she had come searching for Little Gao and probably had passed out from the whiskey. A wave of shame flooded through her, and she fell back against the pillows. Above, the flickering lamplight danced across the ceiling. Below, the bed felt as if it were dancing, too, and she had to grip her roiling stomach to keep from throwing up.

Moaning, she slid her legs over the side of the bed and lifted herself to a sitting position. She sat waiting for the world to stop spinning, forcing her breath to slow down, trying to calm the jumble of thoughts in her mind. Images of the past day came rushing back, and slowly she recalled not just the drinking and fighting but the reason for it all.

"Ta-na . . ." she sighed, the tears flowing again as she lowered her face into her hands.

"Ta-na-wun-da," came the reply. The name repeated in her mind and in the air around her.

Raising her head, Mist-on-the-Water looked around. She heard the name yet again and turned toward the sound. There he was, her beloved husband, calling to her from just inside the window.

"Ta-na-wun-da," he said once more, raising his arm and pointing through the window into the distance beyond.

She followed his arm and saw only blackness, only night.

"He waits for you. . . . Go to him. . . . Walk at his side. . . ."

Mist-on-the-Water tried to speak, but the words caught in her throat. Slowly she rose from the bed and took a few faltering steps toward the vision. But as she approached, the manitou retreated until it passed through the closed window and hovered just outside.

"Don't go!" she begged. "Please don't leave me, Gao!"

"Go to him. . . . Walk at his side. . . ."

"Don't!" she blurted as the vision faded. Running forward, she reached out to him, clutching at the air, her hands banging against glass. She could see Gao receding into a faint glowing mist as she struggled in vain to open the window. The manitou disappeared; the mist was gone. She stood sobbing, her palms pressed against the panes of glass.

For long minutes Mist-on-the-Water did not move. But as she stared into the night, she slowly grew calmer until at last she pushed herself from the window and turned. Though still unsteady on her feet, she felt stronger, and she walked to the dresser and raised the wick of the lamp. As the room filled with light, she confirmed that she was alone, then glanced down to see that she had been put to bed in her clothes.

Ta-na . . . I must go to Ta-na, she told herself, uncertain how to begin. Drawing in a calming breath, she picked up the lamp and quietly left the room.

As she made her way down the hall, fleeting images came back to her. She remembered some sort of fight on the verandah and then racing up the stairs. After that, everything was a blur. But now as she approached the doorway to Michael Soaring Hawk's room, she slowed her pace, feeling a curious shudder in her heart.

"Little Gao," she whispered, knowing with certainty that her boy was in that room.

Turning, she passed through the doorway and stood in the middle of the room, lamp raised in her hand as she gazed at Michael, asleep on the bed. She noticed his old cradle at the foot of the bed and moved toward it, her breath catching in her chest. But the cradle was empty.

She was about to leave the room when Michael stirred. Anxious not to wake him, she lowered the lamp and waited for him to settle back down. And then she saw a little boy cradled in the bigger boy's arm.

My son!

Mist-on-the-Water hurried forward and stood looking down at the sleeping baby. His eyelids were fluttering, and he sucked gently on the back of his hand, as if dreaming about nursing. Placing the lamp on the dresser, she knelt beside the bed and reached for her son but held back before her fingers touched him. Little Gao looked so peaceful lying in Michael's arms, like a child under the protection of his older brother. She wanted to pick him up and take him away with her, but something stayed her hand. She did not even know if she was going on a long journey or only as far as the next bottle of whiskey. One part of her yearned to hold her son close, but another shouted that he was happy and safe and that she must leave him here and never look back.

Fighting the tears, Mist-on-the-Water rose and took up the lamp. Turning away from the bed and her son, she walked out into the hall and down the stairs to the foyer. She reached for the front door, her hand trembling, her heart aching. She started to turn back, then stood immobile, torn between her son upstairs and the darkness outside.

Help me! she begged, yearning for Gao to return and show her the path to take. As she stood there, unable to move, she caught sight of the open doorway that led into the formal parlor. Another voice called to her, promising clarity, offering an answer. Without conscious awareness, she began to walk toward that doorway. As she passed through it, the golden lamplight sparkled across facets of crystal sitting like a cluster of jewels against one wall.

She hardly felt herself moving; it was as if the jewels were coming toward her. And then she was reaching out, taking them in her hand, pouring nectar from one crystal to another, raising the jeweled goblet to her lips.

"No!" she exclaimed, slapping the glass back onto the side table. She stared back and forth between it and the decanters of whiskey, sherry, and rum. "You can't," she whispered, closing her eyes and walking back across the room.

She made it only halfway before the pull, the voices, grew too strong. The lamp shook in her hand, and she had to grasp her wrist to keep from dropping it.

"One," she promised, her lips quirking into a small, self-deceiving smile. "Just one to steady myself."

She found herself back at the side table, decanter in one hand and goblet in the other. She raised the glass to her lips, thrilling as the warm liquid poured down her throat, drowning all doubt. After draining the glass, she refilled it and drank greedily, then put aside the glass in favor of the decanter itself—all the while telling herself she needed only to calm her nerves and then be on her way.

The job was not finished until the decanter was empty and her indecision gone, replaced with the sure courage of whiskey. Snatching up the lamp, she sauntered from the room and back through the foyer. She did not hesitate as she climbed the stairs to the second-floor bedroom where Little Gao was sleeping. Resting the lamp on the floor, she pulled back the blankets and lifted her son into her arms.

"Shh, little one," she hushed, holding him against her breast.

He squirmed but did not wake up as she snatched up the lamp and moved out into the hall. She almost stumbled on the steps but caught her balance and continued down to the foyer. She started toward the front door, then thought better of it and entered the parlor, where she traded the lamp for a full, corked bottle of rum. Placing Little Gao on a sofa, she searched the room and gathered up a few items—a small serving tray, a pair of candlesticks, a set of spoons—all made of silver. Removing a silk runner from one of the side tables, she placed the items in the center and carefully folded and knotted the cloth.

Gathering up the bundle, the bottle of rum, and her

child, Mist-on-the-Water strode through the foyer and out the front door to the verandah. She stood a moment looking out across the fields. No lights winked from Rusog's Town, but she could see the line of lodges in the faint predawn light. Turning to the east, she saw the sky lightening and knew the sun would soon rise.

She hurried down the verandah steps, then circled the manor house to the stables. Leaving her son and her supplies on top of a pile of hay outside, she let herself into the barn and felt her way down the stalls. It was extremely dark, but she had been there often and knew which stall held her favorite horse, a gentle but fleet gray mare named Ononta. Reaching up along the wall, she removed the bridle from its peg and entered the stall. She eased the bit into the animal's mouth, then led it outside.

She considered riding bareback, then thought better of it and returned to the barn, reemerging a minute later with an old but serviceable saddle, a pair of blankets, and a set of saddlebags. She threw one blanket over the horse's back, added the saddle, and cinched it in place. Gathering up the bundle of silver and the bottle of rum, she stuffed them into the saddlebags and fastened them behind the saddle. Then she wrapped the second blanket around her son.

Little Gao was waking now, searching for his nurse. Cradling him in her arms, she whispered, "I'll feed you soon. I promise." Then she took hold of the saddle with her free hand and lifted herself onto Ononta's back.

Kneeing the animal forward, Mist-on-the-Water rode away from the manor. She passed between the long rows of pecan trees and alongside the split-rail fences that lined the pastures. She had gone about halfway down the broad, straight lane when she abruptly reined in the horse, uncertain which direction to take. To the west was Rusog's Town and Ma-ton-ga, who would mourn the loss of Little Gao and not understand the reason for her friend's flight. Behind her to the south sat Huntington Castle, which Ta-na-wun-da had once called home. She knew there was

nothing to the east for herself or her little boy. That left
the north, where she had last seen her husband alive and
laid his body in the ground. Surely Ta-na-wun-da, in spirit,
would have gone there, to walk beside his cousin and
closest friend.

"Ta-na . . ." she whispered, listening for a response,
peering into the darkness for a sign.

Holding her child to her breast, Mist-on-the-Water
kicked the horse into a trot, riding swiftly to the north, to
Ta-na-wun-da and to Gao.

Eight

Beth Harper hurried from room to room in the big manor, beside herself with worry. Also searching were Ben and Anna White Eagle. But there was no sign of Mist-on-the-Water. Even worse, Little Gao was gone. Beth tried not to show her fear to her grandson, but Michael Soaring Hawk knew that something was wrong, and he, too, wandered through the house, calling out his little cousin's name.

When it became clear that the young woman had taken her son and left, Beth sought out the stableman, who was checking the bedrooms again.

"Ben!" she called as she started up to the second floor. A moment later he appeared at the head of the stairs.

"Yes, Mrs. Harper?"

"Would you harness the buggy? I'd like you to take me to Rusog's Town."

"Certainly." He started past her down the stairs, then paused. "You think she went home?"

"I hope so. Where else would she have gone?"

She followed him down to the first floor. As he went

outside, she turned and called into the parlor, "Anna, will you take care of Michael? Ben is taking me to the village."

Her grandson came running out of the parlor, breathless with excitement. "Look, Grandma, what Anna found!"

He tugged at Beth's sleeve, pulling her into the parlor. As she entered, she saw Anna examining some items near the corner of the room.

"What is it, Anna?" she asked, approaching.

The Seneca woman looked up with a frown. "She come here," she said in passable English. "See." She pointed to a decanter lying empty on its side. A crystal goblet held a small amount of whiskey, and nearby one of the bedroom oil lamps was burning low. "Bottle missing," she added, gesturing toward the open cabinet below.

Michael continued to tug at his grandmother's sleeve until she looked down at him. "Where's Cousin Gao?" he prodded.

"He went home," she told the boy, hoping it was the truth.

"Home?" Anna put in, looking more than a little skeptical.

"She must have. That would explain why Ma-ton-ga hasn't come yet." She knelt in front of Michael and placed her hands on his shoulders. "I have to go to the village," she told him. "I want you to stay here with Anna. She'll make you breakfast."

"Come," Anna said, taking the boy's hand.

"Thank you, Anna." Beth stood. "Ben is taking me in the buggy."

Anna nodded, then turned at the sound of someone knocking on the front door. Before she could respond to it, the mistress of the house had rushed past her into the foyer to see who it was.

"Ma-ton-ga!" Beth exclaimed as she pulled open the door. "Where's Mist-on-the-Water?"

The Creek woman seemed confused as she looked from Beth to Anna and Michael, who stood across the foyer at the parlor door. Turning back to Beth, she said, "See her last night. She run off."

"Yes, I know. She came here."

"Not here now?" Ma-ton-ga asked, entering the house.

"I'm afraid not. Nor Little Gao."

"Little Gao gone? But where?"

"I was hoping you'd know."

"Mrs. Harper!" a voice called, and Beth glanced back through the open door to see Ben White Eagle leap up onto the verandah. "Ononta's gone!"

"What?"

"The gray mare—she's gone," he announced. "And one of the saddles."

"Mist-on-the-Water . . ." Beth shook her head in dismay.

"Looks that way," Ben agreed. "Do you still want the buggy?"

Beth thought a moment, then nodded. "We'll look for the mare in the village. If we don't find Mist-on-the-Water, we'll go to Chief Rusog." She was referring to the Cherokee leader, who was married to Renno's older sister, Ena. "Will you come with us?" she asked Ma-ton-ga, who nodded. "I want Chief Rusog to know exactly what's happened. He can send a search party to pick up her trail."

The sun was almost overhead by the time Renno caught sight of his bay gelding among a bank of cottonwoods along a small stream. The animal was munching contentedly on a patch of clover and appeared to be paying little attention to his surroundings. Leaning upon a makeshift walking stick he had fashioned from a stout branch, Renno approached as quietly as his weak leg would allow, keeping the trees between himself and the horse. Every once in a while the gelding's ears pulled back, his head lifting slightly to take in the sounds around him. Each time, Renno halted and waited until the animal returned to his grazing.

After several minutes that felt like an eternity, Renno reached the first of the trees. He debated whether to try sneaking all the way up to the animal, then decided against it for fear of spooking him again. Instead he gently whispered his name: "Kowa . . ."

The horse lifted his head and took a nervous step back from the stream.

"Kowa!" Renno repeated more forcefully, stepping from behind the tree.

Several more times he called the animal's name, which in English meant Great One. Kowa reared back slightly, then caught Renno's scent and turned toward him. He cocked his head, as if examining the intruder and weighing how to respond. Then he wickered and walked toward his master.

"Good boy!" Renno murmured, patting Kowa's neck and completely forgetting his anger at having been forced to walk several miles on his bad leg. "It's not your fault, Kowa."

He waited until the animal had completely calmed, then grabbed hold of the horn and pommel and, lifting his bad foot into the stirrup, hoisted himself into the saddle. He sat there a moment, getting his balance, then talked Kowa forward, first at a walk and then a trot. He had lost a good portion of the day, and he wanted to be home before dark.

Far to the north, someone else was losing much of the day, though to neither poor luck nor mishap. Mist-on-the-Water was sacrificing it to the bottle. She did not drink so much as to become unable to function, only enough to drown her fears and doubts. Enough to fool herself into thinking there was some purpose to this journey—that somehow her dead husband was calling her to his side.

She had no milk, no food of any kind, and when her son's crying grew more frantic, she sought out a stream and fed him water from her cupped hands. When that proved insufficient, she gathered berries and herbs and chewed them into a paste, which he ate hungrily. A small dab of rum on his lips eased him back to sleep, and she was able to continue her ride, her left hand propping Little Gao on her lap, her right cradling reins and rum.

At midday she rode up to Newby's Trading Post just north of Cherokee land. The owner was out back chopping firewood, and his wife was minding the store. Mist-on-the-Water had been there only once before with Ta-na and Ma-ton-ga, and she was relieved that today no one from Rusog's Town was on hand. She slid down from the saddle, tied Ononta to a post, retrieved the cloth bundle from the saddlebags, and carried it and her son inside.

The proprietress was seated at a long deal table in the corner. She glanced up from her needlework and gave a perfunctory smile, then returned to her work. As Mist-on-the-Water surveyed the shelves and counters, she noticed that the woman kept a close eye on everything she did.

"What're you lookin' for?" the woman finally said, putting down her needlework and rising from the table. She walked to where Mist-on-the-Water was examining some shelves of food, then stood tapping her foot impatiently.

"I, um, have some things for trade."

The woman's brow raised skeptically, and she nodded toward the objects in Mist-on-the-Water's hands. "What kinda things? We don't need any young uns."

Mist-on-the-Water forced a smile, then held out the cloth. She gestured for the woman to open it.

The woman placed the makeshift sack atop the counter and undid the knot. As she unfolded the silk runner, her eyes widened in surprise.

"Silver?" she commented, more a statement than a question.

She lifted one of the candlesticks and brought it to the window to view it in the sunlight. Returning to the counter, she placed it back on the cloth with the others and wrapped the silk around them. Laying one hand on the bundle, she eyed Mist-on-the-Water suspiciously.

"Where'd you steal these?"

"No," the young woman insisted, shaking her head. "They are mine."

"Injuns don't have silver like this."

"It . . . it belonged to my husband," she lied, lowering her gaze.

"Husband?"

"His father is Renno Harper."

"I figured as much," the proprietress replied, nodding. "And you stole it and are runnin' off with the money."

Mist-on-the-Water struggled to come up with a reasonable explanation, and she was relieved when the woman's attention was drawn to the sound of a door opening at the back of the store. A moment later Jack Newby emerged from the back room.

"What is it, Henrietta?" he said as he came over.

"This squaw's got silver to sell."

"Stolen?" he asked, and his wife shrugged. He glanced at the young woman, who kept her eyes lowered as she shook her head.

Little Gao started to whimper, and Mist-on-the-Water lifted him to her shoulder. The proprietor was whispering to his wife without bothering to keep his voice down, and Mist-on-the-Water heard him say, "We can always sell it back to the Harpers and earn double." She pretended not to hear and waited patiently for the couple to make their decision.

"Tell you what," Newby finally said with a false smile. "We'll take this stuff off your hands. But there ain't much market for silver in these parts. Can't give you money in return, but we'll pay in goods, if'n you'd like."

Mist-on-the-Water had expected as much and nodded her approval. Under their watchful eyes, she circled the room and chose a small slab of dried meat, then requested some milk. Newby was about to object, but his wife nodded toward the baby and said she'd fetch some.

She headed outside, returning a few minutes later with a bottle of fresh goat's milk.

"I'd say that makes us even," Newby declared as his wife placed the bottle on the counter.

"That, too," Mist-on-the-Water said, pointing to a sheathed hunting knife in one of the cases.

"Not the knife," he declared with a shake of the head. "You've already too much here." He indicated the few meager items on the counter.

"No. I must have the knife, too." She fixed him with her dark, unwavering eyes.

"Only if you put back some of the food." He started to remove the bottle of milk.

"The milk is for my baby, and the meat is for me," she said. "I need a knife to cut wood for a fire to keep my baby warm." Coming up to the counter, she reached for the bundle of silver. "You give me all of it, or I sell my silver in Nashville."

Newby glanced at his wife, who frowned but nodded. "All right," he said at last, putting down the milk. "But only 'cause it's for the little'n."

He took the knife and sheath from the case and added them to the pile. Then he gathered it all up, carried it outside, and loaded it into the saddlebags. When he went back into the trading post, she took out the bottle of milk and pulled the cork stopper. Cradling Little Gao in her arms, she carefully tipped the bottle to his lips. Some of the milk dribbled down his chin, but he drank eagerly. She gave him only enough to appease his hunger, then stoppered the bottle and tucked it into the saddlebags. Climbing into the saddle, she held her son in the crook of her arm and continued north toward Nashville and beyond.

The sun had already set by the time Renno reached Huntington Castle. He had hoped to ride up to the stables unseen and perhaps even have Ben bring him a change of clothes before making an appearance in the house. But his

grandson was sitting out on the verandah, and he gave a
whoop of delight when he recognized the approaching
rider.

"Grandpa Renno! Grandpa Renno!" he shrieked.
Spinning around, he jerked open the door to the house
and shouted for his grandmother to come quickly. Then he
raced down off the verandah and stood waiting impatiently for Renno to dismount.

Realizing his entry would not go unnoticed, Renno
pulled up in front of the house and eased down from the
saddle. Michael Soaring Hawk was instantly in his arms,
and he gave the boy a bear hug and tousled his hair.
Straightening up, he wrapped his blanket tighter around
himself to cover his tattered shirt, then took Michael's
hand and ascended the steps to the verandah, trying his
best to conceal his limp.

"Renno!" Beth exclaimed as she came rushing
through the doorway.

He could see the worry in her eyes—and the shock at
his appearance. But he knew she would say nothing with
their grandson on hand, and so he smiled and embraced
her, careful to keep himself covered with the blanket. A
moment later, Ben and Anna White Eagle emerged from
around the corner of the building.

"You're all right?" Beth asked, caution in her voice.

"Yes, I'm fine."

Michael was eyeing his grandfather with great curios-
ity. "You look all . . . dirty."

"You can thank Kowa for that," he said with a nod
toward the horse. "She spooked when I was mounting up
and dragged me a ways."

Beth gasped and reached out to touch him.

"I'm fine," he insisted, waving off her concern. "But
how are all of you doing?"

Renno noticed his wife share an uncomfortable
glance with Ben and Anna. Michael, on the other hand,
was eager to speak, but when he began, Beth grasped his
shoulders and said, "Let your grandfather rest awhile.

There will be plenty of time to talk later." She turned to Anna. "Would you take Michael upstairs and help him prepare for bed?"

"Do I have to?" the boy whined.

"Yes, you do. You can see your grandfather in the morning, after you've both had a good night's sleep."

Michael frowned but did not protest further as the housekeeper led him into the house. Before he disappeared inside, he twisted around and called out, "Did it hurt when you fell?"

"It certainly did," Renno replied with a wince. "But it hurt my pride a lot more. Now, go on up to bed. I'll be there shortly to say good night."

Michael nodded and scurried after Anna.

Ben walked over to the gelding and gathered up the reins. "I'll take care of Kowa for you, sir," he said, leading the animal away.

"Thanks, Ben."

"And I'll take care of you," Beth announced, slipping her arm through Renno's.

"You don't believe me, do you?" he said with a mock pout. "I'm perfectly—"

"You are no such thing," she exclaimed. "But it's nothing a hot bath and a night in your own bed won't cure."

Renno allowed himself to be led into the house and up the stairs. Although he did his best to cover his limp, he knew it showed, and he could feel in his wife's tense grip that she was more worried than she let on.

When they reached the bedroom, Renno tried to think of an excuse to get Beth to leave while he changed out of his clothes. But there was no putting her off, and she sat down beside him on the bed and eased the blanket from his shoulders. He tried to turn away, but he could not hide the condition of his shirt—or the blood-encrusted wounds.

"Renno!" she gasped, reaching toward his chest, then holding back in fear of hurting him.

"It looks far worse than it is." He stood and lifted the shirt over his head. "I haven't taken a tumble like that since I was a boy."

"Please, sit down," she urged. "Let me clean it off."

Realizing it was no use to protest, Renno sat back on the bed and waited as she gathered up fresh water, salve, and bandages. It stung terribly as she cleaned the wounds, but he remained impassive, even forcing a smile when she looked up at him.

"These aren't scratches," she said, shaking her head. "How did you—?"

"I got a bit cut, that's all," he said, warning with tone and expression that she should pursue the matter no further. Apparently she heeded the warning—at least for the moment—for she returned to her ministrations and said no more about it.

"I think we'll forgo the bath tonight," she said as she finished wrapping a wide cloth bandage around his chest. "But I want you under those covers."

"I need to say good night to—"

"I'll tell Michael you're resting." Her tone was so firm that Renno knew better than to argue. She went to the armoire and chose one of his nightshirts. "Now put this on and tuck yourself in."

"Yes, Mrs. Harper," he replied meekly, taking the nightshirt. Circling to his side of the bed, he sat down and began unlacing his moccasins.

Beth stood in the bedroom doorway, watching as her husband changed out of his clothes. She never failed to be stirred by the sight of him. But tonight she sensed something different, and it frightened her. She knew he had aged during the past year and a half, that the bullet in his back had slowed him significantly. But it had never weakened his spirit. Now the shock of Ta-na-wun-da's death seemed to be doing what the bullet could not. His limp was much worse, and she noticed the way he favored his right hand and held the left almost woodenly at his side.

And those wounds . . . she thought with a shudder. They were not the jagged gashes that would have resulted from being dragged by a horse. They were deep, straight slices—the kind of injuries produced by a blade. In her heart she knew they had been inflicted in combat, not with a mortal enemy but with himself.

As Renno pulled the nightshirt over his head, Beth backed from the doorway, turning slowly and retreating down the hall. She folded her arms in front of her, feeling suddenly cold, seeking the comfort of a small boy's room.

Michael was still awake, staring at the doorway in anticipation of his grandfather. He looked momentarily dejected upon seeing Beth, then brightened and lifted himself on one elbow. "Is Grandpa coming?" he asked eagerly, looking beyond Beth. "Will he tell us about the horse?"

Beth sat beside him and squeezed his shoulder. "He'll tell you all about it in the morning," she promised. "But tonight I'm afraid he's a little tired."

Michael frowned. "Isn't he coming to say good night?"

"He wanted to, but I told him he had to lie down. Just like you." She eased the boy back onto his pillow.

He did not question her statement. It was apparent that he accepted it as the prerogative of grandmothers to tell boys—even full-grown boys like Grandpa—what they must do.

"Can I go see him when I wake up?" he asked, looking up at her expectantly.

"Only if the sun is up. And I don't want you to wake him if he's asleep."

"Yes, ma'am," he muttered with a sigh. He rolled onto his side and closed his eyes.

"Michael, I want to speak with you about something."

The boy opened his eyes cautiously, as if fearing some sort of directive he did not want to hear.

"Can you keep a secret, Michael?"

His expression lightened considerably. "What se-cret?" he asked, lifting himself up off the pillow.

"We have to keep it just between the two of us."

"And Grandpa?"

"No, not even Grandpa. You see, our secret concerns him."

Michael drew his finger across his chest in an *X* and whispered, "Our secret, Grandma."

"Good." She paused, gathering her thoughts, then began, "It's about your cousin."

"Little Gao?"

"Yes. And his mother. Remember when he slept in your room?" she asked, and he nodded. "And do you re-member when Mist-on-the-Water came to see him?"

"When she got sick on the floor?"

Beth suppressed a smile. "That's right."

"And ran away?" he added. "And stole Little Gao?"

"She didn't steal him. He's her son. She just took him home."

"But, Grandma, you said she didn't go home."

"I know, Michael. It's . . . well, it's a bit compli-cated."

"Compli . . . ?" He struggled with the word.

"Hard to explain. Yes, she left without telling anyone, and we're not sure where she went. But she's fine. Proba-bly visiting friends, that's all."

"Maybe Grandpa knows where she went," he sug-gested.

"No, he doesn't. And that's where the secret comes in." She leaned toward him and took his hands. "Michael, your grandfather isn't feeling very well."

"He's sick, like Little Gao's mother?"

"Well, not like her. But he's not well. That can hap-pen when people get older. And right now he needs to get lots of rest. Do you understand?"

"I won't jump on him, I promise."

"Good." She gave him a hug. "But there's something else I want you to do. I want you to keep a secret about

Little Gao and Mist-on-the-Water. I don't want you to tell him that Little Gao spent the night here in your room. Or that his mother came and took him away."

"Why not?"

"It would worry him. And even worse, he might ride off again and try to find her. That could make him sicker."

"I won't tell."

"That's my boy. Your great-uncle Chief Rusog already sent some of his friends to bring her home, so the best thing is for your grandfather to stay here, where he can rest up and play with you."

Michael drew his hand across his lips. "Our secret, Grandma. All locked up." He pretended to turn a key in a lock.

She gave him another hug and kissed his forehead. Rising from the bed, she turned down the lamp and started from the room.

"Grandma?" he called after her.

"Yes, Michael?"

"Is Little Gao all right?"

Her heart caught, but she forced calm into her voice. "He's fine, Michael. He's perfectly fine."

"Good," the boy replied, pulling the blankets to his chin and rolling over.

Nine

After a full day's rest, Renno felt remarkably better, his left side stronger and less numb. He suspected this relief might be only temporary, as in the past. The physician in Nashville had warned him that symptoms would come and go, that his condition could worsen at any moment and leave him permanently paralyzed or worse. He understood that was the reason Beth tried so hard to get him to moderate his activities. But it was precisely this fear of being paralyzed—not so much physically as mentally and emotionally—that kept him from fully complying.

The second morning after returning to Huntington Castle, Renno decided he had lain in bed long enough. He waited until Beth went downstairs, then rose and began to dress. He was putting on his boots when his grandson appeared in the doorway, a pair of books tucked under his arm.

"You're up!" Michael Soaring Hawk exclaimed. "Grandma told me not to bother you."

"You're never a bother," Renno declared, smiling at the boy. "How about helping with my boots?"

Michael hurried across the room and dropped the books on the bed. Kneeling in front of his grandfather, he grabbed one of the boots and tried to yank it up Renno's leg. Renno pretended to struggle and finally let his foot slip into place. They repeated the process with the other boot.

"Will you read to me, Grandpa?" the boy asked, picking up a book.

Renno walked to the dresser and picked out a shirt. "How about reading to me while I finish dressing?"

"All right." Michael climbed up on the bed and spread the book open in front of him. Marking his place with his finger and carefully sounding out each word, he read:

> "John is a good groom. He is very kind to his master's horses. 'If you please, John, will you give the horses a good feed of corn?' his master asks. 'Oh, yes, I will give them a good breakfast. They have to work very hard, and it would be cruel not to feed them well.' Is not John a good groom?"

Michael looked up from the book. "What's a groom, Grandpa?"

"Someone who feeds and exercises horses," Renno replied, lacing his shirt.

"Like Ben?"

"That's right. On a big plantation, there might be a stablemaster in charge of all the horses, a groom to clean and exercise them, and even a trainer. We don't have so many horses, so Ben is stablemaster, groom, and trainer all in one." He examined himself in the mirror, then turned to the boy. "Would you like to take one of the horses for a ride?"

"Grandma said you shouldn't be riding," Michael said, his gaze fixed on the book as he flipped through the pages.

"She worries too much. But she's usually right. I'll have Ben ride you around, and I'll come outside and watch."

"All right," Michael declared with a broad grin. He slapped shut the book and slid off the bed. "Do I have to ride one of the ponies? Can't I ride Kowa?"

Renno hesitated. "Not today, I don't think. Kowa doesn't like others to ride him. When I'm feeling stronger, we'll take him out together." Seeing his grandson's dejected pout, he quickly added, "You don't have to ride one of the ponies if you don't want. Some of the horses are more gentle than Kowa, like the gray mare."

"I can't ride Ononta," Michael said matter-of-factly.

"Why not?"

"Because Little Gao's mother—" Michael caught himself and threw a hand over his mouth.

Renno eyed him a long moment, then asked, "What about Little Gao's mother?"

"I, uh, I'm not supposed to talk about it."

"About what?"

"It's a secret. I promised Grandma."

"Oh, you mean about Mist-on-the-Water," Renno commented, sounding as if he knew all about it. "Yes, the secret. She didn't want to worry me, I suppose."

"She said you were sick and we shouldn't worry you."

"She was right," Renno declared, kneeling and clasping the boy's shoulder in his firm grip. "But I'm not sick anymore. Isn't that so?"

"I guess not."

"So it's all right for me to know about Mist-on-the-Water and Ononta."

Michael's eyes widened in surprise. "You know?"

Renno felt a twinge of remorse twisting the truth with the boy, and he tried his best to avoid a direct lie as he replied, "That's what I said, isn't it?"

The boy let out a sigh and replied cryptically, "So that's why I can't ride Ononta."

Renno decided to try another approach. From his

grandson's earlier comments, he guessed that the horse might not be around and that Mist-on-the-Water might somehow be responsible, so he asked, "Did your grandma say when Ononta will be back?"

"When they find Little Gao and his mother," Michael replied with a shrug, fidgeting as if he wanted to move on to some other activity.

Renno felt his stomach tighten, but he did not let Michael sense his fear. Instead he cupped the boy's chin and tilted his head up until their eyes met. "Michael, I need you to tell me what you know about Little Gao and his mother. I want to find them, too, but I need your help."

Apparently the boy's concern about how much he could say had been relieved when he accepted that his grandfather was already aware of the recent events. And since he was used to repeating things numerous times for adults, he simply shrugged again and let it all out in a stream:

"Little Gao slept in that cradle I had when I was a baby, and his mother came to get him, but she got real sick and Ben carried her away, but when I woke up he was missing, and we looked all over, and Ben said Little Gao's mother took Ononta." He drew in a sharp breath and continued, "So Grandma and Uncle Rusog sent a bunch of men looking for them, but they haven't come back yet, so I can't ride Ononta."

"Thank you, Michael." Renno tousled the boy's hair.

"I *told* Grandma I could keep a secret," he announced, beaming.

"You did really fine. Now, why don't you run out back and tell Ben I'd like him to saddle up Kowa."

"Kowa? But you said—"

"We'll ride him together. Then I've got a bit of riding to do by myself."

Renno watched his grandson race from the room and down the hall. Then he strode back to his wardrobe and began laying out his buckskins on the bed.

When he had changed into his trail outfit, he sought Beth and explained the ruse he had played on Michael and what he had gleaned regarding Mist-on-the-Water's disappearance. It proved a simple matter to ferret out the rest of the story, including the young woman's destination. This information had been provided by one of the Cherokee whom Chief Rusog had sent in search of Mist-on-the-Water and Little Gao. Apparently the search party had split up in different directions, with one of them heading to Newby's Trading Post, where the proprietor admitted having seen a woman with a small child, who stopped for supplies on her way to Nashville. When the Cherokee returned with this report, Chief Rusog consulted with Beth, who decided they would not force the young woman to return against her will.

Renno assured Beth that he understood why she had conspired to keep him in the dark. However, he would not abandon his nephew's widow to the streets of Nashville— at least not without trying to convince her to return home—and would set off at once on her trail. By way of explanation, he told Beth, "It is the will of the manitous."

For her part, Beth was far from pleased, but she knew that arguing with Renno was pointless. With a good measure of fatalism she accepted his decision, although she made him promise while in Nashville to visit Dr. Stuart Fass, who served as the city's physician and dentist. Renno readily agreed and went to the stables to oversee preparations for the journey.

While Ben loaded a packhorse with enough supplies for an extended journey, Renno rode Michael around the yard on his big bay gelding. An hour later he was ready to depart. He tied the packhorse's line to Kowa's saddle, then embraced Beth and his grandson. Mounting up, he rode north from Huntington Castle.

Mist-on-the-Water's arrival in Nashville did not go unnoticed. As she led her gray mare through the town's business district, she made an impression on quite a few men, who gathered at the doors and windows or out on the porches of the many taverns that lined the street. While it was not uncommon for the Cherokee and Seneca of Rusog's Town to visit Nashville, it was unusual for an Indian woman—especially a young, attractive one—to be traveling alone. Word of her arrival spread quickly up the street, and she was met by a variety of colorful remarks as she went past.

She avoided looking at the men, who were no different from the saloon patrons who had traded whiskey and coin for her mother's services in Vincennes. She did not want anything to distract her, for she had come to Nashville only as a stop en route to the Seneca homeland far to the north, where she had helped place her husband, Gao, beneath the earth.

Such had been her intention and her desire upon seeing the vision of her husband. But now as she walked through Nashville, her resolve weakened. She wondered if Gao had actually been summoning her—if indeed she had really seen him or if it had been a trick of the whiskey and the night. And what did she expect would happen when she reached his grave? she asked herself. Would he be there waiting for her, restored to flesh and blood? She could not answer these questions, yet she sensed that she and her son would not return from their quest.

Mist-on-the-Water shook away her doubts. *You have set out on a journey,* she told herself. *You must see it to the end.*

And to do so she required much more than her remaining strip of jerky and the single bottle of milk, which she had managed to refill at a farm just outside Nashville. She needed warmer clothing and supplies. She knew but one way for a Potawatomi woman to obtain these things— a path made all too familiar by her mother. She shuddered at the idea, then forced down her disgust and fear. Gao and Ta-na were gone and had taken her heart with them. She could be defiled no further.

"Running Mink . . ." she whispered, calling to her mother for strength.

She walked over to one of the taverns and tied the mare to the hitch rail. This establishment appeared quieter than the others; there was only one patron out on the porch, and he seemed too inebriated to be of much concern. She glanced up at the sign—THE MOCKINGBIRD SALOON—but could only guess what the strange letters meant from the picture of a bird beside the words.

Little Gao was strapped to her back in a makeshift pack she had fashioned from a blanket. He was awake and seemed content to wave his hands at the people and animals on the street, all the while making cooing sounds as if trying to speak. Mist-on-the-Water rummaged through the saddlebags, then reached up and handed him the remaining strip of jerky. Clenching it in his fist, he eagerly stuffed the end into his mouth and began to suck.

Mist-on-the-Water mounted the steps to the porch and walked past the drunken man, who looked at her questioningly but did not speak. Pushing open the door, she entered the saloon. It was dark and smoky inside, but she noticed a pair of men playing cards in one corner and another at the bar nursing a half-empty glass. The barkeep was a burly gent with a handlebar mustache and only a fringe of curly hair.

She approached the bar, keeping her distance from the man with the drink. She saw him eyeing her with some surprise and apparent pleasure. The bartender, on the other hand, paid little attention as he continued wiping a row of glasses laid out on the counter. Finally he put down his cloth and sidled over to where she stood. He glanced at the child on her back and frowned.

"Want something?" he mumbled.

"I want whiskey," she replied.

He looked at her skeptically. "Got any coin?"

She shook her head and looked away. Grumbling something under his breath, he turned his back on her and returned to his duties.

"Give the pretty lassie a shot," the patron at the counter called out in a thick burr.

"You can buy her one, if you want," the barkeep replied.

"Hell, I kin hardly pay for this'n." Lifting the glass to his lips, the Scotsman tossed it back, draining it completely.

"This ain't no charity ward, McTeague," the barkeep muttered, taking up his cloth again.

"You dinna want her goin' o'er to Morty's, d'ye? Why, a fine filly like this'n will bring in plenty o' folks, mark me words." As if on cue, the door pushed open and a pair of men strode into the tavern. "See?" McTeague nodded at the new customers as they came up to the bar.

"Who's the new girl you hired, Samuel?" one of the men asked, eyeing Mist-on-the-Water with evident approval. Like his friend, he was wearing a dark suit with matching waistcoat and appeared to be a businessman.

"She ain't one of my girls," the barkeep replied.

The man chuckled. "Course not. Hell, you haven't got any girls." He glanced around the room. "Nor any customers worth speaking about." He turned to his companion. "Isn't that right? They're all down at the Black Dog, where there's whiskey and women aplenty."

Samuel approached and placed a glass on the bar. "Then what're you doing here, Hanrahan?"

"Just thought I'd see if the little lady was lost." He turned to Mist-on-the-Water. "I'll take you down to Morty's Black Dog, if you'd like."

"Here's that drink you wanted, ma'am," Samuel cut in before Mist-on-the-Water could reply. He filled the glass halfway and pushed it toward her, then shot an annoyed glance at the man named Hanrahan. "She don't need Morty. She's fine right here."

Again Hanrahan chuckled. "She'd be a whole lot finer upstairs, wouldn't you say?" He reached into his waistcoat pocket and withdrew a pair of silver coins. One he pressed down onto the bar and pushed toward Samuel. "For the room upstairs," he explained, nodding upward. He held the second coin toward the woman. "And this one, pretty lady, is for you." When she hesitated, he added, "Go on, take it."

Mist-on-the-Water stared a moment at the coin, then abruptly pushed his hand away and snatched up the glass of whiskey. She downed it in a single gulp, then slapped it back onto the counter.

Steeling herself, she turned to Hanrahan and announced, "Not silver. I want gold."

Obviously taken aback, Hanrahan looked her up and down, then turned to the other patrons. The cardplayers had put aside their game and come over to see what was happening, and several other men were filing through the front door and gathering around.

"Says she wants gold," he declared in mocking disbelief. "I haven't had a squaw yet who was worth gold."

Samuel had already pocketed Hanrahan's money and must have decided Mist-on-the-Water was a worthwhile investment, for he refilled her glass—this time to the top. He watched with amused appreciation as she downed it almost as quickly as she had the first.

"Forget her," Hanrahan's partner suggested, tugging at his arm.

"Pay the lassie her gold," McTeague prodded. "Hell, ye have eno' in them pockets t'see us all to a throw." He leered at Mist-on-the-Water. "Would ye like tha', lassie? If'n ye take us all upstairs, there'll be gold aplenty for ye t'feed the li'l bairn."

"You can have her when I'm finished," Hanrahan told the Scotsman. "But you'll have to pay her yourself." He stuffed the silver coin back into his waistcoat pocket and pulled out a gold one, which he held out to Mist-on-the-Water. "I'll give you your price. But if you aren't worth it, the second throw's for free."

He grabbed her forearm and pulled her toward the side of the room, where a narrow staircase led to the upper floor. She went a few feet, then jerked her arm free

and walked ahead of him. Reaching the stairs, she started
up but halted on the second step. Turning, she looked
across the room at the leering faces of the men, then down
at the man who had paid for her, and finally at the coin in
her hand. At her back, Little Gao started to whimper, and
she realized he had dropped the jerky near the foot of the
stairs. Stepping back down, she knelt and retrieved it,
brushing it off before handing it to her son.

"Come," Hanrahan snapped as he pushed past her
and started up the stairs.

Mist-on-the-Water turned to follow but found herself
unable to take the first step. She stared down at the gold
coin, suddenly feeling dirty and ashamed.

"Gao . . ." she whispered, telling herself that it did
not matter what this crude man did to her body, so long as
she earned enough to make the journey back to her husband's grave. But despite the drinks at the bar, her head
was much clearer now, and she knew that Gao would not
want her to come to him this way.

"Get over here!" Hanrahan demanded, reaching for
her as he descended the stairs.

"No . . ." she muttered, shaking her head and backing away.

"I paid you!" he blared, rushing foward to grab her.

Still clutching the coin, Mist-on-the-Water spun
around and ran right into the Scotsman, who was sided by
several other patrons. He chortled as he grabbed hold of
her and spun her back around.

"Bitch!" Hanrahan spat, grabbing her arm. "Steal my
gold, will you?" Sneering, he drew back his hand and
slapped her full force across the cheek.

More stunned than hurt, Mist-on-the-Water fell
against the Scotsman. She heard Little Gao crying and
wanted to reach up to him, but the others were pawing at
her, pushing her from one man to another.

"Upstairs with her!" Hanrahan shouted, and several
of the men grabbed her arms and dragged her across the
room, the others cheering them on.

"Enough!" a voice yelled above the noise of the mob. "Enough, I say!" The shout was punctuated by a loud thunderclap.

The men stopped in place but still held on to Mist-on-the-Water, who struggled to turn and see what was happening. Across the room, the barkeep held some sort of club, which he had just smacked down on the bar. On the other side of the counter stood a stocky man with a bushy beard. He was dressed far better than the other patrons, who seemed to defer to him.

"Thank you, Samuel." The man nodded to the barkeep, then approached the group. "Having a little sport?" he asked with a conspiratorial grin.

Hanrahan stepped in front of Mist-on-the-Water. "She tried to run off with my gold."

"I think not," the man said.

Coming up beside Hanrahan, he motioned for the others to release their captive. They immediately complied, and Mist-on-the-Water quickly lifted her son off her back and comforted him. When she looked back up at the person who had come to her rescue, she realized with a start that he was the same man who had brought the liquor to Rusog's Town on New Year's Eve. She recalled his giving her whiskey that night but had little memory of anything afterward.

"She took my gold, all right," Hanrahan repeated.

"She dropped it." Victor Coughtry gestured at one of the other men. "He picked it up. Didn't you, Lewis?"

The man named Lewis started to shake his head, then sheepishly produced the gold coin, saying to Hanrahan, "I was just holding it for you."

Hanrahan snatched it from him, then turned back to Coughtry. "She was trying to steal it. So I think I'll just take a bit of what I paid for."

He reached for Mist-on-the-Water, but Coughtry stepped forward and grabbed his arm. "You'll leave her alone," he declared, his eyes narrow slits.

Hanrahan looked genuinely confused. "What d'you care about a squaw?"

"This isn't any squaw. She's a friend of mine." He smiled at Mist-on-the-Water. "Aren't you?"

The young woman stared at the two men, then at the others crowded around her. She did not trust the man her people had named Etutu Ekwa, but at this moment she feared the others more. She lowered her head and nodded.

Coughtry produced a coin and pressed it into Hanrahan's waistcoat pocket. "This was all just a misunderstanding. Why not find yourself someone more willing."

Hanrahan hesitated, but from his expression it was clear he was not going to challenge Coughtry. Finally he patted his pocket and nodded. "Come on," he told the others. "There's a lot better to be found down at the Black Dog."

As he strode toward the door, first one and then another of the men followed. The Scotsman, however, remained at the bar, grinning, as if waiting to see what Coughtry would do next.

"Run along with your friends, McTeague," Coughtry told him.

"I didna come wi' them," he protested, puffing himself up with importance.

"Aye," Coughtry replied, imitating the man's burr, "but ye be leavin' wi' them. Isna tha' so, me laddie?"

The man's smile faded. He glanced across the room and saw the scowling barkeep still gripping the club. "Well, I s'pose I should be headin' on home." He gave a respectful nod. "G'night t'ye, Mr. Coughtry."

"Good night, Mr. McTeague."

Coughtry watched as the Scotsman exited the saloon. Then he turned to Mist-on-the-Water. "I apologize for their behavior. I only wish I'd come sooner."

"Th-thank you," she whispered, forcing back her tears and clutching her child closer.

"We'd best get you out of here."

"I . . . I'll be all right."

"Not here," he replied. "Not alone in Nashville." He gently took her arm and brought her out onto the porch.

"My horse," she blurted as he started to lead her away from the Mockingbird Saloon.

Coughtry walked to the hitching rail and untied the reins. Taking the horse by one hand and Mist-on-the-Water by the other, he headed across the street.

"Where are we going?" she asked in confusion.

"Don't be afraid. I'm taking you to my office. No one will hurt you—not as long as you're with me."

Mist-on-the-Water stared through the glass door at the curious machinery that filled the outer room. She had never seen a printing press before, and she wondered why such a huge contraption was needed to create little indecipherable marks on a piece of paper. Turning away, she examined the office, noting the rich furnishings. The chair in which she was seated was upholstered in black leather as supple as the finest deerskin, and the desk that dominated the room was of a rich, polished mahogany. She glanced at the small velvet sofa against the wall and confirmed that Little Gao was still asleep. Then she looked back at the desk—at the bottle of imported whiskey Victor Coughtry had placed in front of her.

The office door opened, and the newspaperman entered carrying two glasses. "Here they are," he announced with a broad grin as he placed them on the desk.

Mist-on-the-Water thought he would go to his chair on the opposite side, but instead he perched himself on the edge of the desk. She felt uncomfortable being so close to him but tried not to show it.

"Thank you again," she said, looking down. "But I should be going—"

"Nonsense. You must have a drink first."

He uncorked the bottle and poured a generous portion into each glass.

"I really shouldn't . . ."

"That was quite a shock you had." He offered her one of the glasses. "Go on—just a little to calm your nerves."

Lifting her gaze, she saw the lamplight glinting through the amber liquid. She wished just then that she was back in the safety of her cabin in Rusog's Town. *Yes, I must go back,* she told herself. *Just as soon as I calm my nerves.*

She reached out a tentative hand and felt the cold, moist surface of the glass as he pressed it into her palm. Drawing it to her lips, she took a sip, closing her eyes as it warmed her throat and chest. Real Scotch, imported from Edinburgh.

Her eyes blinked open, and she looked up at Victor Coughtry. He sat two feet away from her, smiling as he drank from his own glass. She shuddered, feeling his hands all over her, his body urgent as it pressed down on her. She shook off the image. *No,* she told herself. *Nothing happened. A trick of the whiskey, nothing more.*

"Gold," he said, almost in a whisper.

He opened a box on the desk and withdrew a coin. Leaning forward, he held the coin over Mist-on-the-Water's glass and, before she realized what was happening, dropped it into the liquid.

"I can give you more—a lot more."

Mist-on-the-Water sat mesmerized by the sight of the coin glimmering in the glass. "I . . . I don't want to—"

"Not like those other men," he cut in. "I don't want to buy you. I just want some information, and I'm willing to pay for that information in gold."

She looked up at him questioningly. "What kind of information?"

"I want to know more about the people of Rusog's Town . . . especially Renno Harper."

He took out a second coin and plopped it into the whiskey on top of the first one. Again Mist-on-the-Water stared at it in fascination. Then she raised the glass and took another sip.

"That's the way," he encouraged her. "Just a little to calm yourself. Then you can tell me about Renno."

She took a longer sip, then held forth the glass so he could refill it.

"That's it. . . . Nothing to be afraid of. . . . Just a few questions is all. . . ."

Ten

Little Gao's plaintive whimpers slowly roused Mist-on-the-Water. She felt dizzy and groggy as she lifted her head off the pillow and looked around for her son. Turning toward the sound, she spied him lying on the floor a few feet away, squirming on a blanket between several cushions that had been propped around him. He was drifting in and out of sleep, alternately sucking at the air and crying quietly as he sought his morning meal.

Mist-on-the-Water shook her head to clear it. The room was completely unfamiliar, and she had no memory of placing her son on the makeshift bed. All she could recall was the saloon and those odious men and then being escorted to the newspaperman's office.

Clasping her hands across her breasts, she rolled over and with a start stared at the man beside her. There under the covers was Victor Coughtry, as naked as she. He snored contentedly, oblivious to the crying child in his room. She recalled now how he had plied her with whiskey and asked her questions about Renno and the people of Rusog's Town. It all came flooding back—how the questions had turned into something more. She doubled over, her stomach roiling at the memory of his touch.

Running Mink . . . she thought, trying to conjure an image of her deceased mother. Now Mist-on-the-Water was no better, selling her body for whiskey.

Slipping out from under the covers, she searched the floor and found her dress where it had been tossed the night before. She pulled it over her head and cinched her beaded belt around her waist, then hurried to Little Gao and gathered him into her arms, whispering gently to him. She searched the room for something to feed him and saw a half-empty bottle of milk, apparently fetched from her saddlebags sometime the night before. She held it to his lips, and he drank hungrily, his eyes fluttering open and closed until he finally settled back to sleep.

Placing him back on the floor, she gathered her things, then went to pick him up again. But at the last moment she hesitated. Coughtry had promised her gold, and he had received more from her than mere information. He should at least pay for what he had taken.

She made a quick inspection of the room, but no coins were to be found—not even in his clothing, which lay crumpled on the floor. Growing angry, she considered waking him and demanding payment, but she sensed that she would come out the worse for it. Far better to slip away without being noticed than to risk raising his ire.

Mist-on-the-Water was about to depart when she remembered the hunting knife she had obtained at the trading post. She had worn it the previous evening, and it had probably been removed at the same time as her dress. Dropping to her hands and knees, she searched the floor and found the knife under the bed, still in its sheath, along with the leather thong she had used to strap it to her leg.

Standing, she hiked up her skirt and tied the sheath around her thigh, then drew the knife slightly and let it slide back into place. She was just lowering her skirt when Coughtry yawned and rolled toward her. Mist-on-the-Water froze, watching his eyes to see if he would awaken.

Soon he was snoring again, and for a long moment she stared at him, feeling another flood of anger and shame. Without thinking, she drew the knife and raised it in both hands, wondering bleakly if she should plunge it into his heart or her own.

She realized that her anger was not really directed at Victor Coughtry. After all, he had protected her at the saloon, and he had not forced her to drink all that whiskey.

Her hands trembled as she held the blade over him. *It's me,* she thought, shaking her head. *Me and that damn white poison.*

She was lowering the blade when Victor Coughtry's eyes snapped open and widened with shock. Thinking himself under attack, he let out a furious oath and leaped from the bed, swinging wildly. Instinctively Mist-on-the-Water threw her hands up, and as he barreled into her, she felt the blade slice through flesh.

Coughtry stumbled back onto the bed, clutching the left side of his face, blood oozing through his fingers. He pulled his hand away, revealing a long gash that ran from the bridge of his nose and across his cheek to just below the earlobe. He stared in astonishment first at her, then at the blood flowing down his bare chest.

"I didn't mean to . . ." she muttered, the words dying on her lips. She saw in his eyes that there could be no explanation. She saw also that his attention had shifted to something to her right. Glancing over, she spied it lying on the bureau.

They lunged at the same moment. But she was closer and came up with the pistol first, cocking it as she spun to face Coughtry. He came to a shuddering halt, palms upraised as he stared in fear at the weapon in her hands.

"Put that down," he said, backing away and covering his cheek with one hand. "There's no need for gunplay."

She waggled the pistol, forcing him back to the bed. He sat down and pulled a blanket over his lap to cover himself.

"For God's sake, woman, put that thing down!" he blurted, his voice breaking.

"Be quiet!" She knelt and retrieved the knife from where it had fallen when she went for the pistol. After tucking it back into its sheath, she crossed over to where her son was lying and picked him up, making sure the blanket was wrapped securely around him.

Little Gao was awake again, watching the proceedings with keen interest and babbling in delight. She hushed the boy, all the while keeping the pistol trained on the naked man across the room.

"If it's gold you want, I'll get it for you," he offered, then hesitated, glancing around the room. "It's not here. It's down in my office. Let me get dressed and—"

"Shut up!" she barked.

She moved to the window. The morning was foggy and cold, with a hint of frost on the glass. Wiping one of the panes with her elbow, she glanced down into the street and saw that her horse was still saddled and tied to the rail in front of the newspaper building.

She turned back to Coughtry. "Get under the blankets."

He looked at her questioningly. When she waggled the pistol and repeated the command, he complied, lying down and pulling the bed coverings up to his chin.

She strode to the corner of the room, where a clothes tree held one of Coughtry's greatcoats. Juggling Little Gao and the pistol, she managed to put on the coat, which was much too large but not so long it would get in the way.

Moving to the bed, she pressed the pistol barrel against his forehead for a moment, then backed toward the door. "One move, one sound, and I'll shoot you."

He lay staring at her, blood streaming down his cheek and soaking the sheets.

Mist-on-the-Water opened the door and took a quick glimpse down the narrow staircase that led to another door at street level. She started out onto the landing, then came back into the room. Hurrying to the window, she jerked it open, then snatched up the man's clothes and tossed them out.

"Not one sound!" she exclaimed, waving the gun barrel at him as she returned to the doorway.

Ducking out of the room, she dashed down the stairs, threw open the front door, and sprinted to her horse. She uncocked the gun and jammed it into the greatcoat pocket, then untied the reins and vaulted into the saddle. Coughtry was shouting from above, and she looked up to see the bloody, naked man framed in the open window. He was holding his cheek with one hand and waving his fist with the other as he shouted for someone, anyone, to thwart her escape.

But it was barely dawn, and the street was deserted. Holding Little Gao close to her chest beneath the greatcoat, she slapped the reins against Ononta's neck and took off at a gallop, keeping the sun to her right as she raced toward Kentucky and the Seneca homeland far to the north.

It was growing dark as Renno completed yet another round of the Nashville taverns. He had already traversed nearly every street in the city without any sign of Mist-on-the-Water or the gray mare she had taken from Huntington Castle. A few people recalled having seen an Indian woman, though there was some disagreement as to the type of horse she was riding and whether or not she had a child with her. One man said she had passed through the evening before, while another insisted it had been at least two days. But all agreed she was no longer in Nashville. "Must've gone back to Rusog's Town," offered one fellow. "Perhaps she headed Knoxville way," another suggested. Each time Renno thanked them for the information and resumed his search.

Since it was too late to inspect the various trails leading away from Nashville, Renno decided to take a room for the night. First he sought out a public stable. As he turned the horses over to the hostler in charge, he asked if an

Indian woman had come to the stable seeking feed for her mare.

"No, I ain't seen nothin' like that," the man said, avoiding Renno's gaze as he led the gelding and the pack-horse to the stalls.

Renno followed him inside. "Are you sure? She was riding a gray mare with the Huntington brand."

"You one of the Harpers?" the man asked, and Renno nodded. "I know the brand, but I ain't seen the horse."

The hostler went about his business, uncinching and removing the saddle. He was in his late twenties, and while he did not strike Renno as overly intelligent, he also did not seem dishonest—uncomfortable, perhaps, which raised Renno's suspicions.

"If she left owing you any money, I'd be happy to pay her bill."

"She didn't owe me nothin'," the hostler said with a brusque shake of the head. He seemed to realize that his comment made it sound as if he had seen the woman, and he quickly added, "No, I ain't seen nobody like that."

"Are you certain?" Renno took a coin from the pouch on his belt and turned it slowly in his fingers. "As I said, I'm willing to pay."

The hostler led Kowa into the stall. As he emerged and closed the gate, he caught sight of the gold coin. His eyes widened, and he appeared to be mulling something over. Then he turned away and started unloading the packs from the other horse. "An Injun lady, you say?" he commented almost offhandedly.

"She's Potawatomi. But she speaks English very well."

The hostler turned and eyed Renno, apparently trying to figure out the connection between what appeared to be a white hunter and the woman. "She your squaw?" he finally asked, his lips arching into a crooked grin.

Renno chuckled. "Not quite."

"Didn't think so. Daughter, maybe? Don't mean no disrespect, but you're more'n a bit older."

"Then you *have* seen Mist-on-the-Water?"

The hostler led the packhorse into a neighboring stall and came back out. "That her name? Mist-on-the-Water?"

"Where did you see her?"

The man stood staring at the coin, and when Renno held it forth, he quickly took it and stuffed it into his pants pocket. "Hell, everyone seen her."

"Where?"

"One of the saloons. Not sure which one."

"Weren't you there?"

"Not actually. I was workin' last night." He placed his hand over his pocket, as if afraid Renno might demand the money back. "But I heard some of the fellas talkin' about her."

"Are you sure it was last night?" Renno asked, and the man nodded. "What was she doing at the saloon?"

The hostler's grin broadened. "What else would a squaw be doin' there? Gettin' drunk and earnin' some coin." He saw Renno's expression darken and quickly added, "No offense, mister. It's just what I heard. Wasn't there myself." He chuckled. "Actually, from what folks was sayin', she wasn't earnin' much money."

"How do you mean?"

"Hell, there was those willin' to pay, but I heard that when the time came, she turned tail and ran."

Renno produced another coin and handed it to the man. "Where'd she go?"

"Don't rightly know, but she was ridin' mighty fast." He hesitated, averting his eyes and fidgeting as he considered how much to tell the stranger. Finally he looked up and announced, "I know, 'cause I seen her. Soon as I did, I knew she was the one they was talkin' about."

"I thought you were working."

"Yeah, last night. But I seen her when I was headin' home this mornin'—just after daybreak. She was beatin' quite a trail out of town."

"Which way?" Renno pressed.

"North."

"Are you sure?"

The hostler nodded. "My cabin's on the north side of town, and she almost run me down. She was on the Louisville Trace, headin' for the Barrens."

As Renno considered this news, the hostler began gathering up the various packs and bags he had removed from the horses.

"You wanna leave this stuff here for the night?" he asked as he stowed them against the wall. "I'll watch it personally."

Renno weighed his options. Mist-on-the-Water was a full day ahead of him, traveling north into the rugged country between Nashville and Louisville, Kentucky. But why? he asked himself. Might she be returning to Vincennes, where she grew up? But then another thought struck him, and he whispered, "Gao . . ."

"What's that?" the hostler called. When Renno looked blankly at him, he asked, "Did you want me to watch these bags?"

Renno nodded, uncertainly at first, then more firmly. "Yes, thank you. I'll be back for my horses at dawn."

"They'll be fed and ready," the man assured him, then returned to his work.

Renno emerged from the stables and strode down the street. Could it be true? he asked himself. Could Mist-on-the-Water really be returning to the lake of the Seneca, where she had buried her husband? It seemed a crazy notion, yet somehow it made perfect sense.

He recalled the words of the manitou: *A young woman will show you the way. . . . Find her before she leaps into the darkness, and there your son shall be found.*

But would he have to go all the way to the lake of the Seneca to find Ta-na-wun-da? Was that what the manitou meant? Renno did not know. But he was convinced that when he found Mist-on-the-Water, the answer would be made clear.

There was nothing more he could do about it tonight, he realized. It would be foolish to go traipsing around the countryside in the dark and possibly injure one of the animals. Instead he would take a room at a boardinghouse and get a good night's sleep, then set out on Mist-on-the-Water's trail at first light. If all went well, he would overtake her in a day or two—especially with a small boy slowing her down.

"I'm coming," he whispered. "I'm coming, my child."

As Renno rode from the stables at dawn, he considered visiting Dr. Stuart Fass, as he had promised Beth. However, the physician would not yet be at his office, and Renno did not want to bother him at home. And he felt remarkably well; in fact, there were no signs of numbness or weakness anywhere on his left side. It could wait until he returned, he told himself, turning Kowa and the packhorse north up the street.

"Renno Harper!" a voice shouted.

He twisted around on the saddle and saw a man waving at him. "Two Feathers!" he called, raising a hand to the Cherokee in greeting.

The old warrior came forward on his pinto. Beside him rode a second Cherokee, dressed in similar winter buckskins.

"Tall Grass," Renno acknowledged with a respectful nod. He turned to the first man and said in the Cherokee language, "What brings you to Nashville?"

"Nothing," Two Feathers replied, smiling cryptically.

"Nothing?"

Tall Grass chuckled. Also speaking in Cherokee, he explained, "What my friend means is that we caught nothing on the trail, so we came here to purchase supplies for the journey home." He shook his head sadly. "Three days we've been on the hunt, but the animals must hear the creaking of our bones as we approach. I told Two Feathers we should leave this work to the younger bucks."

His partner gave a mock frown. "When we no longer can hunt, we no longer can live."

"We can hunt. What we cannot do is capture anything." Tall Grass gestured toward the packhorse. "Are you hunting, too, Renno?"

"In a manner of speaking. I'm looking for Mist-on-the-Water."

"Your niece?" Two Feathers asked.

"Yes. She's taken her child and ridden off somewhere. You haven't seen her, by chance?" he asked, and they both shook their heads. "Where were you hunting?"

Two Feathers pointed to the west. "Along the Tennessee River."

"Then you wouldn't have come upon her. She was seen riding north toward the Barrens, probably headed for Louisville or Vincennes."

"A long journey for a woman alone," Tall Grass noted.

Renno nodded, then inquired, "Are you returning soon to Rusog's Town?"

"Later this morning."

"Will you take a message to Huntington Castle for me?"

"What would you have us say?" Tall Grass asked.

"Tell Beth that I'm feeling well and have taken the Louisville Trace. I will return with Mist-on-the-Water and her son."

The two men assured him they would carry out his wishes. Then they said their good-byes, and Renno reined his horse around and continued his journey north.

As Renno rode down the street, Two Feathers turned to his companion and commented, "This is a strange thing about Renno and his niece."

"Mist-on-the-Water is Potawatomi," Tall Grass replied, and they shared a nod, as if that explained everything.

Tall Grass waited in the main room of the newspaper building, peering through the office door at the strange goings-on inside. Victor Coughtry was seated in a chair, with someone leaning over him, examining his face.

Standing nearby were a couple of other men, who Tall Grass assumed worked at the paper.

The Cherokee tried to be patient, but he didn't want to be kept waiting too long. He had left Two Feathers at the general store on the pretext of going to visit one of the few saloons that served Indians, albeit at the back door. He didn't want his friend to find him here and start asking a lot of questions.

He felt a rush of relief when the office door opened and one of the men motioned for him to enter. As he walked into the office, Coughtry pushed aside the man who was examining him. With a start, Tall Grass saw that a bandage covered the entire left side of Coughtry's face, including his eye.

"Enough!" he snapped when the man again tried to touch the bandage. "Here's your fee, Dr. Fass." He searched his coat pocket for a few coins and thrust them into the physician's hand.

"You really should let me change that bandage—"

"It's fine." Coughtry waved him away. "You can check it again tomorrow."

"If you insist." Fass shook his head in displeasure.

"I do. Now, go see to the patients who need you."

With an exasperated shrug, Fass strode from the office.

"That's better," Coughtry muttered. He looked up at Tall Grass. "And what brings you here?"

The Cherokee glanced at the two other men in the office.

"You can talk freely," Coughtry told him.

He drew in a breath. "You say you want know all about Renno," he said in his broken English.

Coughtry's good eye narrowed. "Is there something I should know?"

"Tall Grass just see Renno."

The newsman leaned forward. "Here? In Nashville?"

"He make long journey north to Barrens."

"The Barrens? Why would he do that?"

"Look for nephew's wife. Look for—"

"Mist-on-the-Water!" Coughtry exclaimed, raising a hand to his cheek. "But why the Barrens?"

"He say Mist-on-the-Water go that way."

Coughtry rose from his chair. "Are you certain?" he asked, and Tall Grass nodded. "As certain as you are that Renno will never support the sale of Cherokee land?"

"Renno die first."

"Yes . . ." Coughtry reached into his pocket and produced another coin. He handed it to Tall Grass, who grinned and tucked it into his pouch. "Have you spoken to the council yet?" he asked the Cherokee, who nodded again. "You told them exactly what I wanted you to say?"

"Tall Grass speak your words."

"But they haven't agreed to sell yet."

"Council will meet again."

"And you're certain you can convince them to sell?"

This time Tall Grass did not look as sure of himself as he had when Victor Coughtry had asked the same question in Rusog's Town. "Chief Rusog old, but his voice strong. He say council must meet with Seneca first."

"But it's Cherokee land, not Seneca."

Tall Grass shrugged. "Seneca our brothers. Council will hear their words."

"Renno's words," Coughtry said with a sneer.

"Renno sachem of the Seneca. His words strong."

"Perhaps . . ." Rising from the chair, he walked to the door and held it open. "Go on back to your village and do what you can about the council. As for Renno, I'll see just how strong he really is."

"Tall Grass your voice and ears," the Cherokee said, following Coughtry to the door. "He speak your words."

"That's right," Coughtry replied distractedly.

He watched as the Indian retreated through the main room and disappeared into the street. Then he shut the door and walked resolutely to his desk. Dropping down into the chair, he folded his hands in front of him and sat nodding. He gestured for one of the men to leave but for the other to remain behind. When at last he spoke, his words were both measured and direct.

"Jim, I want you to take a couple of the boys and follow this Renno fellow out into the Barrens." He touched a hand to his bandage, wincing at the memory of the knife in Mist-on-the-Water's hand. "Wait till he catches up to that squaw and her baby. Then I want you to kill him. Kill all three of them." His lips quirked into a smile. "And when you're finished having your fun, bring me that bitch's scalp!"

Eleven

The wind blew harsh and cold out of the northwest as Mist-on-the-Water entered the stark Barrens of central Kentucky. She drew Ononta to a halt atop a low rise and surveyed the landscape. Only scrub brush and an occasional stunted tree remained of the lush forests that had once covered this region. The Indians had burned off the trees centuries earlier in order to provide grazing for the vast herds of buffalo that once roamed east of the Father of Waters. Subsequent droughts had decimated even that grassland, thus earning the region its name.

Since leaving Nashville, she and her son had survived on plants and water and a single scrawny rabbit she had managed to catch. As she sat her horse and looked out across the forbidding landscape, she wondered if they would find anything to eat here, if they would ever make it through the Barrens to the more hospitable country beyond.

Little Gao was listless and silent, bundled in the pack on his mother's back. He had cried steadily the first day out of Nashville. In time he must have realized that such efforts would not bring food and only made him hungrier, and he had fallen into a fitful silence. Mist-on-the-Water realized he might not survive all the way to Louisville, yet she had refused to turn back, pushing deeper into the wilderness, determined to keep going or to die trying.

But this afternoon, here in the Barrens, she felt a surge of fear. She was more frightened, even, than at that Nashville saloon. More frightened and more ashamed. Her head had fully cleared from the effects of those long days of whiskey, and she saw for the first time how desperate and insane her mission was.

"Gao is dead," she told herself, her words drowned by the swirling wind. "Ta-na-wun-da is gone, too."

And what was she doing? she asked herself. Making a futile journey to the lake of the Seneca, where she hoped somehow to be reunited with them both.

"In death," she mumbled, shaking her head. That was the only way she would see them again.

Is that why I came here? she wondered. *Is this where it must end?*

"No!" she exclaimed, kicking the horse forward, down the incline. She was determined to push on, to complete this quest she had begun.

But each step of the gray mare only added to her doubt. She was without food or money, and she could already feel the life draining out of her child.

"Little Gao . . ." she whispered, her heart aching as she thought of him suffering. "Your father . . . I'm taking you to your father."

The wind whipped harder, mocking her. Black clouds rolled in from the west, obscuring the sun, turning afternoon into night. Mist-on-the-Water jerked upright as a burst of lightning illuminated the horizon and sent thunder rumbling across the Barrens. She could not hear Little Gao above the thunder and the wind, but she felt him trembling against her back.

Shelter! She had to seek shelter before the rains came, before the full brunt of the storm struck them out here in this open wasteland. She struggled to calm the skittish mare, twisting in the saddle as she sought a stand of trees, a hollow, anyplace that might offer refuge.

A series of lightning flashes lit the landscape, revealing a stretch of low, jutting peaks that rose from the arid flatlands to the northeast. She turned the horse toward them, slapping the reins and kicking it into a trot. The wind howled louder; the storm was almost on top of her.

Ten minutes later, Mist-on-the-Water reined in her horse at the base of the nearest of the craggy promontories. This upthrust of land was smaller than she had imagined—no more than fifty feet tall at its peak. But one side was a sheer wall, high enough to offer the salvation she sought.

Leaping from the mare's back, she quickly uncinched the saddle and removed it, then yanked off the saddle blanket and slapped it against Ononta's rump, shouting, "Get going! Get out of here!" The animal hesitated, glancing back at her, then pricked up its ears and bolted into the darkness.

Leaving the saddle and saddlebags where they lay, Mist-on-the-Water started around the base of the promontory, searching with each lightning flash for a suitable path. One side offered a fairly gentle slope, and she quickly started up. There were few boulders and little brush to hold on to—just smooth rock and hard-packed earth. But the climb was relatively easy, and soon she found herself standing on the peak.

Though the rain had not yet struck, the lightning drew closer, and the wind whipped the sand into a blinding swirl. Mist-on-the-Water shielded her eyes as she stumbled across the peak. She stopped near the edge of a shelf that jutted out over the valley floor. She could hear Little Gao wailing against her back, and she undid the pack and drew him to her breast.

"My baby . . ." she whispered into his ear as she

hugged him close. "It is almost over. Soon you will be safe in your father's arms."

She tried not to hear his pained cries, telling herself they would end quickly and he would never suffer again . . . knowing that her pain, too, would pass, and she would be forever with the men she held dearest.

"Gao . . . Ta-na-wun-da . . ."

Mist-on-the-Water closed her eyes and took a step forward, feeling for the edge of the cliff.

"Master of Life, give me strength," she prayed. The only reply was the roar of wind and her son's frantic howling.

She stumbled and went down on one knee, and as she struck the hard stone, Little Gao was knocked from her arms. With a scream, she lunged, grabbing at the blanket, feeling him slipping through her hands. But she managed to catch hold of his thin arm and wrenched him to her. She held him close, sobbing, begging him to forgive her.

The first icy droplets of rain struck her cheek, slapping her like the back of a hand. She looked up at the flashing sky and shook her head in anger and despair.

"Help me!" she cried to her husband, to Ta-na-wunda, to the Master of Life. "Give me the strength to make this journey!"

Again she stood, her foot easing toward the edge of the drop. A wave of nausea swept through her, and she struggled to keep from passing out. She heard distant thunder, but a great veil of darkness shrouded her vision. She was faintly aware of the stinging rain, of the hard stone shifting beneath her feet and drawing her forward into the abyss. Sheltering her child against her breast, she moved toward the darkness, toward her destiny. And then the ground was no longer beneath her feet. She felt only soothing wind. Only the voices calling her home.

"He's coming!" a deep voice boomed from the farther reaches of the manor house. "He's home!"

Beth Harper straightened in the chair, the book slipping from her fingers to the floor. "Renno . . ." she whispered, her heart catching.

"Grandpa!" Michael Soaring Hawk shouted, jumping up from the little table in his room, where he had been playing. He raced past his grandmother and out into the hall.

Beth was close at his heels, and when she reached the top of the stairs, she saw Ben White Eagle grinning at her.

"Renno's home?" Beth called down. "And Mist—?"

"No, not Mr. Harper," Ben replied, his smile broadening. "It's Hawk. He's come home!"

"Hawk!" she exclaimed, clapping her hands.

Michael shouted gleefully for his father and almost tumbled down the stairs in his mad dash toward the front door. When he reached the bottom, Ben scooped him up and carried him out onto the verandah.

As Beth hurried down the stairs and outside, she wondered if it could be true—if her stepson was really home from the war. They had learned only the day before of the Americans' decisive January 8th victory at New Orleans, when the British had tried to charge their well-fortified lines. Two thousand British infantry were killed, against only a handful of American losses.

"There they come!" Ben declared, pointing down the lane.

Shielding her eyes against the sunlight, Beth saw a contingent of about a half-dozen mounted troops leading a single wagon. As one of the riders broke away from the others and spurred his horse forward, Beth recognized her stepson and rushed down the steps to the yard.

Michael squirmed out of Ben White Eagle's arms and ran after his grandmother as they raced down the lane toward the approaching riders. Hawk reined in his mount in front of them, and as he leaped from the saddle and knelt down, Michael vaulted into his arms.

"You're home! You're home!" the boy shouted with glee.

"I missed you so much!" Hawk hugged Michael to him. "You've gotten so big!" he added, and Michael beamed with pride.

Beth waited patiently as Hawk held his son close. She saw the tears in his eyes and felt her own welling up. Hawk was home, and he was safe! If only Ta-na-wun-da could be there with them. . . .

She sniffed back her tears, trying to be strong as the rest of the soldiers rode past, driving the wagon over to the verandah.

Hawk stood, gently set down his son, and handed him the reins. "Bring him to Ben," he said, gesturing toward the stableman, who had come down from the verandah to meet the soldiers.

The boy eagerly complied, standing tall as he led his father's horse to where the others were gathered.

"Beth . . ." Hawk declared, forcing a smile as he embraced her. "It's good to be home."

"How did you get here so quickly?" she asked, pushing away so that she could look at his face. "The fighting ended only a few days—"

"I wasn't there for the final battle," he explained. "I left soon after New Year's. After Ta-na-wun-da . . ."

Beth could hold back her tears no longer. "Oh, Hawk, why did it have to happen? Why Ta-na?"

His eyes narrowed in surprise. "You heard about Ta-na?"

Nodding, she dabbed at her eyes. "One of the couriers came through. He told us—" She started to sob, and he took her in his arms again. "Y-your f-f-father—"

"It's all right," he soothed, holding her close.

Forcing calm into her voice, she said, "I—I'm worried about Renno. He took it very hard."

"Where is he?" Hawk asked, glancing toward the house.

"He's looking for Mist-on-the-Water. I think she took it even worse."

"Mist-on-the-Water?"

Reaching up, she touched Hawk's cheek and shook her head in despair. "She ran off . . . soon after she heard about Ta-na. First the shock of losing her husband, and now Ta-na . . ."

"What are you talking about? Ta-na isn't lost. I brought him home." He nodded toward the wagon.

Turning, Beth felt the breath go out of her as a pair of soldiers lifted something from the wagonbed. At first it appeared to be a corpse, the head completely wrapped in bandages. But then they propped him on the ground, and he stood on shaky legs, holding on to their shoulders to steady himself.

"You thought he was dead?" Hawk said in disbelief. "We almost lost him, but Ta-na's strong, and . . ."

She was no longer aware of what Hawk was saying. She pulled away from him and took one cautious step toward the house, then a second and a third. And then she was running back across the yard, calling out his name.

"Ta-na! Oh, dear God! You're alive!"

The sobbing grew louder, more insistent, rising to a full-throated cry—a scream that shuddered through her, rousing her from the darkness.

My son! she thought with a start.

Is this dark world the place of the manitous? Mist-on-the-Water wondered. *The land of the good hunt?* She struggled to see her son, fighting the shadows, searching the blackness. She felt something stinging her face and realized it was the rain.

There is rain in the next world, she told herself. *Yes, this is as it should be.*

But why so dark? Why such fierce, groaning wind?

Gao! she called. "Little Gao!"

His wailing voice seemed so close, and his body shivered against hers. He was pressed against her, his small fists drumming an incessant rhythm upon her chest.

Did I jump? she asked herself. *Are we lying, bodies*

broken, at the bottom of the cliff? Is this what the next world is like?

She wrapped her arms around her son and wondered if it was her body that had moved or merely an illusion. Just now she did not care, and she held him close, shielding him from the driving wind and rain. As she peered into the darkness, a great flash of lightning burst above her, revealing the rocky ground upon which she lay, the storm rolling overhead.

Can I stand? she wondered. Did she even have a body anymore, or had she and Little Gao already donned their spirit robes?

She tried to raise her head, and the slight effort sent waves of dizziness through her. Fighting the sensation, she lifted herself up off the rocks and sat there, holding her son close, not knowing if they were dead or alive. Another series of lightning bursts lit the sky and the valley below, the dark abyss only inches from her feet.

"I'm still here!" she blurted as the sky shimmered with light.

Indeed, she was seated at the very edge of the cliff, where she must have landed when she tried to leap to her death. The life that flowed through her was strong and sure; it would not let go of her so easily. Through her legs and loins it rose, flooding her chest and throat, crying out, "I'm alive!"

Clutching Little Gao to her, Mist-on-the-Water dragged herself away from the abyss. When she had retreated a short distance, she cautiously pulled herself to her feet and stood facing the north—facing the onslaught of the storm.

"I'm sorry, Gao!" she called, the rain washing her tears. "I . . . I can't . . ."

She had tried, but she was not worthy of the task. And now she was standing in the open, the storm still growing in intensity around her. From the gap between the flashes and the thunderclaps, she guessed that the worst of the storm was still several miles away. She had fifteen minutes, perhaps, to seek shelter before it bore down on her and finished what she had been unable to do.

As she turned toward the path back down to the valley, she caught sight of a small flickering light to the east. She cupped a hand above her eyes, shielding them from the rain, and peered into the darkness. The sky lit up again, and she saw the silhouette of another rocky outcropping, somewhat larger than the one on which she stood. The light was at its base and appeared to be a campfire.

Perhaps even a cave! she prayed as she slid down the trail toward the valley floor.

"Ononta!" she called, trying to remember where she had tied the horse. She searched first to the left, then the right, and almost tripped over the saddle on the ground. With a gasp, she recalled chasing Ononta away, convinced that she would need the gray mare no longer.

She pulled the greatcoat around her child, who had calmed somewhat but was still shivering terribly from the cold. As the lightning renewed, she gazed to the east and caught a glimpse of the faint firelight. Gauging the distance, she decided that she could reach it before the full fury of the storm hit.

Mist-on-the-Water set off at once, moving as quickly as the darkness and uneven ground would allow. She stumbled several times but kept her balance and continued her headlong flight. Then her foot caught on something, and she went tumbling through the air. She managed to protect Little Gao from the impact, but the side of her head struck the ground, stunning her. She fought to keep her senses, shaking her head as she pulled herself to a sitting position.

The thunder roared all around them now, right on the heels of each brilliant lightning flash. In the distance, the fire winked faintly, then suddenly was snuffed out. She pulled up short, staring into the darkness in desperation. She let out an anguished wail and fell forward onto her knees.

"Rise!" a voice commanded.

Her head jerked up in surprise. She peered into the darkness, trying to see who was speaking.

"He waits for you. . . ."

"Gao? Ta-na?" she muttered, though the voice sounded like neither of them.

"Go to him. . . ."

A single bolt of lightning momentarily illuminated the figure of an old man standing a few feet from where she was kneeling. A single eagle's feather adorned his long white hair, and he was dressed in white buckskin and held a medicine shield painted with unfamiliar symbols.

The sky lit up again, and this time the man was standing farther away, near where the fire had been burning. Yet when he spoke, his words were as clear and strong as before.

"Walk at his side. . . ."

Mist-on-the-Water staggered to her feet, clutching her son to her chest as she hobbled toward him. She no longer could see him, but she kept going, guided by the memory of his image and the lure of his gentle voice. Several minutes later she saw what might be men and horses near the base of the promontory. She hurried forward, not caring if they were enemies or friends, and ran right up among them. But they were nothing more than scrub pines, so small and stunted as to give no shelter from the storm. In their midst was a pile of blackened brush, the remains of a fire doused by the driving rain. Looking around frantically, she found no sign of the old man and realized with a heavy heart that he had been an illusion. Yet someone had made camp there and departed, taking her last hope for salvation with him.

She dropped to her knees in front of the wet ashes and grasped them in her hand, lifting them to the sky. The rain beat down against her face, drowning her tears, muffling her tormented cries as she railed against the gods, against the manitous, against herself for having too little courage to make the leap into the abyss.

Burying her head against her son, Mist-on-the-Water fell forward on the ground and lay there, waiting for the storm that was to end her life.

Renno pulled his poncho farther over his head and urged Kowa forward. The gelding stamped nervously, almost rearing with each thunderclap, but he obeyed his master's commands and kept moving. Behind them, the packhorse was even more skittish, and Renno prayed he wouldn't bolt and run.

It had been foolish to make camp in the open, and now he had to ride through the rain in search of more suitable shelter. He had misjudged the storm completely. When he had first noticed it approaching, he realized its strength but guessed it would pass to the north, bringing little more than a passing shower to this part of the Barrens. The winds had shifted, however, drawing it straight toward his campsite at the base of one of the outcroppings that dotted the terrain. And as the winds rose and the sky grew more forbidding, he had made a quick search of the promontory but found no caverns or large enough crevices in which to wait out the storm. So he had repacked the horses and headed north, leaving his campfire to the rain.

As he reached the neighboring outcropping and began circling it, he wondered how far ahead Mist-on-the-Water might be. He had been unable to follow her tracks on the hardscrabble ground of the Barrens, and he could only hope that she was following the northbound trail to Louisville. He also hoped she was far enough ahead to be well beyond the storm.

Renno had completed his circuit of the outcropping and was about to ride away when lightning revealed a narrow fissure along the southern wall. He dismounted and walked the horses toward it. There was enough light to discern the opening, which was only a little wider than a horse. He brought Kowa right to the edge, and when the gelding smelled no danger, he entered and found himself in a dry crevice almost twenty feet deep and wide enough that he could lead the horses inside and even turn them around.

Pulling the poncho hood back from his head, he returned to the fissure opening and stood just in from the rain, watching the flashing storm light up the landscape. As he gazed across the valley floor to the outcrop where he had made camp earlier, a curious feeling came over him. At first he thought it was the numbness returning, but it was not confined to his left side and instead sent tingling waves all through him. The sound of the storm echoing through the crevice grew strangely muffled, and for an instant he wondered if he was going deaf.

But then he heard a voice, as clearly as he had heard the manitou near the banks of the Tennessee:

"Your daughter calls you. Go to her side."

Renno stepped out into the open, blinking against the rain as he tried to see the manitou who had spoken. This time it had not sounded like Gao, and he spied a shadowed image that seemed to float in front of him. As lightning illuminated the sky, he saw the figure standing about twenty feet away, an old man dressed in a white buckskin outfit unlike any worn by the Seneca or Cherokee. His right hand gripped a medicine shield painted with stalks of corn—red, white, and yellow—surrounded by curious symbols. It was clearly a spirit, for each time the sky lit up, Renno could see right through him.

"Who are you?" Renno called into the storm.

"I am not a manitou, but a friend," the white-haired man replied. "I bring tidings from the place where twin rivers run, where you and I shall begin the final journey."

A violent thunderclap shook the valley, the flash blinding Renno. When again he could see, the image of the old man was gone.

"Wait!" Renno called after him.

The spirit voice seemed to reverberate within Renno's mind: *I will wait for you in the west. But first your daughter calls to you. Look! There in the darkness!*

Renno's gaze was drawn to the outcrop where he had

first made camp. As the sky blazed with lightning, he squinted at what appeared to be the silhouette of a woman, arms outstretched, standing at the very peak of the promontory. But this woman was far taller than any normal person, with eyes that glowed like twin pyres. And she was calling to him: "Father! Save me, my father!"

The spirit voice was a whisper of thought: *Go to her. Lead her to the light and your son's darkness shall be lifted. Such is the destiny of the sachem.*

"Forgive me, Father, for I have sinned!" the woman cried out. She leaped into the abyss and was gone.

"No!" Renno shouted, walking into the storm. "My daughter! Don't!"

He broke into a run, ignoring the lightning and the driving rain, forgetting his horses as he sprinted across the muddy, slippery ground. He ran without stopping, like a young warrior, the lightning and thunder raging all around him. He ran without knowing why or where, only that she was calling to him and that he must find her. If he failed, all would have been for nothing. Everything would be lost.

"Mist-on-the-Water!" he yelled as he raced to the base of the promontory. "My daughter!"

There was no answering call, and for an instant he thought it had all been illusion. But as he sprinted toward his former campsite in the pines, he heard a faint whimper, clear and gentle, yet more powerful even than the storm. It was the cry of a child.

Renno dashed forward, halting abruptly in the middle of the pines. At his feet, someone lay buried under an enormous greatcoat, and even as he reached down, he knew whom he would find.

"My daughter . . ." he whispered, lifting Mist-on-the-Water and Little Gao into his arms.

Twelve

Dawn broke crisp and clear over the Kentucky Barrens. It had stopped raining about an hour after Renno carried Mist-on-the-Water and Little Gao to the cave, and he had moved the horses outside and set up a reasonably comfortable camp in the shelter. He had even built a fire, stripping wet bark off brushwood he managed to scrounge, and had hung their wet clothes on a makeshift frame to dry. With the food he had brought on the packhorse he had been able to ease Little Gao's hunger, and the boy slept peacefully through the night. His mother, however, had not yet revived, although she was coughing badly under the blankets where she lay. As Renno went about his morning tasks, he began to worry that she might never regain consciousness.

With some sturdy branches he constructed a pack frame for Little Gao and attached it to Kowa's saddle. He considered various methods for carrying Mist-on-the-Water and decided he would have to build a travois. First he heated water and made a tea of healing herbs. Lifting Mist-on-the-Water's head into his lap, he gingerly dabbed the tea on her lips with a strip of cloth. However, what little he could get into her mouth was soon coughed back up.

Renno was about to stop and tend to Little Gao, who was just awakening, when Mist-on-the-Water began to stir. She gagged several times, her body jerking beneath the blankets, then spit up the last of the tea and tried to rise.

"Lie down," Renno soothed, urging her back onto the ground. Her eyes fluttered open, and she stared uncertainly at him. "It's me—Renno. You're going to be fine."

She opened her mouth to speak and sputtered, "G-G-Gao—"

"Little Gao is all right," he told her, stroking her hair and nodding toward where her son was lying. "He's right beside you."

She managed to turn her head in the boy's direction.

"I followed you to Nashville," Renno explained. "I found you not far from here."

She looked back at him, her eyes narrowing as she tried to focus on his face. Her body stiffened, and she coughed again, then lay still.

"You must have seen my campfire," Renno continued. "When the storm worsened, I left it burning and sought out this shelter. Fortunately I went back."

Again she tried to speak, but the effort proved too great, and she fell against his arms.

"You rest now. I'll make us something to eat."

He eased her head down onto a folded blanket, then went to Little Gao. The boy was in remarkably good spirits, and Renno cleaned him as best he could and dressed him in his clothes, which had dried during the night. He returned him to the blanket beside his mother, and Little Gao began to play with her hair. Renno was about to move him away but changed his mind when he saw how intently Mist-on-the-Water was watching him. After putting additional wood on the fire, he cooked up a pan of beans he had brought, adding dried beef to soften in the liquid.

Renno ate first, waiting for the food to cool a little before serving it to the others. He mashed some of the beans for Little Gao, who took his portion eagerly, smacking his lips at the savory sauce until much of his face was painted with it. Mist-on-the-Water, on the other hand, did not seem interested in the food, and Renno had to force her to chew even a little.

After cleaning up, Renno sat down beside the young woman. "I am going to bring you home," he told her.

She looked up at him but did not reply.

Renno considered what to say to her, then finally gave a solemn nod. "I'm going to make a travois for you. Gao asked me to bring you home."

"G-Gao?" she muttered, her eyes widening in wonder.

"I went to the river to call on the manitous, and Gao spoke to me. He told me to find you . . . to bring you home. He said, 'Find her before she leaps into the darkness, and then Ta-na-wun-da shall return.'" Renno shrugged. "I didn't know what he meant, but I knew I had to come."

"He . . . he spoke to you?" she asked, and Renno nodded. "Wh-when?"

"The night after I learned about . . . about Ta-na." He closed his eyes against the tears.

Mist-on-the-Water raised herself slightly. "Me, too. He came to me that same night."

Renno was taken aback by the statement, but then his expression brightened. "What did he say?"

She shook her head slowly, as if struggling to call back the memory of that night. "Ta-na . . . he spoke about Ta-na-wun-da."

"What about him?"

She shrugged. "I . . . I don't remember." Looking distressed, she suddenly broke into a fit of coughing.

Renno wanted to reach out to her, but he held back, waiting until she regained her composure. Then he stood and gathered her clothes from where they hung near the fire.

"You'll have to wear these again," he told her, placing them beside her on the ground. "They're mostly dry."

She seemed to realize for the first time that she was naked beneath the blankets, and she pulled them tighter around her neck.

"I'll be outside working on that travois." He started from the shelter.

"No," she called after him. "I . . . I can ride."

He debated the idea a moment, then nodded. "Ononta must have run off in the storm; I couldn't find her. But I brought along a packhorse, which you can ride. You can use my saddle."

"Ononta didn't run off," she told him. "Last night—I sent her away."

Renno looked at her curiously but decided not to press the matter.

"But I took off the saddle first," Mist-on-the-Water continued. "I'll show you where."

As she picked up her dress and started to put it on, Renno went outside to fetch the horses.

It remained chilly but fairly comfortable as Renno and Mist-on-the-Water returned to the Louisville Trace and followed it south through the Barrens. Before leaving their campsite, Renno had retrieved the second saddle, disposed of some of the nonessential supplies he had brought, and redistributed the remainder in saddlebags on both horses. Then he had transferred Little Gao's pack frame to the packhorse and strapped the boy in place.

As they rode, Renno noticed that although Mist-on-the-Water's cough had improved, her frame of mind had taken a turn for the worse. He had been encouraged by her mood back at the shelter, but as the day wore on she withdrew into herself, unwilling even to make small talk. When they stopped among a sparse stand of alders for a late-afternoon meal, she not only pushed away her food but appeared wholly uninterested in her child.

"You've got to eat something," he urged the woman, kneeling beside her and holding out some dried beef. She merely lowered her gaze and turned away.

"If not for yourself, then eat something for your son. He needs his mother."

"What does it matter?" she said, almost beneath her breath.

"It *does* matter. Not just to Little Gao but to me."

She looked up at him questioningly.

"You are part of my family," he explained. "Your husband was my nephew. And Ta-na-wun-da—" His voice broke with emotion. "My son loved you as though you were a sister. Even more deeply than that." He reached over and took her hand. Her body stiffened, but she made no attempt to pull away. "My wife and I knew this . . . and we were pleased. You are like a daughter to us. You *are* my daughter."

There were tears in her eyes, but she could not raise them to meet his gaze.

"Your son is my grandson. He has lost a father; he must not lose his mother, as well."

Her lips quivered as she whispered, "I . . . I d-don't know . . . I don't know if I can . . ."

"You *can*, my daughter." He lifted her hand and placed it on his chest. "Feel my heart, how it aches at the loss of my son—and my nephew. Just as your heart aches. But we can go on. Together, we can . . . and we must. It is what your husband wants for you. It is what my son . . ."

Renno let go of her hand and sat in silence. When Little Gao began to fuss and whimper, he waited for Mist-on-the-Water to take him in her arms. But she sat motionless, her cheeks wet with tears. Finally he moved to where the boy was lying and picked him up.

He was about to bring Little Gao to his mother when his attention was drawn to the sound of horses approaching from the south. Still holding the boy, he walked a short way from the stand of trees and shielded his eyes, trying to see the horsemen. They were silhouetted by the glare of the low-hanging winter sun, but as they drew nearer, he counted first two, then three riders.

Although Renno guessed they were fellow travelers, he decided not to take any chances and hurried back to where Mist-on-the-Water was seated. Placing Little Gao on her lap, he said, "Three riders are coming. Wait here."

She looked up at him mutely and took the boy.

Striding to his horse, Renno retrieved his pistols, quickly loaded them, and tucked them behind his belt under his wool coat. He also loaded his rifle but left it in the saddle scabbard. With Kowa and the packhorse in plain view from the trail, he realized there was no point in trying to hide, so he stepped from the trees. As he stood there, a few feet from where Kowa was tethered, his hands rested on his belt buckle, inches from the pistols.

The riders were coming at a trot but slowed to a walk as they neared the trees. The man in the lead removed his hat, revealing curly red hair that matched his several-days' growth of beard. He slapped the hat against his chest, clearing some of the trail dust from his green oilcloth jacket, then hung the hat on his saddle horn. When he was about twenty feet from Renno, he reined in his black gelding and signaled his companions to do likewise.

"Good day, friend," he called out, giving Renno what passed for a friendly smile.

"Hello," Renno replied with a nod.

The man glanced around the area, then asked, "Taking the trail alone?"

"Hell, Jim, you blind?" one of the others interjected, kneeing his horse forward a few steps until he was beside the leader. He gestured toward the stand of trees. "See? He got him a squaw."

The man named Jim gazed into the trees and nodded in acknowledgment. "That he does."

"And a papoose," the other man added.

"She your squaw?" Jim asked, smiling again at Renno.

He had no intention of answering their questions. Instead he asked one of his own. "What do you fellows want?"

"Just wondering if you're taking her up north to Louisville or down to Nashville. I mean, either way, if you're planning to sell her around town, we'd like a first go with her here. Ain't that so?" he called over his shoulder, and his comrades voiced their enthusiastic approval. "What d'ya say, friend?"

Renno's expression hardened. "I'd say we aren't friends, and she's not for sale."

Jim shrugged. "Didn't mean no offense." He gave a conspiratorial grin. "Hope you don't fault us for asking." Twisting around in the saddle, he said to the others, "Let's be on our way. It's a long ride to Louisville."

Renno kept close watch on the three riders as they turned their horses back toward the trail. It was the red-haired man who made the first move, jerking a pistol from beneath his coat and spinning toward Renno.

Pulling open his coat and drawing both pistols, Renno cocked the right one and fired almost simultaneously with the other man's gun. He felt a hot stab along his left forearm, and his second gun fell from his hand. Tossing aside the spent weapon, he dove for the one on the ground just as a second and third shot rang out, both bullets passing overhead.

He came up with the gun, drawing back the hammer as he raised it toward his attackers. The leader had been struck by Renno's first bullet and had fallen from his horse. One of the other riders was struggling to hold steady his rearing horse, while the third man was drawing a rifle from the saddle scabbard. As the man raised it to his shoulder, Renno fired at him, the bullet catching him in the middle of the chest and throwing him backward off his mount.

The remaining rider had his horse under control now

and was reaching for his own rifle. Renno dropped the empty pistol and charged horse and rider, grabbing hold of the rifle barrel as the man tried to bring it into play. Before he could cock the weapon, Renno yanked him from the saddle. He came tumbling down on top of Renno, and both of them landed hard on the ground, the rifle spinning out of their hands.

Stunned by the force of the impact, Renno rolled the man off and scrambled to get up. But his opponent, who was young and wiry, vaulted on top of him, knocking him onto his back. Renno saw a glint of metal and reached out instinctively, grabbing the fellow's wrist and twisting violently. But the man managed to hold on to the knife, and he leaned forward with his full weight, driving it down at Renno's chest.

"Let'm up, Murphy!" a voice shouted. "I'll finish him!"

Renno glanced to the side and saw the man named Jim standing about ten feet away, pistol raised to fire. His left leg was bleeding from where Renno's first shot had struck, but he had managed to get back on his feet and reload his weapon.

With a furious cry, Renno knocked his assailant to the side. The man provided an effective shield against his gun-wielding companion, but he still had control of the knife and struggled to get back on top and drive it home. Jim, meanwhile, hobbled to his right, trying to position himself so as to get a clear shot at Renno.

Just inside the stand of trees, Mist-on-the-Water moved almost woodenly toward where the horses were tethered. It had not been Renno's warning about approaching riders but the first gunshots that had finally roused her from her private suffering. At first she had imagined herself back at Fort Niagara, hearing the volley of rifle shots that killed her husband. But then she had looked down at her son and remembered where she was and all that had transpired. And when more shots had sounded, she had wrapped up her boy and hidden him behind a tree, then crept over to the horses.

As she came up alongside Kowa, she took in the scene before her. Renno was locked in hand-to-hand combat with one of the outlaws. Another lay motionless on the ground, blood soaking the front of his jacket. The third was aiming a pistol at the struggling Renno.

Turning to Kowa, she wrenched the rifle from its scabbard and pulled back the hammer, checking to make sure Renno had loaded it. She stepped from the trees and shouldered the big gun. Seeing that the red-haired man was about to fire on Renno, she let out a piercing wail to call his attention to herself. She drew a bead on his chest and, as he swung his pistol toward her, squeezed the trigger. The big gun slammed back against her. When the smoke cleared, she saw that the slug had struck the outlaw's right arm, throwing it upward and sending his shot harmlessly into the air. He was almost knocked off his feet, but he managed to steady himself and stood clutching his upper arm, staring in surprise at the Indian woman.

Mist-on-the-Water did not have the powder horn or shot pouch, but she drew the ramrod and slid it down the barrel, pretending she was just finishing reloading. The outlaw, having already tasted her marksmanship, seemed less than eager to be in her sights again. Spinning around and dragging his bleeding leg, he staggered to his horse— the only one of the three that had not run off—and with great effort pulled himself into the saddle. He glanced back, saw Mist-on-the-Water shouldering the rifle again, and whipped the horse into a gallop, heading back the way he and his companions had come.

Mist-on-the-Water reached under her skirt and drew out her hunting knife. As she ran toward where Renno and the remaining outlaw were still grappling on the ground, she saw the man break Renno's grip and thrust with the knife. Renno gave a powerful heave, throwing him off, but then stiffened, his arms dropping limply at his sides as he fell back on the ground.

A few feet away, the outlaw pushed himself up and shook his head to clear it. The knife was still in his hand. When he saw Renno lying helpless on the ground, he moved in for the kill but was intercepted by a figure hurtling through the air. Taken by surprise, he raised his arms to ward off the expected blows. He had not seen the knife in Mist-on-the-Water's hand, and he gasped in shock when the blade struck just below his breastbone and angled upward into his heart. The air went out of him, and he rolled onto his side, blood spurting on the hard-packed earth.

Mist-on-the-Water pulled herself off the ground and poked the man's body with her foot. After confirming he was dead, she hurried to Renno and dropped down beside him, lifting his head and shoulders onto her lap. She could see that he was struggling for air, and she stroked his cheek, telling him over and over that everything would be all right. His eyes rolled back, and he lost consciousness.

Summoning her courage, Mist-on-the-Water forced herself to open his coat. She was surprised that no blood had soaked through the front of his buckskin shirt and even more stunned when a closer inspection revealed not a single gash from the knife. The only injury she could find was a slight flesh wound on his forearm, which appeared to be from a bullet. It had already stopped bleeding and certainly did not account for his current condition.

Then she remembered the bullet he had taken in the back more than a year before. She had seen its effect on him in the past, though it never caused anything more serious than a slight weakness in his left side. But Ta-na-wun-da had confided in her about it, and she knew that the Nashville physician expected the paralysis to worsen over time and eventually cripple him entirely—if not fatally.

"No, Renno!" she cried, shaking him gently. "Not now! Not because of me!"

She sat weeping for long minutes that seemed like hours. And then she heard another person crying—her son, Little Gao, whom she had left among the trees. Renno was still unconscious but breathing more regularly now, so she eased his head to the ground and made him as comfortable as possible before heading back into the stand of trees. She gave Little Gao some food to calm him, then strapped him into his pack and propped it against a tree. Returning to where Renno lay, she cleaned the gunshot wound as best she could and wrapped a long strip of cloth around his forearm. A few minutes later she had gathered up their things and tied them to the horses. Then she looked around to see how she might carry Renno.

A travois, she thought, nodding. *It is the only way.*

She retrieved her hunting knife from the body of the dead man and wiped it clean, then searched the stand of trees until she found a couple that were long enough and of suitable diameter. After stripping and cutting them to the right size, she attached them to the packhorse, the upper ends lashed together and the lower ends trailing on the ground, held apart by a short crosspiece. To complete the travois she stretched and tied blankets between the poles to form a bed. It took about an hour to construct and almost as long to drag Renno over and position him on the blankets.

She tied Little Gao's pack frame to the saddle of the bay gelding and spoke to the horse a moment, telling him that Renno was being pulled behind the other horse and that the gelding needed to be gentle, since it was carrying a baby. Kowa wickered plaintively but stood still, as if he sensed something was wrong and would do his part to help.

Mist-on-the-Water checked Renno a final time, making sure he was strapped securely to the travois and would not slide off. His breathing was shallow but steady, and as she felt his forehead, he opened his eyes and looked up at her.

"Renno!" she exclaimed.

He opened his mouth to speak, then grimaced in pain.

"Are you all right?" she asked, patting his hand.

He tried again to speak, but all he could manage were a few grunting sounds.

"Two of those outlaws are dead," she told him. "The third one got away, but he has two bullets in him, one from each of us." She forced a smile, then continued, "You're on a travois. I'm taking you to the Nashville doctor; I think it's the old wound."

He looked up at her and gave a slight nod.

"Can you manage the journey?" she asked, and he nodded again. "Then we must get started." She stood, then leaned back down and kissed his cheek. "Thank you, my father, for coming to get me."

Mist-on-the-Water lashed the lead line of the packhorse to Kowa's saddle, then climbed onto the gelding, gave her son a gentle pat on the head, and started down the trail. As she rode, she kept looking back at the packhorse, making sure the travois was holding and that Renno was not sliding off.

"My father . . ." she whispered, repeating it several times until the words began to settle within her.

Yes, she thought, allowing herself the hint of a smile. *I like how it sounds.*

Thirteen

As the sun dipped below the horizon, Mist-on-the-Water rode off the trail, leading the pack-horse into a sheltered, grassy hollow near the southern end of the Barrens. Leaping down from the gelding, she hurried back to the travois and was pleased to find Renno awake and smiling up at her.

"How do you feel?" she asked, kneeling beside him and taking hold of his right hand. To her surprise, his grip was strong.

"Much better," he told her.

He released her hand and reached for the rope that Mist-on-the-Water had strapped across his chest to keep him from slipping. She noticed he was not using his left hand, and when he fumbled with the ends of the rope, she untied it for him.

"Help me up," he said, grasping the travois pole on his right.

"Shouldn't you rest—?"

"I've been resting all afternoon," he replied, his firm tone making it clear that he would not be dissuaded. "Help me to stand."

Mist-on-the-Water moved to his left side, slipping his arm over her shoulder and assisting him as he lifted himself off the travois. He stood unsteadily, testing the strength of his left leg.

"All right, let me go," he declared, waving her away with his right hand.

She eased his arm from around her shoulder, holding on to him a moment before letting go and stepping away. He straightened and stood nodding with satisfaction.

"Almost back to normal," he announced, gingerly lifting his left leg and bringing it back down.

"Has this happened before?" she asked.

"It comes and goes."

"But this time . . . you couldn't move at all. You could hardly breathe."

He balled his right hand into a fist, then tried to do the same with the left. He was able to move his fingers but not draw them in all the way.

"It was worse than usual," he acknowledged, then gave her a slight smile. "Then again, I haven't been in a fight like that—not in a long time. I'll have to leave such things to younger folks."

"Do you know who those three men were?"

Renno shook his head. "Highwaymen, I suppose. Figured we were easy pickings alone here on the Trace."

"The one who rode off . . . will he come back?"

"I shouldn't think so—not with two bullets in him. That was quick work on your part. And if you hadn't finished off that fellow with the knife, I wouldn't be here."

She felt suddenly ashamed and lowered her gaze.

Renno reached over and took her hand. "It isn't your fault," he told her.

She could not bear to look in his eyes as she whispered, "It is because of me that you are here . . . that you are injured."

"It's barely a crease," he said, indicating the gunshot wound. "As for my back, you had no part in that. It will do what it will; there's nothing that can be done about it."

She felt her eyes welling with tears. "I'm sorry."

"It's all right," he assured her, squeezing her hand. They fell silent a moment, and then Renno asked gently, "Back at Nashville . . . is there anything you want to tell me?"

Her jaw tightened, and she tried to keep her voice steady as she replied, "I was there only one night. I needed supplies. When I couldn't get them, I decided to make the journey anyway."

"Yes, the journey," he repeated. "You were going to the lake of the Seneca, weren't you? To be with Gao?"

Again she lowered her head and gave a slight nod.

"Do you really think that's what he wants?"

"I . . . I don't know anymore."

"It must be something else—something he was trying to tell both of us. About Ta-na-wun-da."

She tensed a little as he cupped her chin and raised her head, forcing her to look at him.

"What I think," Renno continued, "is that we should return home and figure this out together. And if, come spring, you're still determined to go to the lake where your husband lies, I'll take you there myself."

"Yes," she said, forcing a smile. "Let us go home."

They spent the night in the hollow. Come morning, Renno had largely recovered. His left arm and leg were still weak, but no worse than they had been at Huntington Castle. He felt so good, in fact, that he refused to use the travois but instead rode Kowa, with Mist-on-the-Water and Little Gao on the saddled packhorse.

They made slow but steady progress south across the border into Tennessee and on to Nashville. As they reached the outskirts of the city, Renno noted how nervous Mist-on-the-Water became. He did not want to pry further into what might have happened in town, but he sensed she was frightened about returning.

"It's still light, and we've plenty of supplies," he said,

keeping his horse in pace beside hers. "We could skirt the city and push on to Rusog's Town."

"No," she replied with a shake of the head. "You must see the doctor."

"Fass? There's nothing he can do."

"But you said you promised Beth."

"Yes, but there's really no point. He's examined me many times, and the diagnosis is always the same. 'Don't exert yourself. Stay in bed. Hope for the best.' "

"You should tell him what happened."

"I know what's happening. The bullet fragments are putting pressure on my spine—some times worse than others." He raised his left hand and squeezed it into a fist. "See? The weakness is gone."

"It may return."

"Which is why we should push on home," Renno insisted. "That's all Doc Fass would tell me to do: 'Go home and get to bed.' " When she started to object, he cut her off with a raised hand. "Nashville will slow us down. We'll take the fork ahead." He gestured down the road toward a second trail that angled off to the southwest, bypassing most of the city and leading more directly to Rusog's Town and the Cherokee lands.

As they continued down the road and turned onto the right-hand fork, he saw her body relax and her smile return. He decided to take advantage of her mood and said, "Mist-on-the-Water, there is a favor I must ask you."

She turned in the saddle. "What is it?"

"I don't want Beth worrying about me."

"You don't want me to tell her about—?"

"None of it," he said. "Not about the highwaymen, and not what happened to me afterward. I promise I'll put myself to bed—that's the important thing. She needn't know how bad it was."

She hesitated a long moment, weighing what she should do, then replied, "I will not speak of this to Beth. But how will you explain where we've been?"

Renno thought it over a moment. "When I was in

Nashville, I sent Beth word that I was heading north on the Trace. So we'll just say the truth: I caught up with you, and you agreed to come home."

"But where was I going? What should I say?"

"You planned to visit your husband's grave and then return home. Nothing more."

"I . . ." Her voice cracked with emotion, and she pulled her horse to a halt.

"What is it?" Renno asked, reining in beside her.

She shook her head. "I didn't plan to return."

He reached out to her. "I know."

"You don't know. There is more. I—" She drew in a calming breath. "I was planning to meet my husband, not in this world but the next. I tried to—" She could not say the words aloud.

"I know what you tried to do," he told her, and she looked up at him in disbelief. "I learned this from the manitous . . . and from another," he added cryptically. "It doesn't matter any longer. It is the will of the Master of Life that you are here now, riding home."

"But I feel such shame."

Renno shook his head adamantly. Reaching up, he opened his coat and undid the laces of his buckskin shirt, then pulled it wide to reveal the scars that laced his chest.

"I tried to do the same, but with my knife. Yet I, too, am here today. It must be for a purpose." He kicked his horse forward. "Come. It is still a long ride home."

When at last their journey came to an end and they rode up the lane to Huntington Castle, they were greeted by Michael Soaring Hawk, who leaped from the verandah and ran breathlessly toward them. Beth had been sitting outside with him, and she hurried over as they reined in their horses. Behind her, a third person appeared at the front door.

"Hawk!" Renno cried out, easing himself down from the saddle. He embraced Beth as Michael ran to greet his cousin, Little Gao, in Mist-on-the-Water's arms.

"Hawk! You're home!" Renno exclaimed, reaching to pump his elder son's hand, then pulling him into a bear hug. "You're all right!"

Beth embraced Mist-on-the-Water, declaring, "The most wonderful thing has happened!" Choking back her tears, she stammered, "T-tell them, Hawk!"

"What is it?" Renno said, pushing away from his son.

"It's Ta-na-wun-da . . ." Hawk's eyes also filled with joyful tears.

Before he could continue, Michael tugged at his grandfather's jacket and screeched, "He's alive! Uncle Ta-na's alive!"

"It's true, Father!" Hawk confirmed. "That report you received was wrong. He was wounded, but he's alive."

"Ta-na!" Mist-on-the-Water gasped, her eyes searching the verandah. "Where is he?"

Beth came up beside her and took her arm. "He's upstairs. But—"

"What is it?" Renno pressed.

"He was hurt quite badly," Hawk explained.

Mist-on-the-Water moved close to Renno, looking as if she was about to faint. He wrapped an arm around her and Little Gao.

"Take us to see him," Renno declared, helping the young woman up to the verandah.

They entered the house and started up the stairs, Renno both comforting Mist-on-the-Water and leaning on her for support, the young woman clutching her son in fear. Moving down the hallway, they passed Michael's bedroom and continued to the far corner room, where Mist-on-the-Water had seen the manitou of her husband.

As Renno reached for the doorknob, Hawk came up beside him and stayed his hand. "He isn't as you remember him," was all he said to his father.

Renno hesitated a moment, gazing into his elder son's eyes. "Is he alive?" he asked, and Hawk nodded. "That's all that matters."

Pushing open the door, Renno walked ahead of Mist-on-the-Water into the bedroom. He started toward the bed and was surprised to find it empty. Looking across the room, he saw Ma-ton-ga standing near the window, holding what appeared to be a tray of food. Beside her, a gaunt figure sat motionless in a plush chair facing the window. It took a moment for Renno to recognize his son, and then he rushed over to him.

"Ta-na . . ." he breathed. He reached for his son's shoulder, but something held him back. For a moment he gazed down at Ta-na, then slowly came around to stand in front of him. The young man's face was covered with criss-crossing welts and lacerations, which had scabbed over and appeared to be healing. His left hand was bandaged, but Renno could see his fingers and was relieved that nothing had been amputated.

It was Ta-na's eyes that unnerved Renno. They were turned toward the window, as if he were looking out. But they were dull, almost lifeless.

"Ta-na-wun-da," Renno whispered, kneeling and taking his son's right hand.

Ta-na's head cocked slightly, but he gave no sign of recognizing his father. Renno looked up in confusion at Hawk and Beth, who had come up behind the chair and were standing on either side of Mist-on-the-Water, Hawk steadying her and Beth holding Little Gao. Hawk gestured for Renno to continue speaking to Ta-na.

"Son, it's your father. Mist-on-the-Water is with me."

Hawk led the young woman around the chair. She dropped to her knees and placed her head on Ta-na's lap.

"We . . . we thought the worst," Renno continued. "And now, to find you still alive . . ."

Ta-na's lips quivered, as if he was trying to speak. He blinked against the tears, then lowered his head.

"It's all right." Renno stood and placed his hand on his son's shoulder. "There's plenty of time to speak later." He glanced up and saw that Hawk was shaking his head. "What is it?" he asked.

"He can't speak," Hawk replied, keeping his voice

low. He moved to where Ma-ton-ga was standing and wrapped an arm around her, as if seeking her strength. "He hasn't spoken since that cannon blast."

Renno touched his son's cheek, tilting his head upward until their eyes met. Ta-na seemed to be looking through him, and then his eyes drifted to the side, his gaze fixed on something far beyond.

"Blind?" Renno muttered, his own eyes widening at the realization. "My son is blind?"

Though Ta-na-wun-da could not see things around him, his world was not totally dark. At least that was the conclusion of Dr. Stuart Fass when he visited Huntington Castle several days after Renno's return. He spent some time examining the young man in the bedroom, then joined the rest of the family in the parlor.

"How is he?" Renno asked, rising from beside Beth on the sofa as Fass entered the room.

"He's resting." Fass placed his medical bag on a table beside the doorway and approached. He was in his midforties but looked somewhat younger, with curly brown hair and a trim beard. "That young woman is with him," he said, referring to Mist-on-the-Water, who since her return home had spent most of her time seeing to Ta-na's needs. "She's doing an excellent job."

"What about Ta-na-wun-da?" Renno pressed.

"Remarkably better," the physician replied, dropping into a chair that faced the sofa. Seeing Renno and Beth's hopeful expressions, he quickly added, "Not his vision, I'm afraid. But the other wounds. Much improved from when I first saw him. I doubt there'll be much scarring."

"He still hasn't spoken," Hawk commented, coming over from the fireplace at the far end of the parlor.

Fass shrugged. "There doesn't seem to be any damage to the vocal cords, but I can't be certain. There might be some sort of injury to the—" He hesitated, then said resolutely, "The brain."

"Would that account for his vision?" Renno asked.

"I think not. Technically, your son can see." Before they could respond, he continued, "I don't mean he can see you or me—or even enough to walk around on his own. But he most definitely sees light and shadow."

Hawk sat down beside his stepmother. "Is that common?"

"Quite."

"But how can you tell?"

"From the way his eyes react to light. The problem lies with the retinas." Fass cupped his hands together into a ball. "Let's say this is an eye, with my right hand being the front and my left the back." He pulled his hands apart but kept them cupped. "The light passes through the pupil at the front and strikes the inside wall at the back of the eye." He touched his right forefinger against the palm of his still-cupped left hand. "This part of the eye has a covering called the retina, which somehow sends the picture to our brain. Your son's retinas are damaged."

"But you said he can see," Renno reminded him.

"Only light and dark. Perhaps the vaguest of forms. Nothing more."

"What about spectacles?"

"They won't help. Not for this condition."

"Will his retinas heal?" Hawk asked.

Fass shook his head. "They appear to have detached from the wall of the eye. It's not likely they'll reattach."

"But surely there's something you can—"

"Nothing," Fass said, cutting off Renno. "Not even the finest surgeon can operate inside the eye."

"Blind . . ." Renno mumbled. He walked across the room to one of the side tables and poured himself some brandy. He lifted it halfway to his lips, then lowered it and stared into the glass.

"As long as I'm here, I'd like to examine you, too, Mr. Harper," Dr. Fass suggested.

He waved off the idea. "That's not necessary."

Beth rose and went over to her husband. "I want you to," she said softly. "It's been months . . ." She left unsaid that she knew he hadn't visited the physician when he was in Nashville.

"I'm feeling fine."

"And you look fine," Fass put in, rising from his chair. "So this should take but a few minutes." He retrieved his medical bag. "Perhaps up in your bedroom?"

Renno allowed Beth to lead him back across the parlor, then reluctantly followed the physician out through the foyer to the stairs.

After the two men departed, Hawk approached the doorway and placed his hands on his stepmother's shoulders. "He's going to be fine," he said soothingly. "Both of them are."

She dabbed a tear from her cheek. "I hope so, Hawk. I truly hope so."

During the following week, Ta-na-wun-da's health continued to improve. He remained uncommunicative, however, and seemed totally uninterested in anything but sitting in his chair near the window. Though able to walk without difficulty between the bed and the chair, he rejected all efforts to get him to leave the room. He would not eat on his own, but when Beth or Mist-on-the-Water fed him, he accepted the food without complaint.

When the Nashville physician made it clear there was no hope for a cure, Renno turned to traditional Seneca and Cherokee remedies. A succession of healers—men and women alike—visited from Rusog's Town and the neighboring villages, bringing herbs, chants, and potions. None met with success. In fact, the only thing that seemed to brighten Ta-na's mood was Mist-on-the-Water's daily visit. She spent hours with him, sometimes talking, often just sitting in a chair beside him. On occasion she brought Little Gao and spent the entire day in the room, feeding and caring for both of them.

One unusually bright and warm morning, Mist-on-the-Water came to Ta-na's room shortly after he had finished breakfast. Beth was still with him, and the two women spoke for a few minutes, after which Beth took her leave. Mist-on-the-Water approached Ta-na and, instead of sitting beside him, took his hands and helped him to his feet.

"We're going for a walk," she announced cheerfully.

He turned toward her, saying nothing, his eyes narrowing curiously.

"You've been up here too long. We're going outside."

Ta-na tried to pull back his hands, but she tightened her grip, forcing him to take a few faltering steps toward her.

"You don't have to speak, if you don't want. But you're going to walk."

Slowly, Ta-na's muscles relaxed, and after a few minutes he allowed himself to be led out into the hall. It took some perseverance on Mist-on-the-Water's part, but she finally brought him down the stairs and out onto the verandah.

In the succeeding days, they increased the distance and duration of their walks. Ta-na even began to communicate, not with words but with simple gestures, such as shaking or nodding his head and waving away things he didn't want. A week after he first ventured outside, Mist-on-the-Water led him out to the fields between Huntington Castle and Rusog's Town. She held his arm, guiding his steps as they ranged far beyond the manor house to the very edge of Rusog's Town, finally seeking out a shallow stream at the base of a gently sloping hillside.

"The stream is running stronger; spring is near," she noted, sitting down at the edge of the water and tugging his hand until he sat cross-legged beside her. She patted his hand. When she spoke again, it was in the Seneca language of Ta-na-wun-da's people. "I brought you here because there's something I must tell you."

He turned his head toward her, his expression intent.

"When I came home with Renno . . . do you know where I'd been?" She paused a moment, then continued, "Your father found me in the Barrens." She felt his hand stiffen. "No one told you? Well, he did. I was there with my son. I thought I was going to the lake of the Seneca, but really I was trying to find my husband—and you. I carried my son up the highest cliff I could find and was about to leap. And I might have, if something hadn't stopped me. I don't know if it was Gao or some other spirit watching out for me. But it protected me. And it sent me home. To you."

Ta-na pulled his hand free and turned slightly away.

"I thought you were dead and that I could meet you in the next world. But you are alive." She took his face in her hands. "Alive, Ta-na. We are both alive. I never want to lose you again."

"No!" he blurted.

The sound of his voice stunned her. She tried to turn his face toward her, but he jerked free and leaped to his feet. He started forward and stepped into the water, then pulled back and lurched in a different direction. Jumping up, she hurried after him, but he quickened his pace until he was running along the bank of the stream. When he stumbled, she caught up, but as she reached to grab him, he tripped and sprawled into the water.

"Ta-na!" she exclaimed, dropping beside him in the stream. She threw her arms around him, kissing his shoulders and neck and face, all the while whispering, *"Kononkwa,* Ta-na-wun-da!"—"I love you, Ta-na-wun-da"—in his Seneca tongue.

"No!" he shrieked, twisting away from her. "I can't!"

He pulled himself to his feet and turned in place, as if trying to sense the direction home. Then he staggered up the hill, directly toward the distant manor house.

Mist-on-the-Water sat up, sobbing as she watched him disappear over the crest. Slowly she rose and turned in the opposite direction, toward Rusog's Town. She had gone only a few feet across the shallow stream when she thought of Ta-na struggling home and perhaps getting lost along the way. She knew she could not leave him wandering alone, so she climbed the incline after him.

She found Ta-na on the far side, lying in a grassy hollow between two hills. Rushing down to him, she saw with a shock that the side of his face was smeared with blood where he had struck a large rock. She rolled him onto his back and quickly ascertained that he was breathing. She tried to rouse him, and when she failed, she realized she had to go for help. Rusog's Town was much closer than Huntington Castle, so she took off back up the hill.

When she reached the crest, she glanced back toward the hollow to confirm that Ta-na had not moved. Turning to continue her run, she caught sight of a horse and rider just beyond the stream. She waved her arms frantically at what appeared to be a young man, motioning him toward her.

The rider kicked his pinto into a trot, leaping across the stream and thundering up the hillside to where Mist-on-the-Water was standing. As he drew closer, she recognized him as Ho-ta-kwa, a Seneca who had been a friend of her husband's.

"It's Ta-na-wun-da!" she shouted, gesturing down the opposite side of the hill as he reined in his horse.

Ho-ta-kwa stared down into the hollow, then kneed the horse and rode swiftly down the incline. By the time Mist-on-the-Water ran down the hill, Ho-ta-kwa had already dismounted and was checking the wounded man.

"He was running and fell!" she exclaimed, dropping to her knees beside Ta-na. "I was going for help."

"We will take him on my horse," the young man said in English. Rising, he lifted Ta-na in his arms and carried him to the pinto. Draping him facedown across the animal's back, he leaped up behind, steadying Ta-na with one hand and taking up the reins with the other. "To Huntington Castle?" he asked.

"No. My cabin is closer."

The young man nodded.

"Hurry!" she urged. "I will follow."

*   *   *

Ma-ton-ga stood at the bedroom door of the cabin, gazing at Little Gao asleep on his bed. He was Mist-on-the-Water's son, yet Ma-ton-ga felt as if he were her own. She realized her hands were on her belly, and she wondered how it would feel to carry a child—Hawk Harper's child—within her.

Hawk still had not voiced his love or told her of his intentions. But since his return from New Orleans, they had spent much time together, and she knew it was only his concern for his brother that kept him from acting on his feelings. But his heart spoke the truth of his love, and so for the time being she was content to wait.

Ma-ton-ga's thoughts were distracted by shouting voices outside. She glanced at Little Gao to make sure he was still asleep, then strode to the front door and pulled it open. Outside, a rider was approaching with what appeared to be a body slung in front of him across the horse's back. Ma-ton-ga recognized him as the Seneca named Ho-ta-kwa. Running alongside him was Mist-on-the-Water.

She hurried outside as Ho-ta-kwa reined in his horse and dismounted, lifting the body into his arms.

"Ta-na!" she gasped, throwing her hand over her mouth.

"He's alive," Mist-on-the-Water told her, pushing past and directing Ho-ta-kwa into the house and over to the bedroom.

Ma-ton-ga followed them into the room and helped pull back the blankets so that Ho-ta-kwa could place the unconscious man on the bed.

Ho-ta-kwa leaned close to Ta-na's face and felt his breath. Nodding, he turned to Mist-on-the-Water. "I will ride to Huntington Castle," he announced, then hurried from the room.

"What happened?" Ma-ton-ga asked as her friend filled a bowl with water from a jug beside the bed.

Mist-on-the-Water did not reply as she sat beside Ta-na and dipped a length of cloth into the water. Gingerly she wiped away some of the blood, then wrung out the cloth and continued to dab at the jagged gash on his forehead. Each time she touched the wound, Ta-na jerked in pain.

"What happened?" Ma-ton-ga repeated, moving closer.

She tugged at Mist-on-the-Water's sleeve, and the younger woman paused and looked up. Ma-ton-ga was taken aback by her expression, for it held neither fear nor even concern. Indeed, her smile was almost rapturous, as if she were communing with the Master of Life.

"He spoke to me. . . ." Mist-on-the-Water intoned, and for a moment Ma-ton-ga thought her friend had indeed heard the voice of the Master of Life. Mist-on-the-Water's own voice lowered to a fervent hush: *"Ta-na-wun-da spoke!"*

Fourteen

After a quick breakfast, Renno and Beth left their home for the ride to Rusog's Town. They and their elder son, Hawk, had spent the previous evening at Mist-on-the-Water's cabin, sitting with Ta-na-wun-da, praying he would awaken. It had been well after midnight when they finally returned to Huntington Castle for a few hours' sleep. Now the Harpers walked arm in arm to where Ben White Eagle was holding the carriage steady for them. Renno helped his wife aboard, then stood beside the vehicle, looking back at the house and waiting for Hawk to join them. His attention was drawn to the sound of approaching hoofbeats, and he turned to see a rider coming at a gallop down the lane.

The young man wore the uniform of an army regular, and he gave a smart salute as he reined in his horse and vaulted from the saddle. "Corporal Jacob Steen," he announced. At his waist he wore a small courier's pouch, which he opened as he approached.

"Renno Harper," Renno replied, offering his hand.

They shook hands, and then the corporal produced a sealed letter from the leather pouch.

"My business is with Captain Hawk Harper," the man explained. "I was told this is his home."

"Captain Harper is my son." Renno motioned for Ben to summon Hawk, and the stableman hurried off toward the house. "Have you ridden far?"

"From Knoxville. But the letter I carry comes from Washington." The corporal's eyes widened, and he puffed himself up as he declared, "It's from the office of the President."

"I see." Renno turned at the sound of Hawk coming outside. "Here's Captain Harper now."

He led the corporal to the verandah and introduced the two men. Steen immediately handed Hawk the letter.

"I'm to await a reply," he said as Hawk broke the seal and perused the contents.

"Yes," Hawk replied distractedly while continuing to read the message. When he finished, he looked up at the soldier. "If you would excuse my father and me for a few minutes."

"Certainly," the corporal replied with a salute.

"Ben, why not take Corporal Steen to the stables and see to his horse," Renno suggested.

As soon as they were alone, Hawk handed his father the letter, saying, "Look at this."

"Good news?" Renno asked, unable to decipher Hawk's enigmatic expression.

"Yes . . . partly."

Intrigued, Renno began to read. He glanced first at the signature at the bottom and noted that it was from an aide to President Madison. Skimming the preliminary introductions and niceties, he skipped to the heart of the message:

> I am pleased to be able to send official word
> that your brother-in-law, the comte de Beaujo-
> lais, has accepted a position in President Madi-
> son's diplomatic corps and will not be returning

to France. There is every good reason to believe that in time he will be granted American citizenship. Beau has attracted quite a following in the capital, and we are delighted to have been able to influence him to our cause—no doubt with a great deal of assistance from your sister. As you can well imagine, Renna is overjoyed at the prospect of remaining in the States. I am certain she will be sending a more detailed account of her plans via regular post.

"This is wonderful news!" Renno exclaimed, looking up from the letter. "Why, from your expression, I'd have thought you were being sent back off to war!"

"Keep reading," Hawk replied, gesturing at the letter.

Renno started to look back down, then turned as Beth climbed down from the carriage and approached. "The most wonderful news!" he called to her. "Renna and Beau have had enough of European intrigues. They won't be returning to France!"

"They won't?" She came up to him and eagerly took his arm.

He displayed the letter. "This is from one of the President's aides."

"Eli Buchanan," Hawk put in. "We met at West Point and served in Washington together."

"Is it true?" she asked, looking to her stepson for confirmation.

"It appears so. Beau has joined our diplomatic corps."

"Can he do that?"

"So long as the President has confidence in him."

Delighted, Beth hugged first Hawk and then Renno. "Do you think they'll come visit?"

"Not right away." Hawk gestured for his father to keep reading the letter.

"Here it is," Renno said, scanning the letter. "Apparently Beau has already been given a sensitive assignment that will keep them in Washington through the summer." He looked up from the paper. "Negotiating with the French, I'll bet."

Hawk nodded. "With the war with England at an end, our focus may well turn toward the continent. There are few who believe we've heard the last of Napoleon."

"So all that Beau is really doing is crossing to the opposite side of the negotiating table," Renno commented with a snicker. He glanced up at Hawk and noted his somber expression. "You don't seem too pleased for your sister—or for us."

"I'm sorry. I'm delighted—really I am. It's the final paragraph that concerns me."

Beth prodded her husband. "What does it say?"

"Let's see. . . ." He ran his finger down the page and read aloud:

"I relate all this simply by way of prefacing the real purpose of this letter. President Madison has asked me to write to you on his behalf. It seems he will be assigning me to a permanent diplomatic mission that will be stationed in London once a final treaty is secured, which we expect within the month. Therefore it is his fervent desire that you come to Washington forthwith and assume my current post as his administrative aide. A formal presidential request cannot be drafted until the treaty is signed and announced, by which time we hope you will already be on your way to the capital. Please know the high regard in which you are held by the President and know that it is his, and my, sincerest desire that you will accept this offer not merely as a duty to your country and your President but as an honor."

Renno lowered the letter and smiled at his son. "This truly is an honor. Would you consider turning down the President?"

"It isn't the first time he's asked."

"I know." Renno left unspoken the fact that Hawk had resigned his military commission on the very eve of his appointment as Madison's military liaison officer. But his decision had resulted from the deep depression he had suffered following the murder of his wife and one of his twin sons at the hands of Creek renegades. Much time had passed since then, during which he had served with Andrew Jackson's Tennessee militia on two occasions— against the Creeks and most recently against the British.

"What will you do?" Beth asked, touching his arm.

Hawk shrugged. "Give it a few days' thought, I suppose."

"And the courier?" Renno gestured toward the stables.

"I'll send Eli word that I'm considering the offer and will either leave for Washington within the week or send my regrets. Would you tell the corporal I'll have my reply ready shortly?" he asked, and Renno nodded. "You might as well go ahead to the village. I'll join you when I'm done." He started into the house, then halted and looked back at his father. "About Ta-na-wun-da . . ."

"He's going to be fine," Renno said, forcing a smile. "I'll tell him you're coming."

"I don't want you to get your hopes too high. Even if he did say a few words to Mist-on-the-Water, there's no guarantee he'll do so again. Or even regain consciousness—"

"Ta-na is going to be fine," Renno said emphatically. Turning, he led Beth toward the carriage.

Ta-na-wun-da walked out through the golden stalks, across fields that stretched as far as his eye could see. In the distance an old man was kneeling, planting kernels, pausing to look back and beckon.

As Ta-na approached, the man moved farther away, hand to soil, never resting, sowing the sacred mounds, chanting the song of corn planting.

> *High up in the sky,*
> *High up in the sky,*
> *See the rainmaker dancing.*
> *He brings the rain clouds now.*
> > *Heh-yeh! Heh-yeh! Heh-yeh!*

> *Behold the planting fields—*
> *All shall soon be blooming,*
> *Where the young flowers grow.*
> *Tall shall grow the cornstalks!*
> > *Heh-yeh! Heh-yeh! Heh-yeh!*

"Stop, old man!" Ta-na-wun-da shouted.

Old Man looked up at him and smiled. *"Diettino nio Diohe'ko! Diettino nio Diohe'ko!"* In the Seneca language of Ta-na's ancestors, he proclaimed: "We give thanks to our sustainers! We give thanks to our sustainers!"

In every seventh hill he added seeds of squash and bean so that the spirits of the three Diohe'ko—"those that sustain us"—would remain forever inseparable, entwined.

> *High up in the sky,*
> *Behold! The fair rainbow,*
> *Brightly decked and painted,*
> *Sings fair news to the corn.*
> > *Heh-yeh! Heh-yeh! Heh-yeh!*

> *The swallow swooping low*
> *Sings fair news to the corn.*
> *Behold! Hitherward rain!*
> *Hither comes! Hither comes!*
> > *Heh-yeh! Heh-yeh! Heh-yeh!*

Ta-na-wun-da gazed out across the golden stalks. He gazed at the dark sky and saw the lightning flashes. The warm rain brushed his face.

"Old man! Do not leave me!" he called, running across the fields.

Old Man raised a hand in greeting. "I am Corn-planter," he announced.

Reaching down, he picked up a medicine shield and held it in front of his chest. Rays of sunlight glinted across the surface, giving the stretched hide an almost metallic sheen. Emblazoned on the front were stalks of corn, one red, one yellow, one white, surrounded by curious symbols that looked like the spirit animals that filled the night sky.

"I go forth," Old Man proclaimed. "I await you in the west at the place where twin rivers run. Open your eyes! Offer thanks to the Great Spirit, the Master of Life. Offer thanks for the silence of darkness. For therein awakens the light!"

The gray clouds rolled across the sun, casting a shadow that reached out from the west, reaching across Ta-na-wun-da. He lashed out, flailing at the clouds, at the darkness. And the shafts of corn fell at his feet and were trampled into the hard red earth.

He saw Old Man no longer. He saw the corn no longer. And in the distance, a swallow trilled a plaintive song.

> *Behold! The cornstalks murmur!*
> *Everywhere, we are growing!*
> *Heh-yeh! The world, how fair!*
> *Everywhere, we are growing!*
> *Heh-yeh! The world, how fair!*

"Heh-yeh!" Ta-na-wun-da shouted, sweat pouring down his face.

He looked around but saw only the barest shimmering glow, as if he were surrounded by fog so thick that only a flicker of sunlight could get through. He struggled to see the rainbow, the corn, the old man kneeling and chanting upon the planting fields. They were gone, and Ta-na-wun-da was alone—back in the silent darkness that had claimed him that recent New Orleans dawn.

Open your eyes! Give thanks to the silence of darkness!

Ta-na jerked around, trying to see the one who had spoken. He called out to him: "Stop, old man! Don't leave me! Don't go!"

The voice faded into the darkness: *Diettino nio Diohe'ko! Diettino nio Diohe'ko!*

And then he was enveloped by the fog, by the warm rain, by a sweet embrace. A new voice sang to him, soft and gentle. Like the trill of a swallow. Like a lullaby.

"Ta-na . . ." she called to him. "Do not cry. . . ."

He reached out and felt her arms close around him. Her body trembled, and she began to cry. He held her tight, whispering her name. "Mist-on-the-Water . . . Mist . . ."

They stayed there for long minutes, lost in each other's embrace. Finally he reached up and touched her cheek, feeling the texture of her skin, the soft curves of her face.

"Wh-where am I?" he stammered, his eyes filling with tears as he strained to see something more than the vague shadow that loomed in front of him.

"Oh, Ta-na!" she exclaimed. "You're with me! You're awake, and you're here with me!"

"Someone . . . someone was . . ." His voice faded.

"What is it?" she asked, caressing his face.

He fought to keep sight of the image. A field . . . a man . . . shadows, all shadows . . .

"Something about . . . I—I don't remember."

"Don't worry," she soothed. "Everything is going to be all right."

"Where am I?" he repeated, turning his head as if looking around.

"In my cabin. We went for a walk and were sitting by the stream. Do you remember?"

He thought back beyond the dream to their walk across the fields, to the hillside and the stream.

"Yes. I . . . I ran off."

"You fell and struck your head," she explained. "I'm so sorry. It was all my fault."

"When? How long ago?"

"Yesterday."

His eyes widened in surprise, and he started to get up off the bed.

"Lie still," she urged, pushing him back.

"Home . . . I must tell them—"

"They know. Renno and Beth were here all last evening. Your brother, too. They'll be back any moment."

Ta-na's body relaxed, and he allowed her to ease him down onto the pillows.

"Rest now," she whispered. "I will sing to you as you sleep."

He felt her warm lips brush his cheek. And then she began a gentle chant:

> "High up in the sky,
> High up in the sky,
> See the rainmaker dancing.
> He brings the rain clouds now.
>   Heh-yeh! Heh-yeh! Heh-yeh!"

"That song!" Ta-na called out, lifting his head from the pillow. "Before . . . were you singing it before?"

"Singing? No, I was lying beside you, asleep."

"Where did you hear it?"

"As a child, I suppose. It just came to mind."

"But he . . ." Again the words trailed off as the sound of the old man's chant faded from memory. "I . . . I'm sure I've heard that song. . . ."

"Sleep . . ." she urged, kissing him softly, her voice lulling him as he drifted away.

"Behold! The cornstalks murmur!
Everywhere, we are growing!
Heh-yeh! The world, how fair!
Everywhere, we are growing!
Heh-yeh! The world, how fair!"

Fifteen

When Ta-na-wun-da awoke, he could see nothing but a dull glow with no distinct source, leading him to believe it was daytime. Hearing what sounded like a heated discussion, he lay perfectly still, trying to distinguish the words, wondering if he was hearing spirit voices again. Slowly, as the words took shape and form, he realized the language was Seneca and the speakers were his father and Chief Rusog. He remembered then that he was in Mist-on-the-Water's cabin and guessed they were in the next room. From their tone he could tell they were arguing, and he had to listen carefully to understand what it was about.

"The council must not do this!" Renno declared, his voice rising with passion.

"And they will not," came Rusog's measured response. "This I will make certain."

"But can you control the council while you're away? Perhaps you shouldn't make this journey."

"The council will take no action while I'm gone."

"I hope you're right," Renno replied.

"Still, my people do not understand why he seeks land of such little value. And why he offers us so much."

"Today it's but a few hundred acres; tomorrow it will be all of our lands," Renno insisted. "The path of his tongue is not straight."

"That is because he speaks like a white man," Rusog quipped. Ta-na could almost see the smile on his face, for Renno, his brother-in-law, was half white himself. "But his words hold power within the council," Rusog continued.

"He has addressed the council?"

"He sends Tall Grass to speak for him. But his message is strong among the people."

"Because he wraps his words in firewater," Renno said, his voice dripping with contempt.

"Many have been seized by the white man's disease. This is true. But many look at the small piece of land he desires, and they see that it has no water and little game. They say that with Etutu Ekwa's gold, we could buy iron pots for our wives and rifles for the hunt."

"I tell you, Rusog, these are white men's tricks. Don't place your trust in this man."

"I trust no white man."

"Not even me?" Renno challenged.

"You are Seneca." Rusog paused, then added, "I trust the Seneca even less than the whites."

Ta-na could hear both men chuckling. Just then a door opened and closed—he guessed it was the front door of the cabin—followed by footsteps and quiet chatter. He caught only a few words but recognized the voices of Mist-on-the-Water and Ma-ton-ga and what sounded like a baby cooing.

One voice grew closer, and then he heard Mist-on-the-Water say in English, "Is he awake?"

"Not yet," Beth said from afar; apparently she had been out in the main room with Rusog and Renno.

Ta-na-wun-da steeled himself for the moment when Mist-on-the-Water would enter the room. He considered pretending to be asleep, telling himself that he was not ready to face so many people, but he could not deceive his family and resigned himself instead to a barrage of questions. He prayed he would be able to answer them.

Mist-on-the-Water must have paused before entering, for he heard his father announce, "I'm going to see Rusog off. I'll be back in a few minutes."

"Where are you going?" Mist-on-the-Water asked.

Ta-na guessed that she was speaking to the Cherokee chief, for Rusog answered in heavy but precise English, "I journey to the Land Between the Rivers." He was referring to a narrow tract nestled between the Tennessee and Cumberland Rivers northwest of Nashville.

"You go find Tecumseh?" Ma-ton-ga asked.

"But Tecumseh was killed," Mist-on-the-Water reminded her. "My own husband saw him fall."

"They say Tecumseh return."

"Rumors, nothing more," Renno told the women. "Many won't accept that he's gone—that his cause is lost. They'll turn any wandering medicine man into Tecumseh reborn, or more."

"It is said that the healing powers of this medicine man are great," Rusog put in.

"Does he claim to be Tecumseh?" Renno asked.

"He calls himself Cornplanter."

"Gaiantwaka?" Renno used the Seneca name of the brother of the prophet Handsome Lake.

Rusog shook his head. "This Cornplanter is not of your people but comes from far beyond the Father of Waters. Those who have met him claim that he is the spirit of Tecumseh, returned as an old man."

"Tecumseh!" Ma-ton-ga exclaimed. Her people, the Creek, had been among his most ardent followers.

"The young warriors say that Tecumseh planted seed that would ripen into a single nation of all the red people and that now he has returned as Cornplanter to harvest what he has sown."

"You don't believe this, do you?" Renno challenged.

"It is not for me to say. I will go to this Cornplanter

and listen to his words. If he speaks true, he will be welcome in our villages. If not, I will ask him to return to his own land beyond the Father of Waters."

The front door opened and closed, and people were moving about in the far room. But Ta-na-wun-da was aware of none of it. Instead, his mind was filled with a single word, a single name: *Cornplanter*. It had been playing at the edge of his consciousness all night, and now it sounded from the very depths of his being. *Cornplanter!*

"Diohe'ko!" Ta-na-wun-da exclaimed, bolting upright on the bed. His body shook, and his face dripped with sweat.

"Ta-na!" Mist-on-the-Water came rushing into the room and threw her arms around him.

The others crowded in, all speaking at once. Ta-na shook his head against the onslaught of noise. And then a single voice—the voice of Old Man—pierced the babble, sounding within his mind. Ta-na's lips parted, and he repeated the phrase over and over: "Diettino nio Diohe'ko. . . . Diettino nio Diohe'ko. . . ."

"Yes! Diettino!" Renno exclaimed. "Thank God!"

Ta-na turned his head toward the voice. "F-Father?"

"I'm here, son. All of us are."

Ta-na felt Renno's strong hand grasp his own. He cocked his head, trying to listen to the distant, fading voice. "Do you hear it?" he asked, straining to make out the old one's words, to catch sight of him through the shadowed fog.

"Yes, son, we hear you," Renno replied.

"No!" Ta-na pushed away their clutching hands. "Don't you hear him?"

"Who, son? Who?"

Ta-na, rubbing his head, did not answer. No one else spoke for a time, and then Renno whispered to the others, ushering them from the room. Finally the door closed, and a single pair of footsteps approached the bed.

"Ta-na, it's me, Renno."

Ta-na felt the mattress sink as his father sat down beside him.

"Are you all right, son?"

"I . . . I can't see him anymore."

"It's your eyes. Don't you remember? You led an assault on the British lines. A cannon exploded, and—"

"Not my eyes." He turned his face toward Renno, his unseeing eyes searching for a glimpse of his father. "Didn't you hear him? He was speaking Seneca."

"Diettino nio Diohe'ko?"

"Yes!" Ta-na exclaimed. "You heard him!"

"No, Ta-na, I heard you. You were praying."

The young man shook his head. "Not me. It was him. The old one."

"Old one?"

"He . . . he calls himself . . . Cornplanter."

Renno was stunned into silence.

"I heard you and Chief Rusog talking," Ta-na continued. "About a man named Cornplanter."

"You heard us?"

"When I woke up. You were talking about a medicine man. You called him Cornplanter, didn't you?"

"Yes, but—"

"That's the name he told me."

"Who?" Renno asked in confusion. "Chief Rusog?"

"No. The old man. Cornplanter."

"But he's up Kentucky way, if he even exists."

Ta-na reached over and took his father's hand. "Yes, he's there. And he called to me. More than once."

"Are you positive? What did he say?"

"He was chanting some kind of song . . . a song for planting corn. I saw him so clearly."

"Was it before . . . before you became . . . ?" Renno could not bring himself to say the word aloud.

"No—*after* I was blinded," Ta-na replied almost matter-of-factly. "I've seen him several times. Not with these eyes but with this one." He pressed his palm against his chest.

"Did he tell you anything?"

Ta-na struggled to remember. Nodding, he slowly recited the old man's words: " 'I await you in the west at the place where twin rivers run. . . . Offer thanks for the silence of darkness, for therein awakens the light.' "

"Twin rivers . . ." Renno repeated, caution in his voice. "Are you certain you saw this man?"

"As clear as when I had my sight."

"What was he wearing?"

"I—" Ta-na shook his head. "I don't remember. But he was holding a shield. A medicine shield."

"It had symbols on it," Renno declared resolutely. "And three cornstalks—red, yellow, and—"

"White!" Ta-na raised his face toward his father expectantly. "You saw him, didn't you?"

"In the Barrens. There was a storm, and I can't be positive, but . . ."

"It was the old one. Cornplanter."

"Perhaps." Renno fell silent as he thought back to the night in the storm. "It was something he said. It was so . . . so . . ."

"What was it?" Ta-na urged.

"He used that same phrase: the place where twin rivers run. He said he'd wait there for me, too."

"Then we must go."

"Where?" Renno asked.

"To the Land Between the Rivers. Isn't that where the Tennessee and the Cumberland run almost side by side? Isn't that where Chief Rusog said the medicine man Cornplanter is supposed to be?"

"Yes, but—"

"I can't go alone. But together we could."

"You want me to take you there?" Renno said incredulously. "It's a long journey, and your health—"

"I'm blind—that's all. But you can lead me. They say he's a medicine man. Perhaps he can heal my eyes . . . and your back."

"My back doesn't matter. I'm an old man myself.

When the manitous decide to take me, I'm prepared to go."

"Father, you know there's a reason we've had the same vision. You know we must go."

"I . . ." He hesitated, then reached over and touched his younger son's cheek. "Yes, Ta-na-wun-da, I know."

"When can we start?" Ta-na said eagerly.

"First you must regain your strength. And we must wait for Hawk to leave."

"Hawk?"

"This morning he was summoned to Washington. The President wants him to serve as an aide."

"When does he go?"

"He hasn't agreed, but I'm certain he'll leave within the week. That is, unless he gets wind of our plans. He'd insist on coming along, and somehow I sense this is a journey we must make alone."

"Yes," Ta-na agreed, nodding.

"Let's keep this to ourselves for now. In the meantime, Beth and the women can put a little meat on you." He poked his son's ribs. "On the both of us."

Grinning, Ta-na took hold of his father's arm. "I've been lying in this bed long enough. Help me up."

"But—"

"Come on."

He slid off the mattress and stood, his legs shaky. He waited a moment, holding on to his father's arm to steady himself, then walked across the room and out to his waiting family.

Four days later, a trio of riders headed north from Huntington Castle toward Nashville. As Renno had expected, his elder son was going to Washington. Hawk had not yet agreed to accept the position as President Madison's aide, but he had sent word that he would meet with the President to discuss the possibility. The trip would also give him an opportunity to visit Renna and her family.

Renno had not told Hawk—or anyone else, for that matter—the real reason he and Ta-na-wun-da were making their own journey, saying only that they would visit Dr. Stuart Fass and then return home. He had invited Hawk to accompany them as far as Nashville, and Hawk had readily agreed.

When they reached the city, it was too late to see the physician, so they took rooms at a boardinghouse and spent the evening in one of the taverns. In the morning, they had a quick breakfast in the dining room, then proceeded to the stables out back.

"You'll write and tell us your plans?" Renno asked his elder son as they finished saddling their horses.

"As soon as I know what they are," Hawk replied, tying a pair of bags to the back of his saddle.

"If you decide to stay, we'll bring Michael. Beth would love to see Renna and Beau and the children."

"Thank you, Father." He and Renno embraced. "There's one other thing, though." Hawk looked uncomfortably at his father and brother.

"Yes?" Renno asked.

"It's about the job. I . . . well, I won't move to Washington unless . . ."

"Don't worry about me," Ta-na interjected, clapping his brother on the shoulder. "I'm fine. Really I am."

"It's not you," Hawk said with a sheepish grin. "Not that I'm not concerned, mind you. But it's someone else." Again he hesitated.

"What is it, son?" Renno pressed.

"It's Ma-ton-ga. I'll only move to Washington if she agrees to come along." He looked up at his father. "I know I should have told you before, but I—"

"Me?" Renno said, his face lighting with joy. "I couldn't be happier for you. But what about Ma-ton-ga? Have you told her how you feel?"

"Not in so many words."

"Well, you'd better, before someone steals her away."

"You don't need to worry about that," Ta-na assured

his brother. "And I don't think there's any question what Ma-ton-ga will do when you tell her."

"You don't?" Hawk asked.

Ta-na grinned. "Wherever you go, that's where she'll be." He drew his brother into a bear hug. "I couldn't be happier for you, Hawk. For both of you."

"Now, don't forget to write," Renno reminded Hawk.

"And you can reach me at Renna's," Hawk replied.

"I'm afraid I can't write," Ta-na said with a shrugging gesture toward his eyes. "At least not legibly enough to read. My handwriting was bad enough when I could see."

"I'll be able to read it," Hawk assured him. "Or you can dictate a letter to Beth."

"All right," Ta-na relented. "But I've warned you."

"Just write, little brother."

"I will."

Again Hawk embraced his brother and father, then pulled himself into the saddle.

Renno patted the horse's neck. "Son," he called up to Hawk, "I want you to do what's best for you—and for Michael and Ma-ton-ga. But whatever you decide, you always have a home at Huntington Castle."

"Thank you, Father. I'll try to do what's best."

"I know you will."

"Are you sure you don't mind my leaving? I could wait until after—"

"No, we'll be fine," Renno assured him. "And you've got a long ride ahead of you."

They said their final good-byes, and then Hawk turned his horse down the alley that led to the street.

"We'd best be on our way, too," Renno said, taking Ta-na's arm and guiding him to his horse. "It's a good sixty miles or more to the Land Between the Rivers."

Ta-na grabbed the mane of his pinto and hoisted himself onto its back. He did not have a saddle, only a blanket and a pair of saddlebags strapped across the horse's rump.

"There's one stop we need to make first," he told his father.

"Where?"

"Dr. Fass's office."

"There's no reason—"

"We promised Beth," Ta-na reminded him. "And I think he should examine your back before we head out. It's been bothering you more the past day, hasn't it?"

"It's fine," Renno insisted as he mounted up.

"It's worse than when we left home."

"How would you know?"

"I'm blind, but I can still hear."

"Hear? I haven't once complained—"

"It's not what you said. It's the sound of your voice and the way you hold yourself when you walk."

"But you can't see the way—"

"I can hear you walking. It hurts, and you're compensating."

Renno eyed his son for a long moment. He was about to object, then relented and shrugged. "It hurts a little, I suppose. I'm just stiff from the ride."

"And weak. You're dragging that left foot."

"All right," Renno exclaimed, raising his hand in defeat. "We'll visit Doc Fass, if that'll quiet you down."

"Come—I'll lead the way," Ta-na replied with a smirk as he kneed his horse and set off down the alley.

"You'll lead us into a wall!" Renno shouted, kicking his horse forward and taking off after his son.

They reined in at the physician's office and tethered their horses. Renno took his son's arm and led him to the building, a small two-story structure with an anteroom, office, and examination room on the first floor and an apartment on the second. A bell jangled as they pushed open the door and entered the outer room, which held little more than a few hard-backed chairs. It was still quite early, and no one else was on hand, so they sat down to await the physician.

At one side of the waiting room was an open door that led to a narrow staircase. A few minutes after their arrival, they heard someone coming down the stairs, and Fass appeared in the doorway. His curly hair looked more tousled than usual, and his collar was still undone. When he saw Renno and Ta-na, he grinned broadly and strode across the room, hand outstretched.

"I hope we aren't too early," Renno said, rising and shaking the physician's hand.

"Only by a day."

"A day?"

"The office is closed today."

"I'm sorry. I didn't realize—"

"It's all right," Fass exclaimed, clapping Renno on the back. "It's never closed to friends—or anyone in need." He glanced at Ta-na, who had risen from his chair. "So, what brings you boys to Nashville? Friendship or need?"

"A little of both."

"My father wants you to check his back," Ta-na said.

Renno shifted uncomfortably. "Well, we figured that as long as we were in town, we might as well have you take a look at both of us."

"A splendid idea," Fass declared. "Let's go in back."

He led them into the examination room, which was quite a bit larger. The walls were lined with shelves of apothecary jars, and there were a couple of chairs and an examining table.

"Have a seat," Fass said, gesturing toward the chairs.

He opened a cabinet in the corner of the room and took out a tray of instruments, which he placed on the table. He began the examination by lighting a lamp and holding it in front of Ta-na's face, watching the movement of the eyes as he raised and lowered the lamp. Then he took a closer look, using a magnifying glass to view inside the eye.

"No change," he announced, putting down the lamp. "Which is good."

"Good?" Renno asked.

"The retina hasn't detached any further."

"And his sight? Will it improve?"

Fass gave a small sigh. "I doubt it. But there is some vision. Isn't there, Ta-na?"

The young man frowned. "Not much more than light and shadows."

Fass suddenly lashed out with his hand, as if he were going to strike Ta-na. He stayed his hand only inches from the young man's face, causing him to flinch slightly.

"What did you see?" Fass snapped, lowering his hand.

"I . . . uh, not much. It just went dark. And I felt the air."

"Good."

"Good?"

"You saw *something*." He turned to Renno. "We can always hope that in time he'll see more."

"He'll regain his eyesight?"

"I don't think so. But he'll compensate. Perhaps even learn to recognize shapes—enough to walk around without bumping into things."

"What about my father?" Ta-na asked impatiently.

"Yes, let's see about Renno."

Fass looked through his instruments, choosing a small rubber mallet. He began by checking Renno's involuntary responses, then had him do a number of exercises, such as holding his arms outright at his sides as long as possible. At first he joked jovially, but as the examination progressed, he grew increasingly quiet.

"What is it?" Renno finally asked.

"How long has your right side been involved?"

"What do you mean?"

"Your right side. How long?"

"It's my left that acts up," Renno insisted.

"That's what you told me at your house, but I knew it wasn't true. I figured perhaps you were just tired. But it's gotten worse."

"Look, Doctor, I've been on the trail, and—"

"It's more than that." He turned to Ta-na-wun-da. "Your father should be home in bed."

"How bad is it?" Ta-na asked.

"It isn't," Renno insisted.

"Those bullet fragments are lodged in your backbone. Movement serves only to cause further damage—it could even tear the spine, sort of like sharp rocks fraying a cord. Sometimes there's swelling, and paralysis sets in. Then when the swelling goes down, you feel better—but you aren't. Each time the damage gets worse. And eventually . . ."

"I'm not going to spend my life in bed," Renno declared. "Not as long as I can move. When I can't, that's when I'll take to bed."

"It will kill you," Fass said bluntly.

"Let it."

Shaking his head in frustration, he turned to Ta-na. "He shouldn't be on a saddle. Hire a wagon and make a bed of blankets in back. Then get him home."

"We're not going home," Renno said, rising from the chair.

"Good. Take a room here in town. And stay in bed."

"Come on, Ta-na." Renno walked from the room.

"Take your father home," Fass urged as he guided the young man out into the waiting room. "He needs to spend as much time as possible lying down."

"There'll be time enough for that when I'm dead," Renno declared, opening the front door.

"Father, maybe Dr. Fass is right. Maybe we shouldn't—"

"Let's get going; we've a long ride ahead of us." He strode toward the horses.

Fass turned to Ta-na. "If that pigheaded father of yours isn't going to take my advice, there's no point in bringing him all the way here. The ride will only make things worse."

"Well, Nashville was on our way, so we figured—"

"On your way? Where exactly are you headed?"

"To the Land Between the Rivers. We're planning to meet Chief Rusog and—"

"Are you crazy?" Fass stormed outside and glowered at Renno, who was already in the saddle. "Are the both of you crazy?"

"Come on, Ta-na," Renno said.

The young man felt his way over to the hitch rail and untethered his horse.

"The Land Between the Rivers?" Fass said incredulously. "That's way up at the Kentucky border."

"A stone's throw," Renno retorted. "There's a medicine man up there who may know a trick or two you college boys never learned," he added scornfully.

"Medicine man?" Fass scoffed. "Indian witchcraft, is more like it. I might as well put another bullet in your back and get it over with."

"I'm sorry, Doctor," Ta-na said, vaulting onto the pinto's back. He handed the reins to his father, who tied them to Kowa's saddle horn.

"Go on, kill yourselves, for all I care," Fass replied with a dismissive wave of the hand.

As they started down the street, the physician turned and headed into the building. Halting in the doorway, he called out Renno's name. The riders pulled up and looked back at him.

"I want to examine you again on your way back—that is, if you haven't killed yourself first."

Nodding, Renno kneed his horse forward and continued down the street, Ta-na-wun-da following behind.

Fass watched the dust swirl up behind them. "The lame leading the blind," he muttered, shaking his head.

Sixteen

Renno reined in his horse and waited for Ta-na-wun-da to ride up beside him.

"How many are there?" Ta-na asked, cocking his head as if trying to count the approaching riders by their sound.

"About a dozen." Renno noted that his son's hand was resting on the knife at his belt. "You won't need that. There are women and children among them."

"Are they Cherokee or Seneca?"

"I'm not sure." Renno sat his horse, peering into the distance. The travelers were just emerging from a large stand of trees, and as they came across the grassy meadow, he recognized their clothing. Suddenly he exclaimed, "Rusog! It's Rusog!"

He kicked his horse into a trot, leading Ta-na across the meadow. As the band of a dozen Cherokee pulled to a halt, Chief Rusog pulled away and approached at a gallop.

"Renno!" he called, riding up to them in the middle of the field.

The two men leaned forward and gripped forearms.

"Ta-na-wun-da! You are here, too!"

"We have come to see Cornplanter," Ta-na explained.

"Did you find him?" Renno asked.

Rusog let out a sigh. "We found the man called Cornplanter. And now we are returning home."

"Did he speak truth?" Renno said. "Was his medicine strong?"

"Cornplanter has no medicine. He is only an old man."

"Then his words were false."

"No . . ." Rusog replied. "His words were straight. He says he is only an old man, and these words are true. He brings no medicine to our land."

"And what of Tecumseh? Does he claim to be Tecumseh returned?"

"He says only that he has traveled from the Sacred Hills far beyond the Father of Waters."

"Then why do people seek him out?" Ta-na asked.

"I do not know. Three days we spent near his tepee. He shared his food and thanked us for having traveled so far to visit with him. But he had no medicine. And so we return to our village."

"Are you certain it was Cornplanter?" Renno pressed.

"I asked him, 'Are you the one named Cornplanter?' He said, 'That is what I have been called.' "

The other travelers had reached them now, and Renno recognized most of them from Rusog's Town. He greeted them warmly.

"Will you ride with us back to the village?" Rusog asked.

Renno hesitated, looking at his son.

"No," Ta-na said with conviction. He was staring straight ahead, as if trying to gaze beyond the trees to the old man's tepee.

"No, I think not," Renno agreed. "We have made a long journey. We will visit this Cornplanter before we go home."

Rusog nodded. "His tepee is a half-day's ride to the north. It sits along the bank of the western river near Thunder Point. Shall we make camp and wait for you?"

"No," Renno said, shaking his head. "We will see what this old man has to say."

Rusog grinned. "You will find that he speaks little. His grandson even less."

"Grandson?" Ta-na said in surprise.

"There is a boy."

"And a mother?"

"Just grandfather and boy."

"Good," Renno said. "Come, Ta-na. Let us go meet this old Cornplanter."

They said good-bye to Chief Rusog and the others, then continued along the trail, traversing the field and entering the stand of trees beyond.

It took Renno and Ta-na-wun-da an hour to reach the banks of the Tennessee, the westernmost of the two rivers that bordered the narrow tract known as the Land Between the Rivers. Three hours later they were finally within sight of Thunder Point, a spit of land formed by a bend in the river.

"I see a light ahead," Renno called back to his son as they started out onto the point.

"Is it the tepee?"

The sun was just dipping below the horizon, and Renno had to shield his eyes as he stared to the west and examined what appeared to be a conical structure out near the tip of the land. "It appears to be."

They dismounted and walked their animals down a path that had been trampled through the tall rushes. Renno described the tepee, which appeared to be covered in buffalo hide. To the left of it, two horses were tied to stakes near the water's edge. As they drew closer, the tepee flap was thrust aside, and someone stepped out, then darted back in again, jerking the flap closed behind him.

"I think the boy saw us."

Renno called out a greeting, saying that they had come in peace to visit the one known as Cornplanter. At first there was no response, but then the flap was pulled aside and left open as an invitation to enter.

Renno tied their horses to one of the thin alders that lined the riverbank. Returning to where Ta-na was standing, he took his son's arm and led him toward the tepee. He entered first, then helped his son duck through the opening.

A man was sitting cross-legged on the far side of a low fire glowing at the center of the tepee. His head was turned downward, and he was humming a chant and occasionally repeating the phrase, "Heh-yeh . . . Heh-yeh . . . Heh-yeh . . ." At first Renno didn't see the grandson, but then a movement off to the left caught his eye. The boy, who appeared to be twelve or thirteen years old, was huddled against the tepee wall, peering out from under a buffalo robe drawn over his shoulders and head.

When the old man raised his head, Renno's breath caught in an audible gasp.

"Is it him?" Ta-na whispered.

"Yes," Renno breathed in reply.

The old man had long white hair, with a single eagle's feather plaited into one braid, and he was dressed in buckskins so pale they were almost white. But it was his soft, dark eyes that revealed him to be the same one who had come to Renno in the Barrens.

The old man smiled and said something in a language Renno did not understand. Guessing that he had given his name, Renno said first in Seneca and then in English, "I am Renno, sachem of the Seneca."

"Renno," the man repeated, nodding. He gestured toward the space in front of the two visitors. "Please sit." He spoke the words in precise English, but with a clipped accent.

Renno and Ta-na sat down, facing the old man across the fire.

"They call me Cornplanter," the man told them. "This is my grandson, Wind Catcher."

"And this is my son, Ta-na-wun-da."

Ta-na nodded in the direction of the old man's voice.

"What brings you to my tepee?"

"*You* have brought us here," Renno said directly.

"But we have not met before."

"In the Barrens to the north . . . you led me to a young woman who was near death in a storm."

"But I have never walked these Barrens. I have only just come from the Sacred Hills in the land where the sun sleeps at night."

"You came to me in the Barrens," Renno insisted. "You told me you would wait for me at the place where twin rivers run, and we would begin the final journey."

Cornplanter lowered his gaze and did not speak.

"I have seen you, too," Ta-na-wun-da declared, leaning toward the firelight.

The old man looked up and gazed into Ta-na's eyes. "You have seen me, you whose eyes do not see?"

"I see you even now." Ta-na closed his eyes, focusing on the image that hovered before him. "Your hair is white, and a single feather hangs at your right shoulder. A red mark rises from your left breast to your shoulder—a stalk of corn reaching for the sun. It appeared when you were born, and it gave you your name."

Renno looked curiously at his son, then glanced at Cornplanter. The old man's hand was covering the precise spot Ta-na had described.

"Where have we met, my son?" Cornplanter asked Ta-na.

"In darkness. You came to me in the land of shadows."

"You have been blessed with great visions," the old man acknowledged. "But I am sorry. I know nothing of your visions or why they have brought you here. I am only an old man who has journeyed with his grandson from beyond the Father of Waters."

"Why?" Renno asked. "Why have you traveled so far from your home?"

"My own people once lived here between the rivers, in this place of rushes. It was in the time of my father's father's father, when the buffalo roamed these lands. But my people followed the buffalo far across the Father of Waters. And now I have followed my own vision back to the place where my people were born . . . where the sun is born each morning. I have come to show my grandson the land of his ancestors."

"They say you are a prophet and a medicine man. A great healer."

"And that is why you have brought your son to my tepee?" the man asked, his thin lips pulling into the faintest of smiles. "You think that a planter of corn can bring the sight back to his eyes?"

Renno's shoulders slumped. "I know only that the old man in my vision promised my son's darkness would be lifted. I followed that vision, and here I sit."

"I am no prophet. I am a planter of corn, nothing more. All I can do is come to this place of rushes and raise my tepee. And wait for the sun to follow the night."

As he spoke, it grew noticeably darker outside, and the firelight cast shadows that leaped and pranced upon the tepee walls.

"But surely there is another reason you have come here," Renno pressed.

"I came to plant what may be my last kernels of corn. Of those I have sown, only a few will sprout, and even they shall wither. All I can do is sing my song and pray that one or two plants survive the winter and keep our people strong in the days of famine that surely must come."

He started to hum again, and this time Ta-na-wun-da took up the chant. Cornplanter sat in awed silence, listening as Ta-na-wun-da finished the song of corn planting:

"Behold! The cornstalks murmur!
Everywhere, we are growing!
Heh-yeh! The world, how fair!
Everywhere, we are growing!
Heh-yeh! The world, how fair!"

Cornplanter rose, circled the fire, and sat before the young man. "That song is not of the Seneca," he observed. "It is not even of my people in the Sacred Hills. It comes from far to the west, in the hot dry land near the great sea at the edge of the world. In my youth I traveled beyond the Shining Mountains, and I learned this song among the people who call themselves Zuni." He reached up and touched Ta-na's cheek. "Who taught you this song, my son?"

"It was given to me in the darkness by the man named Cornplanter," Ta-na replied. "You taught me this song."

The old man lowered his head again and began to mutter incomprehensibly.

"Surely there must be something you can do for my son," Renno pleaded. "Perhaps some medicine of your people that will return his sight."

Cornplanter looked up, first at Renno, then at Ta-na-wun-da. Shaking his head, he announced, "There is nothing wrong with you, my son."

"But I am blind."

"Blind?" the old man said mockingly. "Did you not see this mark?"

He pulled open his buckskin shirt, revealing a long, jagged birthmark that indeed looked like a tall stalk with several ears of corn hanging from it. He grasped Ta-na's hand and placed the palm upon the mark.

"Do you not feel it? Can you not hear it singing to you in the silence?" He released Ta-na's hand. "You are not blind. You have only lost sight of your path."

Ta-na's lips quivered slightly, and he stammered, "B-but I . . . I—"

"Open your eyes!" Cornplanter exclaimed. Reaching out, he took Ta-na's face in his hands and touched his thumbs to the closed eyelids. "Offer thanks to the Great Spirit, the Master of Life. Offer thanks for the silence of darkness. For therein awakens the light!"

"But it's dark. I . . . I can't see—"

"Didn't you see me when I came to you singing? Didn't you see my eagle's feather and white hair? And wasn't I holding a medicine shield?"

"The shield!" Ta-na exclaimed.

"You *can* see," Cornplanter told him. "If your eyes are silent, look with your heart."

He released Ta-na and turned to his grandson, who had not moved a muscle during the entire conversation.

"Wind Catcher . . . bring me my shield."

The boy scrambled out from under the robes and padded across the tepee to a pile of blankets and clothing. Reaching underneath, he drew forth a large flat object wrapped in deerskin. With some effort he lifted it in front of him and hurried to where his grandfather was seated.

Cornplanter rested one edge against his lap and painstakingly untied the thongs that held the deerskin cover in place. After carefully unwrapping it, he held up a beautiful oval shield, fashioned from hide stretched over a frame. It was larger than most Indian shields and appeared heavier and more solid. Most unusual of all were the symbols painted around the edge, which appeared to be animals fashioned out of stars that surrounded three stalks of corn—one red, one yellow, one white.

"You have seen my shield, have you not?" the old man asked, and Ta-na nodded.

"I have seen it, too," Renno said, his voice a bare whisper.

Cornplanter offered the shield to Renno, who took it and felt its unusual heft. Cornplanter gestured for him to pass it to Ta-na, and Renno quickly complied. The young man also felt its weight and obvious strength, then ran his hand over the surface, touching the painted symbols. Nodding in approval, he held it forth to Cornplanter.

"It is yours," their host declared.

"Mine? But I couldn't—"

"Keep it. What use is a medicine shield to an old man who can no longer raise a lance?"

"But it should be for your grandson," Ta-na said.

"It is not for him. Not yet. The shield speaks to me, and it tells me who must wield it."

"It speaks to you?" Renno said skeptically. "But you said you weren't a prophet."

Cornplanter chuckled. "I spoke the truth—I am only a planter of corn. But like you, I have had a vision. I saw a young man approaching, his eyes blazing like hot coals. He called me to make this journey—to bring my grandson to this place of rushes. He told me to give my shield to him so that he might carry it back to the land where it was born."

"But that wasn't me," Ta-na protested, again offering the shield. "I wasn't the one who came to you."

"The man in my vision sang to me," Cornplanter continued. "It was a song I had not heard since I was young, like him. It was the Zuni song of corn planting." He gently pushed away the shield. "It is yours. In time, you will know where you must take it."

Ta-na-wun-da sat holding the shield against his chest, feeling its power flow through him. Finally he nodded and said, "I must give you something in return."

"Yes," Cornplanter agreed. "There is something of yours that I require."

"What is it?"

"A promise." He gestured to his grandson, and the boy came over and knelt in front of Ta-na. "Reach out," he told Ta-na. "This is Wind Catcher."

Ta-na held forth his hand, and Cornplanter placed it on the boy's shoulder.

"I want you to take Wind Catcher with you. I want you to raise him as a brother."

Ta-na-wun-da was stunned into silence. Slowly he raised his hand to the boy's cheek and felt the smooth, firm skin. A tear moistened his hand, and Wind Catcher lowered his head.

It was Renno who spoke. "We can't take your grandson from you. We—"

"You need not take him today. You can wait until tomorrow, when I have left." Smiling calmly, Cornplanter placed a hand on the back of his grandson, who was crying softly. "Do not weep, Wind Catcher," he told the boy. "I told you we would find your brother before I had to go."

"But why are you leaving him? Where are you going?"

Cornplanter did not respond to Renno's questions. Instead he turned to Ta-na-wun-da and gripped the young man's arm. "You must do as I tell you," he said, his voice solemn, almost grim. "Make a lance to carry with the shield. When you wield the lance and the shield, do so with strength but never in anger or fear. If you do as I say, your vision will be restored. Your path will be made clear."

The old man fell silent. When Renno again tried to converse with him, Cornplanter raised a hand.

"I am tired," he told them, then stood and retreated to a bed of skins at the rear. "We will speak in the morning." He lay down and pulled a blanket over him.

Seventeen

It was pitch black when Ta-na-wun-da jerked himself awake. Shivering in a cold sweat, he lay under his blanket with his arms wrapped around himself, listening to the silence, trying to figure out where he was. *It must be the middle of the night,* he thought, for in the darkness he could hear the breathing of others asleep. And he smelled the musky odor of a fire. *Cornplanter,* he recalled, nodding. He and his father had spent the night in the medicine man's tepee.

The old man's words came back to him: *If you do as I say, your vision will be restored. Your path will be made clear.*

For an instant he wondered if perhaps his vision had already returned. But then he heard the crackle of the fire and turned toward it, only to see nothing but a faint, hazy glow. Beneath the heavy breathing and the snap of burning wood was another, more constant sound. He concentrated on it for several moments and finally determined that it was the water rushing along the nearby riverbank. As he tried to envision the Tennessee, an eerie ripple coursed up his spine, and he saw himself floating down that river, the water bathing his eyes and showering him with light.

He eased the blanket off and sat up. Groping in the darkness for his moccasins, he felt the cool surface of the medicine shield. He pulled back his hand a moment, then drew the shield toward him. Searching the ground again, he found his moccasins and slipped them on his feet. Then he donned his heavy buckskin overshirt, picked up the shield, and turned toward where he remembered the te-pee opening to be.

Ta-na gauged the distance to the flap as well as the positions of the others sleeping around the fire. When he was confident he knew where everything was, he rose and padded across. His foot struck something, and he held his breath, thinking he had nudged his father. But there was no answering movement, and as he gingerly toed the object again he realized it was only one of their saddlebags. Continuing across the tepee, he found the door flap, pulled it aside, and eased himself through.

He stood a moment in the brisk predawn air, his face upraised toward the sky as he listened to the nearby water, then slowly circled the tepee and started into the rushes that lined the riverbank. He had to move carefully so as not to stumble on the uneven ground—or worse, to fall into the river. At last he reached a fairly steep embank-ment and sat down cross-legged on a bare patch of ground, placing the shield beside him.

Shrouded by the cool, damp fog that hugged the river, he sat thinking about the events of the past year: his father's crippling injury, his own near-death and blinding, his growing affection for the widow of his cousin and clos-est friend.

"Gao . . ." he whispered, shaking his head. He missed his friend terribly. And he felt so ashamed of the feelings he harbored for Gao's wife. He knew that Gao would want him to look out for Mist-on-the-Water. But it was not Ta-na who was taking care of Mist-on-the-Water; she was taking care of him. He was a blind man, no good to his family or himself—certainly not the kind of husband a young woman like Mist-on-the-Water deserved.

A cripple like Renno, he thought, closing his eyes in shame for thinking of his father that way. Renno had led a proud and productive life as sachem of the Seneca. Even now, in his final years, when no man would be judged harshly for giving up the struggle, he was refusing to succumb to the effects of a wound that would have brought down a lesser man. Ta-na, on the other hand, had seen only twenty-one summers, and already he was more helpless than the oldest men in his village.

"Why?" he called out. "Why didn't I die?"

His head hung low as he sat on the riverbank, wishing the water would carry him away, fearing that indeed it might. As it rushed past, it seemed to grow louder, filled with power and fury as it raced north toward the distant Ohio. Ta-na felt it pulling at him, and he had to flatten his hands against the ground to still the sensation of being swept away.

The voice of the river sang to him, repeating his name, again and again, layers of sound that urged him out of the darkness, calling him home. . . .

For an instant he thought it was his old friend Gao calling to him. But then the tone grew more desperate, more insistent, and he recognized the voice of his father.

"Ta-na! Ta-na-wun-da!"

"Father!" Ta-na blurted, leaping to his feet and turning toward the tepee. "I'm here!"

He heard hurried footsteps as Renno trampled through the rushes toward him.

"Ta-na?" Renno called out. "Is that you?"

"Yes! Over here!"

A moment later, Ta-na's father came up alongside him and grasped his arm. "What are you doing down here?" he asked, concern evident in his tone.

"I couldn't sleep."

"I heard you leave, and when you didn't come back . . ." Renno let go of his arm.

"I wanted to sit by the river . . . to think."

"Are you all right?"

"Yes, I'm fine," Ta-na said without conviction.

"Come. We'll walk back together." Again Renno took his arm, but the young man pulled free.

"I . . . I'm not ready."

After a long pause, Renno said, "All right. I'll join you awhile."

The two men sat on the riverbank, lost in their thoughts as they listened to the water. Finally Ta-na broke the silence. "Can I ask you something?"

"Of course."

"Are you certain?"

Renno gave a sharp laugh. "I may not answer, but you can ask. What's troubling you?"

"You."

"Me?" Renno said incredulously.

"And me."

"I told you—I'm feeling fine."

"It's not your back," Ta-na told him, then quickly added, "though that concerns me, too."

"Then what?"

"Why did you bring me here?"

Renno thought a moment before replying, "Because you asked me to. Because I hoped . . ." He fell silent.

"That I'd see again?"

"I suppose."

"And what if I don't?"

"That doesn't matter to me," Renno insisted. "Not to any of us."

"It matters to *me*." Ta-na let out a sigh. "And if I never see again . . . I can't bear the thought of having people take care of me for . . . forever."

"Is that why you said you were worried about me?" Renno asked. "Do you honestly believe I think less of you because you can't see?"

"Why not? I do."

"Don't!" Renno snapped. "This . . . this affliction of

yours . . . it's not for us to say why such a thing has happened. Perhaps you're being tested before . . ." His voice trailed off.

"Before what? Before I die?"

"No." Renno's voice lowered to a hush. "Before *I* die."

"You're making no sense."

Renno reached out and gripped his son's forearms. "Ta-na, when you were young, I spent far too little time with you. I should have brought you along on my travels. I should have taught you the things my father taught me."

"You taught me to hunt and to read. So did my uncle El-i-chi." Ta-na forced a smile. "You taught me to see with my heart. If only you could teach me to see with my eyes."

"That's what I mean. I was blind myself, and perhaps that's why you're in this darkness."

"No," Ta-na protested, pulling away his hands. "I was in battle and wasn't careful, and my stupidity took away my sight. It should have taken my life."

"It did, for a time," Renno replied, his tone softening. "When I thought you were dead, I cursed the manitous and the Master of Life for stealing you. For taking back their promise. I had lost faith, and like you, it blinded me to the truth."

"What truth?"

"The truth of who you are."

"I am Ta-na-wun-da, your son."

"And I am Renno, sachem of the Seneca. Yet there is one who is even more Seneca than I am. But I was so blind I didn't recognize that the true blood courses through my younger son's veins." He grabbed Ta-na's arm again. "Not just the red blood of the Seneca people but the blood of the sachem. The blood of my father and his father before him."

"I . . . I don't understand."

"You, Ta-na-wun-da—it was you all the time, yet I did not see. Not until we buried your cousin did I realize the truth."

"What truth?" Ta-na said in a hush, as if he were afraid to hear.

"Up north last year, near the lake of our people, I looked into your eyes and saw what the manitous had revealed. I saw the light of the sachem. I knew then that it is you, not your brother, who is destined to wear the robe. The manitous made me a promise that day, and when I thought you had died, I cursed them for breaking that promise. But now I have learned this truth: We cannot know where our path will ultimately lead, only that we must walk it."

The sky had brightened, revealing the tears in Ta-na's eyes. He shook his head slowly, uncertainly. "Whatever you saw that day . . . it is gone. There is no more light. It has gone out."

"It burns even more fiercely in the darkness," Renno declared with conviction. "Like the blazing coals that Cornplanter saw."

"This . . . this makes no sense. When the time comes for a new sachem to wear the robe, it will be Ow-sweh-ga-da-ah Ne-wa-ah." He used his brother's Seneca name. "He is the true white Indian."

"Hawk walks another path. You're the one the Master of Life has chosen to lead our people when I'm gone."

"Me?" Ta-na said in disbelief. "A blind man? I can lead no one—not even myself."

"Perhaps through this affliction you've been gifted with greater sight. I don't understand it myself. I know only that the light I have seen within you doesn't lie."

"I wish that were true. . . ." Ta-na muttered.

Renno released his son's arm and clapped him on the back. "It's dawn. Let's return to the tepee."

Ta-na shook his head. "Not yet. I want to sit awhile longer." He hesitated, then added, "By myself."

Renno considered the request, then stood. "Don't stay too long."

"I won't."

Ta-na listened as his father's footsteps receded

through the rushes. Turning back to the river, he gazed toward the water, struggling to see something—anything—in the darkness that surrounded him.

He's wrong, he told himself. *He's growing old. Afraid of death.*

"Afraid . . ." he said aloud. "No. He's mistaken. It's not me. I'm no sachem."

As if in reply, he heard his name carried on the morning breeze. He turned to his right, in the direction of the sound. It was a voice, but not a human one. Yet it was so familiar as it called him, summoned him forth.

"Gao?" he whispered, cocking his head and straining to listen. "Is that you?"

The voice urged him to approach. Without realizing what he was doing, he picked up the medicine shield and started to walk along the embankment. He moved swiftly yet did not stumble; it was as if the voice were guiding each step. As he made his way upstream beside the river, he sensed something in front of him and reached out, his palm touching the bark of a tree. He moved through the copse of alders, feeling each one, listening to the words that rode the wind. It was the voice of his dearest friend, Gao, but it spoke the words of the old planter of corn:

"Make a lance to carry with the shield. When you wield the lance and the shield, do so with strength but never in anger or fear. If you do as I say, your vision will be restored. Your path will be made clear."

His hand closed around the thin, sturdy trunk of a young tree. He ran his hand up and down its length, feeling its supple strength.

"Yes . . ." he breathed, lowering the medicine shield to the ground.

Dropping to his knees, Ta-na-wun-da drew the hunting knife from his belt and began to cut.

The first light of dawn was already brightening the walls of the tepee as Renno entered and sat down on his blanket to the left of the doorway. Cornplanter was awake and sitting on the far side, stirring the embers back to life. Just beyond, his grandson was curled under his robes, apparently still asleep.

"The sun will be strong today," the old man commented, looking up at Renno.

"Yes, the sky is clear," Renno said distractedly.

"Do you always walk like that?"

Renno looked at him curiously.

"Like I do," Cornplanter continued, grinning. "Like an old man."

Renno sat up straighter. "I'm just a little stiff this morning."

"Is it not from that wound in your back?"

"Who told you . . . ?"

Cornplanter placed a thin branch on the coals. "I see it even from here. It leaves its marks upon your face."

Renno was about to disagree, but then he nodded and replied, "It really doesn't hurt."

"No," Cornplanter agreed. "As we reach the end of our journey, the old wounds hurt no more."

Renno moved closer to the fire. "In the Barrens . . . you said we'd take the final journey together. Is that why I'm here?"

Cornplanter shrugged. "It is not for me to say why you have come."

"I'm not afraid of dying. I'm only sorry it will be from an old bullet eating away inside of me, rather than on the field of valor."

"Valor . . ." Cornplanter sighed. "You speak like a young warrior, eager to sacrifice himself for his people. But isn't that precisely what you have done?"

"Me? I was stupid and let a drunkard shoot me in the back. That's all."

"Perhaps his bullet was guided by the hand of the Master of Life. Perhaps it serves only to prepare the way."

"The way? I don't understand."

Cornplanter laughed aloud. "Nor do I. But I will tell you of my dream." He closed his eyes and began to rock back and forth. "During the night, you appeared before me as a young warrior. At your side was a brother warrior, and behind you stood your father and your father's father. They were leading you from this world to the next. And below you, your nation sang the ancient condoling rites."

He raised his head toward the smoke hole at the peak of the tepee, his voice deep and mournful as he chanted in the tongue of Renno's people:

> *"Konyennedaghkwen,   onenh   weghniserade*
>   *yonkwat-kennison.*
> *Rawenniyo raweghniseronnyh."*

> "My offspring, now this day we are met
>   together.
> The Master of Life has appointed this day."

Cornplanter opened his eyes, his gaze burning into Renno's soul. "They were singing of a man who died not from the old wound in his back but from the great sacrifice he made for his son and for his people. A sacrifice made on the field of battle, worthy of Ghonkaba and Ja-gonh and the first white Indian. This is the dream the manitous brought me. This is the destiny and the path you have chosen."

Renno shook his head in stunned disbelief, struggling for words. He wanted to ask how the old man knew so much—knew even the names of Renno's father and grandfather. But when he opened his mouth to speak, Cornplanter raised his hand for silence.

"The riders are coming. The journey begins."

Renno heard the approaching hoofbeats of several horses. He turned toward the doorway and was about to see who it was, but he felt someone grab his arm. He looked up to see Cornplanter standing over him.

"They come for me, not for you," the old man declared.

He circled the fire and sharply nudged the robes

covering his grandson. The boy jerked awake. Yanking off the robes, he stared up with bleary eyes at his grandfather.

"Hurry to the river," Cornplanter told the boy, who scrambled into his moccasins. "Seek Ta-na-wun-da among the alders and tell him they have come. Tell him to stay away."

Wind Catcher started toward the doorway, but Cornplanter grabbed him and gestured toward the rear of the tepee. With a nod, the boy scurried to where he was pointing, lifted the hide covering, and crawled underneath. Sensing something was wrong, Renno retrieved one of his pistols from the saddlebag he had used as a pillow and swiftly loaded it.

"No," Cornplanter said, coming over and reaching out for the weapon. "We have no need of that."

The hoofbeats grew louder, then abruptly halted just outside the tepee. Renno glanced down at the gun in his hand, then up at Cornplanter. He did not want to obey the old man, yet there was something in Cornplanter's eyes that commanded obedience, and he reluctantly handed over the gun. Cornplanter carried it partway across the tepee and slipped it under the folds of a blanket, then returned and sat beside Renno.

The door flap was yanked aside, and a white man stepped through, followed closely by two other men. Their pistols were drawn, and they trained them on the two occupants of the tepee as they spread out on either side of the opening. Renno's hand itched for his gun, but he knew it would be a fool's play to reach for it, since it was more than six feet away. He would have to wait and see what these strangers intended.

They weren't *all* strangers, Renno realized with a shock when a fourth man entered the tepee. Renno immediately recognized the red hair and stubble of beard and noted that he favored his left leg—the one Renno had shot during their confrontation in the Barrens. His former comrades had called him Jim. Apparently, after they had been killed, he had made new friends and had come seeking revenge.

Jim was the only one of the four who hadn't drawn his weapon. Instead he was rubbing his right shoulder where Mist-on-the-Water had shot him. He took a step toward Renno, grinning smugly as he said, "I thought that was your horse out there."

"Welcome to my tepee," Cornplanter said. "Will you smoke with us by the fire?"

The outlaw gave the old man a dismissive glance, then turned back to Renno. "I'd say we have a score to settle, wouldn't you?" He looked around the tepee as if expecting someone else to be on hand.

"He ain't here," one of the others said.

"Check outside," Jim ordered, drawing his pistol from his belt and cocking the hammer. "You go with him," he told one of the others, and the pair ducked through the opening, leaving Jim with only one man to side him.

"What do you want?" Renno demanded, shifting slightly so that he would be ready to go for his gun when the opportunity arose.

Jim laughed gruffly. "Don't want nothing, 'cept to kill you and that Injun get of yours."

"Any business we have is between the two of us," Renno declared. "There's no need for—"

"That's true enough," the outlaw agreed. "But there's others with their own scores to settle."

"Others?"

"Don't matter who. All that matters is that you and that 'breed boy of yours end up dead."

"If this is because of the Barrens—"

"Got nothing to do with the Barrens. That just makes the job a damn sight more enjoyable." He shook his head. "No, *Mr.* Harper," he said with mocking disdain, "this has to do with you making the wrong enemies. Why d'you think I trailed you to the Barrens in the first place? And all the way up here?"

"Who wants me dead?" Renno asked directly.

"Like I said, it don't make much difference. But when a fellow goes to meet his Maker, I suppose he oughta know who fired the slug that sent him there. The name's Jim Radison." He nodded by way of introduction, his smirk deepening. "And as soon as my boys drag that blind buck of yours back in here, we'll finish this show."

Eighteen

Ta-na-wun-da stood on the riverbank, leaning on the four-foot length of wood he had been carving into the handle of a lance. He had heard three or four horses ride up to the tepee, and by their shod hooves he knew that the riders were white. He was considering whether or not to return and find out who they were when his attention was drawn to the sound of someone tramping through the rushes off to his right. It was the light step of a boy, and he turned and called out, "Wind Catcher!"

The boy shifted direction and came running over to Ta-na. "They are here!" he said in an excited whisper as he tugged at Ta-na's sleeve.

"Who?" Ta-na asked, keeping his own voice low as he sought in vain to see something in the hazy glow.

"They come to kill you!"

Wind Catcher's English was not as polished as Cornplanter's, but Ta-na understood what he was saying. Gripping the boy's shoulder, he asked, "What are you talking about?"

"Grandfather tell me they are coming. Two days ago,

he say my brother come for the shield, then white men come to kill him and take it away."

"Wait here," Ta-na directed. "I'll go see who they are."

"No!" the boy blurted. Again he grabbed Ta-na's sleeve and tried to pull him farther along the riverbank. "They come! Grandfather tell us to hide!"

Ta-na heard voices now—two men calling back and forth as they beat the rushes in search of him. Cursing the cannon blast that had taken his sight, he crouched low in the heavy bank of fog and allowed the boy to lead him back into the copse of alders. But he knew their trampled path would lead the strangers right to them, so he whispered into Wind Catcher's ear, "We must crawl into the rushes and hide at the river's edge."

They dropped to the ground, and the boy gripped the other end of the lance and used it to guide Ta-na down a steep embankment. Ta-na managed to hold on to the shield and lance as he awkwardly made his way into the rushes and tall grass that lined the riverbank. As he moved, he took care to straighten the vegetation behind them so as to leave as little trace of their passing as possible.

When they reached a relatively flat area beside the river, Ta-na leaned the shield against a large boulder at the water's edge and drew out his hunting knife. He positioned the handle against the end of the lance, then had Wind Catcher hold it there while he removed the leather laces from the front of his shirt and used them to lash the knife in place. When he was satisfied the blade would hold, he handed the shield to the boy and told him to take it and swim to safety if necessary.

The voices grew louder as the men crashed through the brush. Praying the fog bank would keep him hidden, Ta-na-wun-da gripped his makeshift lance and moved up the embankment, putting some distance between himself and the boy, wondering who these men were and how Cornplanter had known they were coming.

*   *   *

Inside the tepee, Jim Radison stood with feet slightly apart, his pistol waist-high as he trained the barrel on Renno. Beside him, his partner kept his gun aimed at Cornplanter's chest, awaiting orders. Renno took in Radison's arrogant smirk and tried to gauge if he would follow through as he had promised and wait to make his play until the other men returned with Ta-na-wun-da.

Renno prayed that Wind Catcher had found Ta-na in time and they had somehow made it to safety. But he doubted his son would try to escape knowing that Renno and Cornplanter were in trouble. Worried that Ta-na might do something foolish, he decided he would have to make some sort of move—before Radison and his partner grew tired of the wait and started shooting.

"How much are you being paid to murder two men?" he asked Radison, trying to buy some time by engaging him in conversation.

"If you're figuring to offer more, don't waste your time," the outlaw leader replied.

"Your boss must have quite a bit of money," Renno surmised. "And he must be generous with it, seeing as how you won't even consider another offer."

"Hell, this is one job I'd do for free."

"What about you?" he called to the other man, who gave him a passing glance. "What's your share? Fifty dollars? A hundred, perhaps? What if I were to double it?"

The comment drew the man's attention. It also elicited a scornful laugh from Jim Radison.

"If you're trying to rile my boys, it won't work. That right, Bascomb?" he called over his shoulder. Without awaiting a reply, he told Renno, "Bascomb and his friends might perk up their ears at such foolishness, but they know better than to turn on me or—" He grinned smugly. "We'll just call him the boss."

Radison stepped back to the tepee entrance. Keeping his eyes on Renno, he leaned toward the open doorway and listened for some sign of the other two men returning. His frown indicated they were not within earshot.

"Hey!" the man named Bascomb exclaimed, waggling his pistol at Cornplanter, who had risen from where he had been sitting on the blankets. "Get down!"

Disregarding the order, Cornplanter stood smiling at the outlaw with palms upraised. In a calm, almost peaceful voice, he proclaimed, "What you have come to do, do quickly."

"Shut up, old man!" Radison snapped as he moved closer to Renno. "Sit down or we'll finish things right now."

Cornplanter extended a bony forefinger toward Bascomb's pistol. "There is no need for that. Give it here." He moved toward the outlaw.

Bascomb turned questioningly to Radison, then glowered at Cornplanter and again ordered him to sit. But the old man kept coming, reaching out for the gun, his hand inches from the barrel as he repeated, "What you have come to do . . ."

Flustered, the outlaw raised the barrel slightly and pulled the trigger. The force of the blast knocked Cornplanter backward several feet, but incredibly he remained on his feet, the same ineffable smile on his face. There was a dark, burnt hole in the center of his white buckskin shirt, and it was already tinged with red.

". . . do quickly," Cornplanter concluded, his voice quavering but strong. He again started forward, arms outstretched.

Nearby, Renno saw that Radison had turned toward Cornplanter. Bascomb, meanwhile, was frantically reloading. Seizing the opportunity, Renno dived toward the blanket where his pistol lay hidden. The sudden movement drew Radison's attention, and the outlaw leader swung his pistol around and fired. The bullet smacked into a pile of robes inches from Renno's head.

Renno rolled once and came up with the gun. Thumbing back the hammer, he swung it around, searching for his target. Radison was reloading now, but Bascomb had finished and was raising his gun on Cornplanter again. Taking quick aim, Renno fired, his slug catching Bascomb on the side of the face and blowing half of it away. His body crumpled to the tepee floor, the pistol firing harmlessly into the ground.

Renno leaped up, smoking pistol in his hand. Ten feet away, Radison was ramming a ball down the barrel. Realizing there was no time to spare, Renno tossed aside the spent weapon and leaped at the man, who jerked up the gun and in one quick motion cocked it and pulled the trigger. The hammer struck the pan with a dull, empty thud, and before he could thumb it back again, Renno barreled into him, knocking him off his feet.

When the first shot sounded from within the tepee, Ta-na-wun-da was crouched only a few feet from the men stalking him. He could hear them talking and knew they were hunting a "blind Injun buck," as one of them had described their prey. Ta-na had no idea why they wanted him, but when the gunshot rang out, he knew it was deadly business.

"What's that?" one of the men shouted, and from the sound of his voice Ta-na could tell he had spun around and was facing the tepee.

"Jim must've gotten tired of waiting," the other replied, a hint of humor in his tone. "Figured he'd start the party without us."

"Where is that Injun bastard?" the first one muttered, turning again toward the river—toward where Ta-na was hunkered low among the rushes. "I can't see anything in this goddamn fog."

"He came this way, that's for damn sure."

Ta-na gripped the lance, waiting for the right moment. Just then two gunshots rang out, one on the heels of the other. The sound drew the men's attention, and they momentarily turned their backs on Ta-na.

"Party's finished," one of the men remarked with a chuckle.

"That leaves us the blind buck to have our fun with."

Gauging where the nearer man was standing, Ta-na-wun-da rose up from the rushes and turned toward him, eyes opened wide as he struggled to see. He sensed a shadow in front of him but couldn't tell if it was the man's back or just an imagined form. But then the shadow moved, and he knew he had to strike. With a prayer to the manitous to guide his hands, he rushed forward, jabbing out with the lance.

The shadow seemed to loom over him, and then he heard a shuddering groan and felt the knife blade strike something hard, like bone, and then slip through. The lance was yanked downward and was almost pulled from his hands as the outlaw dropped to his knees, then fell forward and lay writhing on the ground, the knife blade firmly planted in the small of his back.

Ta-na was jerking the lance free when he heard the other man spin around and shout. The rasping snap of a pistol hammer was followed by a thunderous boom, and as Ta-na tried to dodge to one side, the bullet slammed into his head. The world exploded in a blaze of light as he was lifted off his feet and sent tumbling down the embankment and into the river. His body struck the surface, and he was pulled under, the frigid water closing around him. He tried to cry out, but the water poured into his lungs as the current carried him away, as the flashing lights swirled and faded into the distance.

Renno and the outlaw leader rolled across the tepee floor, locked in hand-to-hand combat. Renno had managed to get in several solid punches, but they had little effect on Jim Radison, who apparently had seen his share of barroom brawls. With a sharp cry, the younger man thrust his arms out and managed to break Renno's grip. Kicking upward, he knocked Renno off, throwing him backward several feet. Scrambling to his feet, Renno was about to leap again at Radison when he saw a knife in the outlaw's hand. He had drawn it from his boot and was grinning maliciously as he motioned for Renno to come at him.

"Wanna piece of this?" he challenged, waving the knife blade in front of him.

Renno looked around, trying to remember where he had left his own knife the night before. Radison moved in, lashing out with the knife, the sharp tip slicing through the front of Renno's shirt.

Renno stumbled as his weak left leg buckled under him. He dropped to one knee, then jerked to the side, away from the slashing blade. But it caught him on the shoulder, laying open a deep gash, and he fell onto his back. He started to rise but was met by the outlaw's boot as Radison gave a violent kick to his head, stunning him and knocking him over onto his belly.

Radison let out a cold laugh. Lowering the knife to his side, he moved behind his victim, ready to deliver the coup de grâce. Bending over, he gripped a handful of Renno's hair and yanked back his head, baring the neck. Reaching around with the knife, he was about to draw it across the jugular when a *whoosh* of air caused him to turn. He was met by something hard and heavy smashing into the side of his head, knocking him off his feet. A second blow sent him sprawling unconscious on the ground.

Renno looked up through bleary eyes and saw Cornplanter standing over him, an iron kettle in his hand. The old man was still smiling, but he dropped down heavily and sat holding his chest. Renno shook his head to clear it, then pulled himself to his knees and examined the wound on Cornplanter's chest just below the heart. Although it was large and gaping, surprisingly little blood was flowing from it.

"The . . . the gun . . ." the old man muttered, gesturing across the tepee.

Renno remembered there were two other men outside, and he dashed to where his pistol was lying. Snatching it up, he opened his saddlebag and retrieved the powder horn and shot bag. He hurriedly reloaded and had just returned to Cornplanter's side when a figure appeared in the doorway.

Spinning around, pistol in hand, Renno found himself facing one of the remaining outlaws. His finger itched to pull the trigger, but he held back. The man had the barrel of his pistol shoved up under the chin of Wind Catcher, who was squirming in his arms.

"Lower that hammer and toss it away," he ordered Renno, who looked back and forth between Wind Catcher and his grandfather, then hesitantly complied.

Keeping a tight grip on the boy, the outlaw moved over to where Bascomb was lying and grimaced when he saw what was left of the man's face. Dragging the boy along, he approached the other body and nudged it with his foot. Radison stirred and began to moan, and the outlaw backed away and waited for him to come around. Slowly Radison roused and sat up, rubbing his head and blinking against the pain. At last he opened his eyes and glanced up at his partner, then turned to Renno and the old man, his expression a blend of hatred and triumph.

Ta-na-wun-da fought the raging current, fought the darkness that had descended upon him. He gagged on the water that filled his lungs and struggled not to draw in a breath, for that would mean drawing in his own death. He was dizzy, and his head throbbed with pain. But he would not give in easily. There was the boy to think about—and his father and the old medicine man.

Don't let me die! he called within his mind. And with the paralyzing fear, he felt the current tighten its hold.

No! he railed against the river, flailing out at the water. But it only served to draw him deeper, closer to death. *You won't take me!*

He remembered the words of the old man: "Never in anger or fear . . ." He had been speaking about the lance and the shield, yet the words reverberated now with power. He felt his lungs close to bursting but forced himself to relax his arms and legs, to let the current carry him where it would.

As he stopped flailing about, he felt his body start to rise, the river carrying him upward toward what appeared to be a shimmer of light.

No anger . . . no fear . . .

The current bore him swiftly to the surface, and his head broke through into the sweet, life-giving air. He tried to take in a breath but ended up gagging on the water he had swallowed. Fighting for air, he began to swim toward shore. He was soon in the gentler shallows and was able to pull himself up onto land, where he lay choking and spitting.

When he finally could breathe again, he sat up and took stock of his situation. His head continued to pound, and he gingerly touched the long gash just above his temple. Apparently the bullet had struck only a glancing blow and had not shattered the skull. But the wound was a nasty one, and blood streamed down the side of his face.

When he felt strong enough, he stood and turned in place, trying to figure out how far he had been carried and which way to go. He wiped the blood and water from his eyes and noticed that the light was brighter than before, broken by occasional shadows. He moved toward one of the shadows and bumped into a tree. Turning away from it, he started upstream along the river, keeping the water to his right and the shadows to his left.

The boulder, he told himself. All he had to do was make his way upstream to the boulder where he had left Wind Catcher. *Perhaps he's still hiding there. Perhaps . . .*

A feeling of dread came over him as he remembered the gunshots from the tepee. He quickened his pace, breaking into a run as he made his way up the riverbank. Several times he bumped into trees or tripped on projecting roots and almost slid into the water, but each time he scrambled to his feet and continued to run. He noticed that the shadows were moving past him at a speed that matched his pace, and as he calmed his fear and began to trust his vision, he realized he could make out the shapes of objects around him. Soon he was weaving in and out among the trees that lined the river, leaping over obstructions almost as easily as when his vision was whole.

He came to an abrupt halt when a dark round form loomed in front of him. Reaching out, he moved slowly forward until his hand pressed the cool surface of the boulder.

"Wind Catcher?" he whispered. He called the name again, but there was no answering sound.

Turning away from the river, he sensed something directly in front of him, and he knelt and picked up the medicine shield where Wind Catcher had dropped it. Clasping it to his chest, he headed into the rushes, following a beaten path up the embankment in the direction of the tepee. As he neared the top of the rise, he smelled death in front of him. He moved cautiously forward until his foot struck the body of the outlaw he had killed. He reached down, searched the man's back, and found the protruding lance. Yanking it free, he gripped the lance in one hand and the shield in the other and crept stealthily through the rushes toward the tepee beyond.

Renno watched the eyes of the outlaw who held the pistol jammed up under Wind Catcher's chin. It was obvious the man was nervous, and Renno worried he would pull the trigger.

A few feet away, Jim Radison stood rubbing his head where Cornplanter had struck him with the iron kettle. He gestured at the young boy in his partner's grip. "Wh-who is he?" he muttered, blinking his eyes to clear his vision.

"Found him hidin' in the grass after I killed that blind Injun."

Renno shuddered but forced himself to remain calm.

"He's dead?" Radison asked. "You sure?"

"Shot him in the head. Last I seen, he was floatin' down the river."

"Good. What about Elliot?"

The outlaw shook his head. "The buck had some sort of lance. Snuck up behind us and got Elliot in the back."

Radison winced slightly but did not otherwise seem concerned. He turned to Renno. "Who's the boy?" he demanded, indicating Wind Catcher.

Renno was debating whether or not to respond, when Cornplanter answered in a weakening voice, "M-my grandson."

With a brusque nod, Radison moved past his partner and over to where his pistol was lying. Retrieving it, he checked the charge and stuffed it behind his belt, then snatched up Renno's pistol and saw that it had been reloaded, as well. He cocked the hammer and walked toward Renno. With a glance to his partner, he said, "Let the boy go."

The man hesitated, then did as ordered. Wind Catcher rushed into his grandfather's arms. Renno saw how feebly Cornplanter held on to the boy and knew he would not last much longer.

Radison motioned for his comrade to keep his gun on Cornplanter and the boy, saying with a smirk, "I want the white Indian for myself."

As he raised the pistol, he was distracted by a loud thud, followed by a guttural moan. He spun around to see the other outlaw stagger forward, the gun slipping from nerveless fingers as he dropped to his knees and fell facedown on the ground. Standing beyond him, just inside the open doorway, was Ta-na-wun-da, shield upraised in one hand, bloody lance in the other, a stream of red blazoning the side of his face. He gave a fierce shriek as he drew back the lance and let it fly.

Radison swung up his pistol and jerked the trigger, the gun bucking in his hand a split second before the lance struck him in the chest, piercing his breastbone and his

heart. Ta-na-wun-da was struck, as well, the bullet piercing the center of the leather shield and knocking him off
his feet and back against the tepee wall.

Even as the outlaw was crumpling to the ground,
Renno was on his feet, running to his son. The shield lay
on top of him, the front torn open by the blast. As Renno
tossed it aside and reached for his son, he feared the
worst. To his joy and surprise, Ta-na was stunned but un-
scathed, and he sat up and rubbed his chest where the
force of the impact had struck him.

Renno picked up the shield and examined the hole.
The bullet had pierced the outer skin but had not emerged
from the other side. Confused, he jabbed a finger in the
hole and widened it, revealing twisted metal where the
lead ball had imbedded itself in a layer of tightly woven
chain links.

On the far side of the tepee, the boy was sobbing as
he cradled his grandfather's head in his lap. Renno helped
Ta-na to his feet, and they hurried over. The blood was
flowing freely now from Cornplanter's chest, and it was
obvious the life was pouring out of him, too. Still, he
managed a smile.

"I . . . I was not ready before . . . but now is a
good time to die. . . ."

"No!" the boy shouted, tears streaming down his
face.

"You . . . you must be strong. I will see you again
one day. Until then, you must go with . . . with your
brother." He looked up at Ta-na-wun-da, who knelt and
took the old man's hand.

"I wish I could see you," Ta-na said, choking back his
own tears.

"You have already seen me . . . and you will see me
again." Reaching up, he touched his own forehead, then
placed his hand over Ta-na's eyes. "I . . . I give you my
grandson. And I give you my sight." He looked beyond
them and saw the twisted metal where the medicine
shield had caught the bullet. "The shield . . . it serves

you well," he said, withdrawing his hand from Ta-na's eyes. "Remember," he whispered. "Never in anger . . ."

His gaze seemed to shift to the far distance, and his smile grew stronger and surer.

"Build my platform here by the river . . ." He closed his eyes, and the breath went out of him in a hush.

Nineteen

"I will make the sky clear for you,
so that you will not see a cloud.
I will give the sun to shine upon you,
so that you can look upon it peacefully
    when it goes down.
You shall see it when it is going.
Yeh! the sun shall seem to be hanging
    just over you,
and you shall look upon it peacefully as
    it goes down."

Renno and Ta-na-wun-da completed the Seneca song for the dead, chanting in English, their common language with Wind Catcher. They stood a few moments in silence in front of the burial platform, which they had constructed out of the tepee poles so that Cornplanter could be laid to rest in the manner of his people in the Sacred Hills. Then they moved back, leaving the boy to have a few moments alone with his grandfather. He dropped to his knees and looked up at the platform of blankets and robes, fighting back tears as he whispered something. Then he rose and walked solemnly to where they were waiting.

"I am ready," was all he said. It was one of the few things he had spoken since Cornplanter's death the day before.

"Your grandfather will rest peacefully here," Renno told him. "He can look out upon the river that was once home to his people."

Wind Catcher walked past Renno and took his new brother's hand. "Did you see him?" he asked.

"Cornplanter?" Ta-na-wun-da looked down at the boy, trying to discern his features in the dark image that appeared before him.

"Last night. I see him standing outside the tepee."

"Yes, that was your grandfather," Ta-na-wun-da declared, though in fact he had seen nothing—either real or in vision.

"He . . . he was smiling."

"He walks with his ancestors now," Renno explained. "It is the great gift that awaits us at the end of life." He placed a hand on the boy's back. "Come, we must be on our way. It is a long ride to our village."

The two men started toward where their horses were packed and waiting. But Wind Catcher held back, releasing Ta-na's hand and taking a last look toward the river where his grandfather was lying.

"Ta-na-wun-da," he called, still gazing at the burial platform.

"Yes?" Ta-na walked over to him, Renno remaining a few feet away.

Wind Catcher turned toward the man who was to be his new brother. "Before you come here, Grandfather say, 'When I am gone, tell them of my vision.'"

"What vision?" Ta-na asked, placing a hand on his shoulder.

"The vision bring us to Land Between the Rivers."

"Tell us of this vision," Renno said, coming up alongside them.

Wind Catcher closed his eyes, his brow furrowed with concentration as he summoned the images his grandfather had described. At last he nodded and began:

"Grandfather in the Shining Mountains many days without food or water. The sun rise one morning, and visions come. Grandfather see many people, not our people in the Sacred Hills but from all the red nations that lie on this side of the Father of Waters. They are marching toward Sacred Hills and toward our brother lands to the south. Many hundreds coming—all the warriors and women and children. Even little ones creeping on the ground and babies tied to their cradle boards. They stream across the Father of Waters and through the tall grasslands. Grandfather say it is the final journey. All must make the journey, and the blood of many will soak the ground. It is a great trail of blood and tears. Even the buffalo cry out to see them passing. The hearts of the buffalo are broken, and in a few winters they vanish from the land."

Wind Catcher opened his eyes and looked up at the two men. Ta-na touched his cheek and felt it moist with tears.

"Cornplanter was able to see what many of us cannot," Ta-na told him. "We cannot know why he had such a vision."

"Why did this vision lead you to journey here?" Renno asked.

"Grandfather see the vision many times. Each time the same. All the red people must make the great trail of blood and tears. But then new vision come, and it bring him hope."

"What did he see?" Ta-na pressed.

"A few warriors make the journey ahead of the people. They travel to the Sacred Hills, to the Shining Mountains, to the dry lands in the south. They know their brothers and sisters are coming, and they go ahead to smoke the pipe and prepare the ground. Grandfather say one of these warriors has great vision but eyes that do not see. He say we must find this warrior and give him medicine shield to make him whole again."

Wind Catcher walked away from Ta-na and Renno to where the horses were tethered. There were four horses; Cornplanter's carried the supplies. The medicine shield was suspended from one of the saddlebags, and the boy removed it and brought it to them.

"Medicine shield have great power," he declared, holding it forth.

The skin stretched across the front had not yet been repaired, and Ta-na clearly saw the sunlight glint upon the chain-mail lining that gave the shield its weight and strength.

"Grandfather say medicine shield contain spirit power of the men who brought horses to our land."

Ta-na took the shield and ran his hand across the surface, feeling the torn leather and the metal underneath, wondering if it was possible that this chain mail might have been worn by the conquistadors who had invaded and conquered the New World.

"Grandfather want you to have medicine shield," the boy continued. "He say it will lead my new brother to the land where his people will live one day."

Ta-na hefted the shield, feeling its undeniable power. Already it had saved his life, and he sensed it had done even more. He drew in a breath and realized he was trembling slightly, and he wrapped his arm around Wind Catcher for support.

"Let's go," he said, gesturing with the shield toward the horses. "Our journey is a long one."

The boy glanced back at the platform where Cornplanter was lying, then nodded and walked at Ta-na's side.

The trio rode steadily through the day and into the next, taking only a few hours' sleep as they bypassed Nashville and made directly for Rusog's Town. As they traveled, Ta-na-wun-da's eyesight continued to improve. His vision was still quite blurry, but he was able to recog-

nize larger objects and could keep up with the others
without being led. In fact, he was getting so good at negotiating the trail, even riding out in front on occasion, that
his father joked that the bullet that had creased his scalp
had knocked the sense and the sight back into him. For his
part, Ta-na suspected Cornplanter might have been correct in suggesting he had not been blind but had simply
lost sight of his path.

They were still a long distance from home when they
saw a pair of horsemen riding hard from the south. They
pulled up, and Renno took the precaution of loading his
pistol and rifle as they waited for the strangers to arrive.

"Their hooves are unshod," Ta-na-wun-da declared.
His hearing had been heightened since his accident, and
now he could see—even at a distance—the faintest of
forms as the riders approached.

"Yes," Renno said, leaning forward in the saddle and
shielding his eyes against the sun. "I think they are Seneca. . . . Yes, Seneca and—" He gave a gasp of surprise.
"It looks like . . . yes, it is! Mist-on-the-Water!"

Tucking his pistol behind his belt, he kicked his horse
into a trot. Ta-na and Wind Catcher were close behind as
they swiftly covered the ground between them and the
riders.

"Mist-on-the-Water!" Renno exclaimed as the two
groups pulled to a halt. He turned to her companion. "Ho-
ta-kwa! What are you doing here?"

Mist-on-the-Water leaped from her horse and ran to
Ta-na-wun-da, who also dismounted. As they embraced,
she saw the poultice that had been applied to his temple.
"You're hurt!" she cried, gingerly touching the wound.

"It's only a crease," he insisted, pulling her hand
away and smiling at her. "You look wonderful."

"You can see?" she said excitedly.

"A little. Enough to see how beautiful you are."

As they embraced again, Ho-ta-kwa announced, "I
bring grave news from the council." Ho-ta-kwa was one of

the youngest members of the combined Cherokee and Seneca council.

"What news?" Renno asked.

"We sent runners to Nashville to find you, but when Chief Rusog returned to the village, he told us you had gone to the Land Between the Rivers to find the medicine man." He glanced at Wind Catcher but did not ask who the boy was. Turning back to Renno, he continued, "I was sent to carry this news to you." He gestured toward Mist-on-the-Water. "She would not be left behind."

"What is it?" Renno pressed, his voice tense with impatience.

"Much has happened since you left. While Rusog was away, we met in council to hear the final offer from the white man from Nashville."

"Victor Coughtry?"

"Yes. The one we named Etutu Ekwa. We shall call him the Great Grandfather no more, for he has proved an enemy to the Cherokee and Seneca people."

"I knew Rusog shouldn't have left the village." Renno shook his head bitterly. "So the council finally gave in to Coughtry's bribes?"

"No. I feared some would be swayed. But we remembered the words of our chief and our sachem, and we remained firm in our resolve not to sell any of our land."

"Good," Renno declared with the hint of a smile. "Then what is this grave news?"

"The man from Nashville did not accept the council's decision. He found others who would sell the land."

"Others? I don't understand."

"Who sold our land?" Ta-na-wun-da demanded as he and Mist-on-the-Water walked over to where the others were still sitting their horses.

"Three members of the council rode secretly to Nashville and put their marks on papers turning over the land."

"But that's ridiculous," Renno exclaimed. "Three men can't go off on their own and sell a tract of Cherokee land—even such a small one. Only the full council has that right. No court would uphold—"

"It's worse than that," Mist-on-the-Water put in. Frowning, she looked up at Ho-ta-kwa. "Tell them."

The young Seneca gave a sigh, then nodded. "Mist-on-the-Water speaks the truth. It is worse."

"How?" Ta-na asked.

"The land is not the small tract near the trading post. It is much larger."

"How large?"

"They have sold all of our land."

"To Victor Coughtry?" Renno's face was a mask of disbelief.

"Much of it. We are told the papers give half to the Tennessee government."

"But council members can't act on their own," Ta-na pointed out. "Only the full council—"

"Who are these three men?" Renno cut in, his jaw set in anger.

"Tall Grass—"

"I should have guessed," Renno blurted with a sneer.

"Joining him were the brothers Black Otter and Running Turtle."

"What ever would induce them to sign?" Ta-na wondered aloud.

"Running Turtle has the whiskey disease; he will do anything to keep it fed. And Black Otter does whatever his older brother says."

"Where are they now?" Renno asked.

Ho-ta-kwa shrugged. "In Nashville, perhaps. They have not returned to Rusog's Town."

"Well, it should be a simple matter to resolve this," Renno mused. "First, all three of them will have to be removed from the council."

"This has already been done. It is as if Tall Grass, Black Otter, and Running Turtle had never been council members . . . as if they do not exist. Our people will speak of them no longer."

"Good," Ta-na-wun-da said.

His father nodded in approval at the news that the three had been ostracized from the community. From that moment on, they were banished from Cherokee land, and no one would speak their names—except when necessary in matters of council.

"Has the council issued some sort of proclamation disavowing the land sale?" Renno continued.

Ho-ta-kwa nodded, but his expression made it clear that the action had not produced the desired results.

"What response did you receive?"

"The Americans insist the sale is legal. One of their judges has issued an order."

"What kind?"

"We have been told we must approve the transfer of land and make preparations to leave or risk having the council arrested and the people removed by force."

"This will not stand," Renno declared, tightening the reins to steady Kowa, who stamped in place as if sensing his master's fury. "Let us hurry. There's no time to spare."

Ta-na and Mist-on-the-Water mounted back up, and the group rode off to the south.

Late that night they made their final camp in a wooded glen about forty miles from Rusog's Town. They built a fire and had a light meal, then set up their bedrolls. Since the glen was well off the trail and there was little risk of attack in this region, they decided against posting a watch.

An hour or so after they had gone to sleep, Ta-na-wun-da was awakened by the sound of someone moving near the fire. His body tensed with anticipation, and he slipped his hand under the jacket he was using as a pillow, his fingers tightening around the handle of a knife. The fire flared up slightly, and he was able to discern a shadowy figure. He strained to focus on the person, then relaxed when he recognized the silhouette of Mist-on-the-

Water. She stirred the fire a moment longer and moved back toward her bedroll.

Ta-na had just eased his hand from under the jacket when someone touched his shoulder from behind. He flinched with surprise, then heard Mist-on-the-Water whisper, "It's me."

Before he realized what was happening, she had lifted his blanket and slid up against his back, her arm slipping around his bare chest. She was clothed, but he felt her heat through the supple deerskin dress.

"I feared you would not come home," she said softly, her breath warming his neck.

"Where did you think I would go?" he asked, keeping his voice low so the others would not awaken.

"When you left the village, I knew you'd seek the medicine man. I was afraid you might go with him beyond the Father of Waters."

"And that's why you came?"

"Wherever you go, I will be at your side."

"Even beyond the Father of Waters?"

"Do not leave me again, Ta-na-wun-da." Her hands clutched his chest, pulling him closer. "Never again."

He lay in silence, feeling her body pressed against his. Mist-on-the-Water had been the wife of his cousin and closest friend. And now she wanted to walk with him forever. He wondered if Gao could see them now . . . if he could feel the heat between them.

Yes, the breeze seemed to answer. And Ta-na-wun-da was certain that wherever Gao might be, he knew they were together and smiled on their love.

"Yes . . ." Ta-na whispered, placing his hand upon hers. He closed his eyes and let himself drift to sleep in her arms.

Twenty

Within an hour of arriving home, Renno and Ta-na-wun-da were ushered into a hastily arranged meeting of the combined Cherokee and Seneca council. In a lodge near the center of Rusog's Town, the two dozen members seated themselves on the floor around a low-burning fire. After passing a pipe around the circle, Chief Rusog rose, holding in his right hand a two-foot-long stick covered with intricate beadwork. Lashed to one end were several long eagle feathers and tassels strung with shells and bones. He addressed the assembly in his native tongue:

"We welcome home our Seneca brother, Renno, and his son, Ta-na-wun-da." He glanced at Ho-ta-kwa and said, "We thank you for bringing them so quickly," then turned in place to take in each council member. "Today we must speak of the traitors who have tried to sell something they do not own. They have been tricked by the white man's words and his whiskey. He tells them that one day we will be forced to leave our land and make a new home across the Father of Waters. And they think that by speeding this day in coming, they alone will be allowed to

stay behind when we have gone. They have proved themselves unworthy of the name Cherokee, and they are no
longer of our people. This has been done, and it is good.
But still the whites say that our land has been sold and we
must move. How are we to undo this treachery?"

Rusog walked forward a few steps and bent to place
the stick upon the ground. Straightening, he said, "I have
spoken," then returned to his seat in the circle.

There was a long silence as the council members
looked from one to another. Finally a man about thirty
years old rose from his place on the far side of the circle,
walked around the fire pit, and took the talking stick in his
hand. Carrying it back to where he had been seated, he
stood facing the others. He was Seneca but spoke in Cherokee, the language of the council.

"And we greet our sachem," he began, nodding to the
man some called the white Indian. He nodded in turn to
Ta-na-wun-da and Rusog. "And we greet the son of the
sachem and the chief of the Cherokee. The words of
Renno and Rusog have always been wise. But we did not
listen, for we let the white man bring his wagon filled with
firewater to poison our men and women, our old and our
young. And we let the white man speak his lies through
the mouth of one of our own. Perhaps if we had heeded
the words of Renno and Rusog and had refused to receive
this white man and his lies, Tall Grass and his friends
would not have been so bold. But they have shown the
true color of their cowardice, and so we have made them
nonpeople among us. But is this enough? Do they not sit
with their white masters, laughing at our weakness? They
knew we would cast them from our lodges and our council
fires. Yet this did not concern them, for in truth they were
the ones who have exiled us, making us nonpeople in the
land of our ancestors. This I ask: Is banishment enough for
those who would destroy their own nation? I have spoken."

He stepped forward, put down the talking stick, and
resumed his seat. After another silent wait, the old Chero-

kee warrior Two Feathers rose, took up the stick, and brought it back to his place in the circle.

"And our Seneca brother speaks words that are wise beyond his years." He acknowledged the previous speaker with a rattle of the stick. "I have known Tall Grass these many years. When I reached manhood and took my place among the warriors, he was like a younger brother to me. Yet he said nothing of the darkness growing within his heart. His greed for white men's ways and white men's gold has made him turn his face from his brother and his people."

He stepped forward and bent down as if to return the stick to the ground, then straightened back up and shook his head in anger.

"The Cherokee are a proud and forgiving people. We have suffered weak men and scoundrels among us. But never must we allow one of our own—a man we let sit with us in council—to escape unpunished after committing an act as traitorous as that which Tall Grass and his followers have committed. The Cherokee reserve their harshest penalty for a single crime alone. Treason such as theirs must not be answered with banishment but with death. This is the counsel of a man who once called Tall Grass 'friend.' " He put down the talking stick. "I have spoken."

Two men rose simultaneously, but when the younger saw the older one stand, he quickly resumed his seat. The older man retrieved the stick and carried it back to where he had been seated.

"And my brother Two Feathers speaks with the long sight of an elder. These three traitors—I cannot bring myself to utter their names—are truly enemies of the Cherokee and the Seneca. So is the white man who paid them gold and whiskey to obtain their marks on a piece of paper . . . a paper that is nothing but an excuse for the white soldiers to steal our land, as they have stolen the land of the Creek to our south. Our enemies must taste the sting of our bullets and our blades. I would consider it an honor to be the one who sends each of them from this world. I have spoken."

The next to address the council was a middle-aged Seneca named Gray Wolf: "And so we must decide if banishment is a fitting punishment for the crime of treason. Like my elder brothers who have spoken before me, I ask the council to place the most serious judgment on the three who have made themselves traitors to our people. And the same punishment should be meted out to the one we named Etutu Ekwa and any who stand at his side. I have spoken."

"No!" declared an elder Cherokee named Spotted Horse as he bolted to his feet. All eyes turned to him, and there was a flurry of whispers, for he had spoken without taking up the talking stick. Furthermore, he had openly disagreed with the previous person and had disregarded the custom of beginning with the word *and*, which served to show a speaker was not discounting the prior comments but was simply adding his own.

Spotted Horse seemed to realize his breach of etiquette, for he turned to the younger man who had just spoken and said, "Forgive me, Gray Wolf. It is not your words but my own fears that have loosened my tongue."

He walked to where the talking stick was lying and picked it up. He did not return to his seat but stood where he was, turning and looking at each council member.

"And the many voices of my brothers have taught me much this day. But there is another voice that rings true within me, and I must speak to this truth. I have no fear of voicing the traitors' names: Tall Grass . . . Black Otter . . . Running Turtle. I have heard the counsel of my brothers, and it is strong. These three have done worse than one who would sneak into a man's lodge and murder his family. They seek to destroy a nation—indeed, two nations, for the Seneca and Cherokee have lived in peace these many years. But my fear, and my loose tongue, is that we might go beyond our own law in seeking justice.

That we might give the white soldiers reason to finish
what three traitors could not."

He turned to Chief Rusog. "It is true that our law
calls for death to any who betray our people. Thus Tall
Grass and his friends should be ferreted from their hiding
places, with no mercy shown. But the man we called
Etutu Ekwa is not of the Cherokee, and he is not of the
Seneca. He is white, and what he has done should be no
surprise to any sitting around this fire. He is an enemy,
but he is no traitor to our people. If we were to face him
on the field of battle, his death would rightly be sung of by
our children and our children's children. But to take him
in the night would bring us no honor. He has wounded us
only because Tall Grass and Black Otter and Running Turtle wielded the knife."

He fixed each council member with his unwavering
gaze. Then he returned the talking stick to the floor and
intoned, "I have spoken."

The silence lasted longer than usual as each man
looked around the circle at his companions. One by one
they turned their eyes toward Renno, eager to learn his
opinion on the matter. He waited until he felt he could
remain silent no longer, then slowly rose and walked to
where the talking stick lay.

With the stick raised in his right hand, he circled the
fire, pausing to shake it first to the north, then the east,
then the south, and finally the west. Returning to his seat,
he stood looking from one man to the next, gauging the
sense of the meeting.

"And I am pleased to be sitting among my brother
Cherokee and Seneca," he began, his voice so soft that
many had to lean forward to hear. "I listened to the words
of my friends, and they were filled with wisdom. And as
they spoke, I looked into the eyes of each of my brothers
seated around the fire. I saw that they heard the words
and thought them good. Like Two Feathers, I feel be-
trayed by Tall Grass and his followers and agree that justice would be served by their deaths. Like Gray Wolf, I

would sleep more soundly if the white man named Victor Coughtry were no longer on this earth. But like Spotted Horse, I know we must not condemn a white man to Cherokee justice. This man is no different from the mudminnow that always swims to the bottom of the river. If we deal with him, we must expect treachery to follow. But when three of our own bring that treachery to our village, they are indeed traitors and must expect a traitor's fate."

Renno walked to where Chief Rusog was sitting and placed the talking stick before him. He did not say "I have spoken," and so the others remained silent as he returned to his place in the circle. When he reached his seat, he did not sit but instead turned to address them again.

"I have put down the talking stick because I must speak to you not as a Seneca but as a white. As you know, half my blood flows from the same source as that of the one named Victor Coughtry, who seeks to use his gold and his influence to remove us from our land. I understand the ways of men such as he. And I understand the workings of the councils of the whites. I must tell you that Spotted Horse has spoken with great wisdom this day. If we were to carry out a sentence of death upon Victor Coughtry, there would be nothing we could do to keep the white soldiers from forcing us off our land. But there is more I must tell you. I see that it is the sense of this council that Tall Grass and Black Otter and Running Turtle must pay the ultimate penalty for their treason. I will not speak against this, but I must ask you to wait before carrying out their sentence."

A murmur of disapproval and impatience rippled through the gathering. Renno waited a few moments, then raised his hand until the council members quieted again.

"These men will not go far. Surely they are in Nashville, and they expect to return to this land once we are gone. Let them have their days of victory. Give me time to speak in the white councils against this injustice. Give me time to unmask Tall Grass and his friends for the liars and scoundrels that they are. Do not let Victor Coughtry turn them into martyrs to his cause, but rather give me time to defeat him at his own game. If I succeed, the whites will have no more use for these traitors and will turn them away. Then the death sentences can be carried out. If I fail, I give you my word that I myself will see that they do not escape Cherokee and Seneca judgment."

Folding his arms in front of him, he said, "I have spoken," and sat down.

The council members sat looking at one another, some without reaction, others nodding slowly. At last Chief Rusog lifted the talking stick to his chest, remaining seated as he declared, "And the words of my brother speak to the heart of the matter."

He paused, watching for signs of dissent. Sensing that all were in agreement, he continued, "Tall Grass and Black Otter and Running Turtle have been found guilty of treason, and the council pronounces sentence upon them: From this day forth, their names are stricken from the tongues of the people. And for their crime they shall pay with their lives. When one moon has passed, the council shall meet again to determine the day and the manner in which this sentence shall be carried out. Until then, our brother the sachem of the Seneca is free to seek redress from the whites." He put down the stick, concluding, "The council has spoken."

The members rose and filed solemnly from the lodge. Ho-ta-kwa was one of the first to depart, but a few moments later he ran back in and went straight to where Renno and Ta-na-wun-da were standing with Chief Rusog. "Runners report a force of soldiers approaching from the north," he announced when they turned to him.

"How many?" Rusog asked, his eyes narrowing in thought.

"Several hundred, more than half on horseback. And they have artillery. They will reach the village within an hour."

"I'll go out and speak to them," Renno said.

Nodding, Rusog said to Ho-ta-kwa, "Bring my horse. I will ride with my brother." He hesitated, looking back and forth between the young men, then added, "Ta-na-wun-da will join us." His words drew a smile from Ta-na.

"May I ride at your side?" Ho-ta-kwa asked.

Rusog reached out and clasped his forearm. "I want you to gather the warrior chiefs and prepare the village for attack."

"I don't think it will come to that," Renno said.

"If it does, we will be ready," Rusog proclaimed as he led them from the lodge.

Renno and Ta-na-wun-da flanked Chief Rusog as they rode across the open grassland toward the approaching military force. Rusog had not had time to change into full war dress, but he donned a ceremonial headdress of eagle feathers and held a lance upraised in his left hand. Renno had on his usual buckskins, cut in the style of the whites, while his son had removed his outer hunting shirt and wore the breechclout and leggings of a Seneca warrior. Slung on his right arm was Cornplanter's medicine shield, and his hand gripped the lance he had fashioned from a length of alder and his knife.

Pulling up, the trio sat their horses and waited for the army to approach. As Ho-ta-kwa had reported, most were on horseback, with perhaps two hundred infantry marching in formation at the rear. There were more than a dozen supply wagons and several small fieldpieces. Ta-na could see them spread out across the field but could not make out any details, so his father described the flags and clothing, which was a mix of official and homemade uniforms. From the description, Ta-na confirmed Renno's assessment that this was a combined force of militia and regular army.

One of the officers gave the order to halt, then rode forward with two soldiers at his side. They reined in about ten feet away, the officer and Rusog raising their right hands in greeting.

"I am Rusog, chief of the Cherokee, brother of the Seneca sachem, Renno"—he dipped his lance toward the man to his right—"and uncle of the sachem's son, Ta-na-wun-da." He indicated the man at his other side.

The officer was an extremely tall, lanky man with salt-and-pepper hair and a clipped mustache. He eyed his opponents closely, his cool blue eyes holding a bit longer on Renno. Finally he raised his forefinger to his temple, giving Rusog what passed for a salute. "I am Captain Morrisey," he announced, not bothering to introduce the junior officers who accompanied him. "Am I to assume you can speak for your people? The Seneca and the Cherokee?"

Rusog and Renno both nodded.

"Then I must inform you that my men and I have been sent to uphold this order from the Tennessee court." He reached into a leather bag hanging from his saddle horn and removed a scroll tied with a black ribbon.

"May I see it?" Renno asked, kneeing his horse and moving closer.

The captain handed him the scroll, and Renno undid the ribbon and rolled it open. His jaw clenched as he read the order that the Cherokee and Seneca surrender their land and remove themselves west of the Mississippi River. The order included a detail of the terms of the sale made in the name of the Cherokee by Tall Grass and his fellow conspirators.

"You and your people must vacate this land," Morrisey said without emotion when Renno looked up at him. "I am authorized to offer generous terms, including food and supplies and a military escort to the river. Furthermore, we will allow you up to a month to prepare for the journey. This will leave your people plenty of time to find suitable hunting grounds before next winter." He gave Renno a perfunctory smile. "I am told that you and your family are citizens of the United States. As such, you will be allowed to remain here in Tennessee, if you so choose.

You will note that the terms of sale expressly exclude Huntington Castle and its land."

"This sale is illegal," Renno declared, thrusting the paper back into the captain's hand.

"The court has deemed otherwise."

"The men who affixed their marks to that bill of sale had no authority under Cherokee law."

"Apparently they do under ours."

"And what if we will not move?" Renno asked.

"You will," Morrisey said adamantly. He twisted in the saddle and gestured at the force massed behind him. "These troops are here to demonstrate the fullness of our resolve and to observe what we hope will be a peaceful exodus. The fact remains that your people are residing illegally on American soil. If you have not vacated within one month of this day, a force many times this size shall carry out the court's edict."

"With cavalry and cannons?" Renno said, his tone laced with sarcasm and anger.

"With whatever it takes."

"And where would you have us go?" Ta-na-wun-da demanded, moving his pinto forward a few steps.

The captain looked the young man up and down before replying, "There is boundless land beyond the Mississippi. America has few interests there and has deemed it the proper home for all natives—not only for our protection but for your own."

"The only protection we need is from those who would steal our land!"

"It is your land no longer," Morrisey reiterated. "And if you are not gone within a month, you'll need a lot more than that lance and shield to protect you."

Ta-na was about to shout something back, but Rusog raised a hand to silence him. With his other hand, he lowered the tip of his lance to the ground.

"You speak the truth when you say this is not Cherokee land," he declared, drawing the captain's attention and surprise. "Though my people have hunted its game

and grown our corn and beans in its soil and lived sheltered in its valleys for generations beyond remembering, it
truly is not our land. But neither is it yours. We cannot
own the land, like a pair of moccasins or an iron pot. It
belongs to the Master of Life, and we live upon it only for
a time."

"And the time has come to leave," Morrisey replied
with a smug grin.

"If the Master of Life decides we must leave, so we
shall. But not because of a white man's paper." He dis-
missed the captain's scroll with a wave of the hand. "And
not because of treachery and lies."

Rusog pulled back on the reins, turning his horse and
riding away. Ta-na hesitated, watching him go, then
wheeled his horse and took off after him at a trot. Renno
alone remained behind with the captain.

"You say we have a month?" he asked, his tone somewhat softer than before.

"There hardly seems a point," Morrisey commented,
shaking his head as Rusog and Ta-na-wun-da rode back
toward the village. "I doubt that one'll ever change his
mind."

"It doesn't matter what Rusog or I or any other single
person thinks," Renno told him. "The final decision will
be made jointly by the people. And whatever it turns out
to be, everyone will go along with it."

The captain stroked his mustache and chin, his eyes
narrowing as he weighed the truthfulness of Renno's re-
mark. "Are you saying you can get them to go?"

"I don't want bloodshed."

"Neither do we."

"Then give me a month to see what I can do," Renno
said, hoping the captain would assume his intention was to
convince the people to leave, when in fact it was to get the
white government to change its policy.

The captain considered Renno's request for a long
time, then finally nodded. "I'll give you a month. Not a
day more." He started to turn his horse, then added, "But

there must be some indication that preparations are under way. We'll be staying right here on Cherokee—I mean Tennessee—land. And if there isn't any movement by next week, I'll be forced to call in the rest of the militia."

"I'll do my best."

"I hope you do," the captain muttered. He kicked his horse into a gallop and raced back to his waiting troops.

Renno watched as the force split into two groups and pulled out. Half turned southwest, the rest southeast, apparently planning to take up positions on opposite sides of Rusog's Town.

"Come on, boy!" Renno called to his horse as he jerked the reins to the left. Kowa made a sharp circle and shot forward, setting a brisk pace back to the village.

For two days Renno considered his options. He had hoped to enlist General Andrew Jackson's aid, for Jackson held great influence not only with the military but with the Tennessee and federal governments. But Jackson had not yet returned from New Orleans. Fortunately Renno knew another who could press their case with the government: his own son, Hawk Harper, who had the ear and the confidence of President Madison himself. And it was becoming increasingly apparent that it would take action by the federal government to forestall a disaster, especially given the intransigence of the Tennessee authorities. From what Renno had been able to determine, some of those officials privately conceded that the bill of sale had been obtained through fraudulent means and was of dubious legality. But their public stance was to insist the sale was legal and that the Cherokee and Seneca must depart as ordered by the court. And Renno knew all too well they were being backed by a vociferous press, which continued to whip up anti-Indian sentiment in the wake of the recent Creek War, and by a public that increasingly believed all native peoples should be resettled west of the Mississippi.

Renno realized that if he were to have any hope of getting the federal government to intercede, he would have to send word to Hawk in Washington. He could not trust such a message to the post and certainly did not expect the military to carry it for him. He would be willing to make the long journey to Washington himself, but he knew it was essential that he remain close to home and continue to seek avenues of redress with the local authorities. Ta-na-wun-da's poor eyesight precluded him from undertaking such an arduous mission. And while many of the young men of the village—Ho-ta-kwa, for instance— would be eager to assist, Renno knew a white man would have an easier time traveling to Washington unhindered. He still had quite a few friends in Nashville who could be expected to help in an emergency, so he decided upon one more trip north.

A visit to Nashville would serve a second purpose. Ever since Cornplanter's death—even before learning of the bogus land purchase—Renno had intended to personally confront Victor Coughtry. Though Renno had pretended to have no idea why Jim Radison and his cohorts had ambushed him, he had a strong suspicion that Coughtry was behind it all. After all, it was the perfect way for Coughtry to remove the one person who could effectively lobby against the land scheme not only with the Cherokee and Seneca but with the whites.

As soon as Renno's course was set, he decided not to delay putting it into action. He knew Ta-na-wun-da would insist on accompanying him, but he was determined to make the journey alone. For the moment, no one knew of his conviction that Coughtry was behind Radison's deadly attack. And while Renno was loath to deal with the newspaperman, he might be able to convince him to cancel the land sale by threatening to expose him as a murderer. If that didn't work, he could always bring more forceful pressure to bear. It was a dangerous move, Renno realized, and it had the best chance of success if he and Victor Coughtry alone knew of it. Ta-na-wun-da, with the moral certainty of youth, might demand vengeance for Cornplanter's death. Renno, on the other hand, had lost some of that strength of conviction and was willing to make a pact with Satan himself if it meant the Cherokee and Seneca people would be left in peace on their land.

The day before he was to depart, Renno felt strangely invigorated and suffered virtually none of the numbness or paralysis that had plagued him the past year. That night he made love to Beth with great passion and urgency, as if he were doing so for the very first time. She could not help but note the change in him, and as they lay in each other's arms, she reminisced about their first night together.

"Are you sorry?" he asked, his voice almost tentative.

She looked up at him curiously. "Good heavens, sorry about what?"

"That I'm no longer that young man you fell in love with."

"You aren't?" she teased. Shifting onto her side, she ran her forefinger down his chest. "You fooled me tonight."

"Maybe. But what about tomorrow when you have to watch this old man drag his body down the stairs?"

She giggled. "One thing you aren't, Renno Harper, is an old man. A foolish one, perhaps."

"Are you calling me a fool?" he said, feigning offense.

"The biggest there is." She brushed her lips across his cheek. "Only a fool would put up for so many years with me and with this big house—when I know full well you'd like nothing better than a campfire and a cabin in the woods."

"You are my cabin—and my hearth." He pulled her close and kissed her long and full.

"And you aren't sorry, my dear, dear husband?" she whispered, her eyes misting. "I'm not the young woman you—"

"Shh . . ." he hushed, touching her lips softly. Pulling back slightly, he caressed her cheek. "I'm the happiest man alive. And the most thankful. I wouldn't change one moment of our lives together—not even the painful ones. I couldn't bear even the risk that I might not be here tonight with the woman I love more dearly than my own life."

She started to speak, but he covered her lips with his own. This time their passion built slowly, with tenderness and joy, their love pouring one to the other and back again, completing the circle they had embraced so many years before.

Renno held his wife close, feeling her breath slowing down and deepening as she drifted to sleep. He wanted to stay there forever in her arms. But he knew that in a few short hours he would be riding away from Huntington Castle, away from her hearth, one more time. He realized he should tell her about his impending journey, and indeed he had tried when he first came to bed. But now, as he lay beside her, he could not bring himself to say the words. He had never been a fearful man—at least not when facing danger or defeat. But with a woman—with this woman he loved so deeply—the fear was more paralyzing than the bullet lodged in his back. He was afraid that he might lose her—that he might not see her again. And most deeply, he dreaded seeing the look on her face when he told her he was not only leaving her again but was riding off alone.

I'll write her a note, he told himself, wincing at the thought of taking the coward's way out. *She'll be angry, but she'll understand.*

Tilting his head toward her, he kissed her gently on the cheek and whispered, "Kononkwa, Beth Huntington Harper . . ."

She stirred and gave a murmuring sigh.

Twenty-one

Ta-na-wun-da woke up reeling from the power of the dream that had visited him during the night. For a moment he did not know where he was, so real had the vision seemed. There was a dull glow in his sleeping area, and he heard movements nearby and saw what appeared to be the glimmering lights of several fires.

The longhouse, he remembered, nodding as he pushed the robe off his shoulders and raised himself on one arm.

After the recent arrival of the soldiers, now bivouacked on the outskirts of Rusog's Town, he had wanted to remain in the village rather than at Huntington Castle. Mist-on-the-Water had offered to let him stay in her cabin, but it was already crowded, for not only were Ma-ton-ga and Little Gao there, but Wind Catcher, as well. Furthermore, he did not feel it proper to sleep under her roof until he fully declared his love and his desire that she be his wife. And a celebration such as that would have to wait until this immediate crisis was resolved.

Ta-na sat up on the platform bed he had been provided in one of the Seneca longhouses in the village. The large building consisted of a central corridor with compartments on either side. Most were large enough to hold a family of four or five, but a few, like Ta-na's, were little more than a sleeping area, suitable for one or two. The side walls of the compartment were made of stretched hide, and at night a blanket was hung between them to close off the compartment and offer some privacy. This morning the blanket was partly open, and Ta-na could see the lights of the communal cooking fires spaced along the corridor. From the glow on the outer wall and ceiling he guessed it was an hour or so after dawn, and he reached for his clothing, which lay piled in the corner.

The dream! He dropped his clothes and sat rubbing his eyes as the images reemerged. Stunned by the force with which they came flooding back, he fell back onto the robes and lay curled on his side, his hands covering his eyes, his chest heaving as he struggled for breath. . . .

The sky lightens with the approach of dawn. Alone on horseback, my father rides away from Huntington Castle. He kicks his bay gelding into a gallop, Kowa's hooves pounding as he thunders across the grasslands. Suddenly the horse rears up, spooked by something in his path. A bearded man stands there in a black suit with crimson waistcoat and white cravat. My father twists around and sees the buildings on all sides of him. Men are crowding into the doorways and on the porches of stores and taverns, shaking their fists, shouting obscenities.

I look for Renno and see him sitting tall, not on Kowa but on the bare back of a pinto. He wears only moccasins, loincloth, and leggings. His head is shaved like that of our ancestral warriors, leaving only a topknot with a feather hanging in front of his shoulder. His right hand holds my lance, his left the Old Man's medicine shield.

Men rush into the street, grabbing at Renno, pulling him from the horse's back, pinning his arms against his sides. The lance and shield fall at his feet and are crushed by the crowd. But my father stands proud, chest thrust forward, smiling as the bearded man draws his pistol and fires.

The bullet pierces Renno's chest. He slumps to his knees, face turned upward, breath releasing in a sigh. I move closer, trying to hear his final words, to gaze into his eyes a final time. A single word escapes his lips: "Ta-na-wun-da." And as I beg my father not to go, I look down at him and see my own face, my own eyes. . . .

"Ta-na-wun-da . . ."

He jumped as a hand touched his shoulder. Opening his eyes, he gazed up at the face suspended above him.

"Ta-na . . . are you all right?"

"Mist-on-the-Water?" He blinked, straining to see her in the thin light.

"It is morning. I've brought you something to eat."

He sat up, pulling the robes around him. Mist-on-the-Water knelt beside him and gently ran her hand across his forehead, feeling the cold beads of perspiration.

"What is wrong?" she asked. "Are you all right?"

"A . . . a dream. That's all." He reached for his clothes and pulled his shirt over his head.

"A dream or a vision?" she pressed, concern evident in her tone.

Ta-na shrugged. "I'm not sure. It was very real."

"Tell me about it."

He hesitated, staring down at his hands, uncertain what to say. She asked him again, and finally he nodded and recounted the images he had seen.

"You saw this twice?" she asked when he had finished.

"First while I was sleeping. Then when I awoke I

tried to remember the dream, and it all came back just as real as before."

"While you were awake?"

"Yes. That is, if I really woke up and didn't dream that, too."

"And what does this vision mean to you?"

"I'm not sure." He fell silent a long moment, rubbing his brow as he tried to sort the jumbled thoughts and images. "I'm certain of one thing: My father's in trouble. If not now, then soon."

"He's home, isn't he?" she asked, and he nodded. "Then you must see him. I have a pot out on the cooking fire. Finish dressing while I tend to it. You'll have some food, then go speak with your father."

Ta-na nodded distractedly. He watched as Mist-on-the-Water climbed down from the platform and pulled the blanket closed behind her.

"Father . . ." he whispered, shaking his head against the sudden fear that rushed through him.

Ta-na-wun-da listened as his stepmother read aloud the letter Renno had left behind when he had departed Huntington Castle before dawn. When she finished, Ta-na shook his head and said incredulously, "You had no idea he was going?"

"None," she insisted. "Do you think something's wrong?"

"I wonder why he didn't tell you."

"He knows I wouldn't want him to leave—especially not by himself." She clutched the letter against her chest in worry. "You don't believe him, do you?"

"I just don't know." Rising from the sofa, he walked across the parlor to the fireplace, then turned to look back at his stepmother. "It makes sense that he wants to see the judge. But why ride off alone without telling anyone?"

"Perhaps he woke up with his back troubling him again. He says he's going to see Dr. Fass while he's there."

"All the more reason to have taken someone along. He knows I would've gone."

"Perhaps I shouldn't have told you," she mused aloud. "He didn't want me to say anything."

"That's what bothers me most." He gestured toward the letter in her hand. "He makes it clear I'm not to know. It's almost as if . . ."

"What?" she asked when he did not continue.

Ta-na shrugged. "I suppose I shouldn't take it personally. It's obvious he doesn't want anyone along who looks . . . well . . . less than white."

Beth's face reddened, and she looked away.

"It's all right," he assured her. "I'm proud I look Seneca." Coming back across the room, he sat beside her and took her hand. "He's right, you know. Just now it isn't safe to leave the village, let alone go to Nashville. The army's making it difficult for us to move about on our own land, and anyone trying to ride away from Rusog's Town is stopped and questioned. I came over here the back way to avoid that very thing."

"That's terrible," she declared, looking up at him with tears in her eyes.

"I can only imagine the kind of reception we'd get in Nashville."

"But you have every right to go to Nashville, or anywhere else, for that matter."

"I know," he said, patting her hand. "It's all right— really it is. Renno's doing the proper thing. I just wish there were some way I could help. I'm sure he'll have this whole mess straightened out soon enough, and things will settle back to normal." He rose again. "I'd best be getting back to the village."

"You can stay here, if you'd like."

"I know. And thank you. But with the way things are, I may be needed in the village."

"You don't think it will come to fighting, do you?" she asked, standing and taking his arm. Together they walked out to the foyer.

"Not yet—provided cooler heads prevail. Some of our younger warriors are getting impatient, however. And with so many soldiers in the area, one bad incident or misunderstanding could lead to catastrophe. That's why I want to be there."

"You'll be careful," she entreated as he opened the front door.

"I always am," he reassured her, then chuckled. "Except that one time in New Orleans," he added, gesturing at his eyes.

"How are they?"

"Much better." His smile broadened. "I can see well enough to know my father married the most beautiful woman in the world."

She blushed. "The second most beautiful, maybe. Don't forget Mist-on-the-Water."

He winked. "I never do."

"Good," she replied. Leaning up, she kissed his cheek.

They embraced, and Ta-na started from the house. He halted halfway across the verandah and turned to Beth. "As long as I'm here, I think I'll get a few of my things from upstairs."

"Of course." She held the door wide as he headed back in and took the stairs two at a time.

As he hurried down the hall to the room he used when staying at Huntington Castle, he thought of the letter his father had left that morning. He told himself it was exactly what it purported to be—a simple announcement that Renno had gone to Nashville to lobby the military and civil authorities on behalf of the Cherokee and Seneca and to see the physician while there. But a stronger voice insisted the journey held a darker, more perilous purpose. Ta-na did not know what it was, but he sensed that his father was riding into danger and might need a friend at his side.

Ta-na recalled the dream of that morning. He guessed it had come around the time Renno was riding away from home, and thus he could not easily discount its clear warning that something ominous was afoot. He was determined Renno would not face it alone.

Realizing he would draw less attention in Nashville dressed as a white, Ta-na rummaged through his clothes and found a suitable outfit. Folding it into a bundle and tucking it under his arm, he returned downstairs and again said good-bye to Beth, then went out to his pinto. At the stables he borrowed a lighter-weight saddle, then rode off across the fields toward Rusog's Town. He would stop in at Mist-on-the-Water's cabin to change clothes and leave word where he was going, then set off at once on his father's trail.

"I'm coming with you," Mist-on-the-Water announced, emerging from the cabin as he strapped the last of his supplies to the saddle.

Ta-na-wun-da turned, his eyes widening in disbelief at what he was seeing. Instead of her usual Potawatomi buckskins she was wearing a prim, matronly traveling dress in the style of the whites. Also gone were her braids, replaced with a fashionable upsweep held in place with a tortoiseshell comb.

"I borrowed this dress from Anna Two Dogs," she explained, naming a Cherokee woman who emulated the whites in all things—especially clothing. "Can you see my hair?"

He walked closer, squinting as he took in the vision in front of him. "You look . . . different," was all he could say.

"I look white," she replied. "White enough to ride into Nashville with you."

"No," he said, shaking his head adamantly and walking back to his horse.

She came up behind him and grabbed the sleeve of his wool jacket. "I'm coming whether you agree or not. Your eyes are much better, but there's still much you cannot see."

He turned and eyed her dubiously, uncertain how she meant the comment. "I can see enough to find my father."

"And enough to get yourself killed."

"No one's going to die."

She firmly gripped both his arms. "I am coming with you," she declared. "I'll be eyes if you need them and counsel if you want it."

He glanced past her and saw Ma-ton-ga standing in the doorway with Mist-on-the-Water's son in her arms. "There's Little Gao to consider," he said feebly, sensing that she was not going to be dissuaded.

"It is Little Gao I'm thinking of. He has lost his father; I don't want him to lose you, as well." She hesitated, then leaned close to his cheek, whispering, "Nor do I, my love."

"I'm going to be fine," he insisted, holding her close.

"You will not leave me again," she said, her tears moistening both their cheeks. "We will ride together to Nashville, and we will bring your father home."

He gave a sigh of defeat. "You'll have to hurry," he told her. "We must leave as soon as possible."

She pulled back, smiling up at him with combined relief and surprise. "My things are already packed. All I must do is find a saddle."

"There are plenty in the village. We can borrow one easily enough." He wrapped an arm around her shoulder and led her to where Ma-ton-ga and Little Gao were waiting.

Twenty-two

Ta-na-wun-da and Mist-on-the-Water entered Nashville under cover of darkness. They had hoped to overtake Renno before he reached the city, but he had gotten a good head start and had clearly set a blistering pace. Still, Ta-na estimated they had made up some of the time and were only an hour or two behind.

Keeping themselves out of the light that spilled onto the streets, they managed to avoid notice as they rode through town. Ta-na decided to visit Dr. Fass's office first, on the chance his father had followed through with his stated intention of visiting the physician while in town. The office was closed, but Fass was still at his desk, and he came out into the waiting room and greeted them warmly.

"You didn't happen to examine my father today, did you?" Ta-na asked, getting straight to the point.

"No . . ." Fass muttered as he stared more closely at Ta-na. "How are those eyes of yours?"

"I'm not here about that," Ta-na replied, waving off the man's concern. "But my father—"

"Come here into the light," he said, tugging at the

young man's arm and leading him into the examining room. Ta-na started to object, but Mist-on-the-Water gestured for him to go along.

"Let's take a look." Snatching up the small desk lamp, Fass held it in front of Ta-na's eyes and peered into them with a magnifying glass. "Just as I thought—no real change. I knew that old medicine man would do you no good. Hell, Renno was just trying to goad me, insisting you could see."

"My father was here? But you—"

"Those eyes look the same as the day you got back from New Orleans."

"But he *can* see," Mist-on-the-Water put in.

"You can?" Fass said dubiously, putting down the lamp.

"Fairly well. But that's not why I've come—"

"How well?" Fass spun around and pointed to the shelves on the far wall. "What's up there on top?"

Deciding it would be quicker to go along with the man, Ta-na glanced toward where Fass was gesturing and squinted as he tried to discern the objects. "Books, of course, though I can't read the titles from here. And a hat. Beaver, I'd say."

"I'll be damned! You *can* see." Again he picked up the lamp and took another look in Ta-na's eyes. "They mustn't have been as bad as I thought. The explosion may have caused only superficial damage to the retina and temporary shock to the system."

Ta-na pushed away the raised lamp as politely as possible. "My eyes don't concern me, Doctor—at least not right now. I'm looking for my father. Did you examine him today?"

"No—"

"Then when did he tell you I could see? This is the first time he's come to—"

"I didn't *examine* him," Fass cut him off. "That doesn't mean I didn't see him."

"He was here?"

Fass nodded. "Barged in like you pups, less than an hour ago."

"Did he say where he was going?"

Fass considered the matter a long moment, then slowly shook his head. "Can't say that he did. Though a good guess would be over to the newspaper office."

"Why do you say that?" Ta-na pressed.

"Well, he seemed keen on learning everything I did that day the two of you last visited. When I told him about the card game, he took off rather quickly."

"Card game?"

"I always spend my free afternoon playing cards with a few of the boys."

"Victor Coughtry included?" Ta-na guessed.

Fass grinned sheepishly. "That's just what your father asked. He wanted to know if I told V. J. where you two boys were heading when you left Nashville, and I suppose I did, though I can't say V. J. paid particular notice. I hope that wasn't wrong of me."

"No," Ta-na replied. "Thank you, Doctor." He took Mist-on-the-Water's arm and led her back through the outer room.

"Renno was a little peeved, I must confess," Fass commented, opening the front door for them. "I suppose your whereabouts weren't anyone else's business, but I didn't think it a secret. Anyway, that's why I figured you might find him at V. J.'s."

"You did nothing wrong," Ta-na assured him, ushering Mist-on-the-Water outside.

"When you find that father of yours, I want you to bring him to see me. He looked strong enough, but I know his back is hurting. He's just too pigheaded to admit it."

"I will," Ta-na declared.

Fass watched as they mounted up. "And I want to give your eyes a more complete examination," he called, giving a brusque wave as he closed the door.

"Where are we going?" Mist-on-the-Water asked as they started down the street.

He shook his head bitterly. "I think Renno has gone to confront that scoundrel."

"Victor Coughtry?" she said, an edge of fear in her voice. "Why would he do that?"

"I suspect Coughtry has been up to a lot more than stealing our land. The doctor tells him we're going to find Cornplanter, and the morning after we arrive there, those gunmen come to call. Who else knew we'd be there? Nobody."

He kneed his horse into a brisk trot and headed toward Nashville's business district.

Ta-na-wun-da found his father's horse tethered in front of the darkened offices of *The Nashville Sentinel*. He signaled Mist-on-the-Water that they would ride past the building and pull up at a hitching rail farther down the street. After they dismounted, he looked around and satisfied himself that they had not attracted the notice of the few people on the street.

"Wait with the horses," he told her, and she nodded.

Opening one of his saddlebags, he withdrew a pistol and tucked it in his waistband, then tied a small shot pouch to his belt. He felt to make sure his knife was still at his side, then started with purpose down the street. Reaching the building, he peered through the front windows and confirmed that no one was on hand, then ducked into the alley on the right side of the building and checked the windows there and around back. Everything was dark in the first-floor offices. However, he could see lights burning in the front room upstairs and heard what sounded like voices.

Ta-na quickly loaded the pistol, then came back around the building, checking the various doors, all of which were locked. There were two at the front of the building, one leading into the offices and a second, near the left side of the building, that opened onto a staircase to the second floor. He considered kicking it in or breaking the glass but realized that would draw attention. Instead he decided to climb the outside of the building.

Returning to the alley, he saw it would be a fairly simple matter to scale the building, since there was a narrow overhang between the first and second floors. By climbing a post on the front porch, he was able to grasp the ledge and pull himself up. It took some maneuvering, but at last he found himself standing on the ledge at the right front corner of the building.

Hugging the building, he followed the ledge back along the alley wall, where he would be protected by the darkness, until he was next to the side window of the front room. He stood there a moment listening to the voices, his jaw setting in anger as their words became clear.

". . . and I doubt you've got the stomach for it," one of the men was saying. Ta-na drew in a sharp breath, for it was the voice of his father.

Someone gave a deep, throaty chuckle. When the man spoke, Ta-na did not recognize the voice but knew at once it belonged to Victor Coughtry. "Is that what you think? That *I'm* going to do it?" He laughed again. "Don't presume you can goad me into a fair fight. I gave up such notions the first time I paid good money to have a man killed. Believe me, he ended up just as dead as if I'd pulled the trigger myself. Felt just as good, too."

There was a pause, and Ta-na heard booted footsteps that did not sound like his father's. *Coughtry*, he told himself, easing the pistol from his waistband.

"No, I'm not fool enough to fight the likes of Renno Harper. I just want you gone—permanently—which is where you'd be if Radison hadn't made such a botch of things. Use your knife."

This last comment seemed directed at someone else, and Ta-na jerked his head to the side and peered through the glass. It took a moment for his eyes to adjust to the flickering light from three lamps positioned around the room. And then he saw his father sitting on a chair in front of the bed, his gaze focused on the pistol in Victor

Coughtry's hand. But it was the other men who drew Ta-na's attention. The brothers Black Otter and Running Tur-tle stood on either side of Renno's chair, with the traitor Tall Grass directly behind.

"The knife!" Coughtry ordered, waggling the pistol at Tall Grass.

The older Cherokee came around the chair and reached for something at his side, then looked up at Coughtry in some consternation. "He sachem of Seneca," he said in broken English as he looked back and forth between Renno and the white businessman. "Not good kill sachem."

Coughtry gave the old man a malicious grin. "You want him to live? And how long do you think *you'll* be alive after he gets back to the village and announces where you are?"

He motioned to the brothers, who apparently were less concerned about murder, for they grabbed Renno's arms and hauled him to his feet. Renno made no effort to resist. It was almost as if he were challenging them to kill him . . . as if he knew his death would somehow bring their conspiracy crashing down.

"Go on, Tall Grass," Coughtry prodded, waving him forward with the pistol. "Trust me, you'll sleep better. We all will."

The Cherokee hesitantly drew the knife from his belt and took a step toward Renno. He muttered something—an apology perhaps—and started to bring up the weapon. The Seneca sachem did not move but merely stared at him and said cryptically, "What you are going to do, do quickly." The comment seemed to unnerve Tall Grass, and he started to lower the knife. Then he gave a sharp, angry growl and raised the blade to Renno's throat.

Drawing in a breath, Ta-na leaned away from the building, then launched himself shoulder-first at the window, shards of glass exploding around him as he dove into the room. He rolled once, cocking the pistol and bringing it up in one smooth motion. The hammer struck, and the gun bucked in his hand, filling the room with black, acrid smoke. Tall Grass had time only to spin around and catch a glimpse of his executioner before the slug smacked into his chest and sent him reeling backward against Running Turtle.

As Ta-na clawed at the knife on his belt, Renno pulled himself free and leaped across the room at the man with the pistol. There was a thunderous explosion, and Ta-na could only pray Renno was all right, for he found himself confronted by Black Otter, who picked up the chair and swung it at his head. Ta-na ducked below it and lunged toward the big Cherokee, knocking him off his feet and across the corner of the bed. He sprawled onto the floor, the breath going out of him as he landed hard on his back.

Gasping for air, Black Otter struggled to get up, then suddenly noticed the knife protruding from his belly. He let out a mournful wail and clutched at it, but his nerveless fingers would not close around the handle. And then Ta-na was kneeling above him, grabbing the knife with both hands and jerking downward in a sweeping arc, slicing open Black Otter's abdomen from rib cage to groin.

Ta-na sensed a movement at his back and swung around just as Running Turtle hurtled through the air, knife in hand. Ta-na managed to grab his wrist, twisting the blade to the side as the two men tumbled across the floor. But Running Turtle held on to the knife, maneuvered himself on top of Ta-na, and drove it hard toward his chest. Ta-na pushed up against him, the tip of the blade hovering inches from his chest as he fought to knock the man aside. He succeeded in forcing Running Turtle's hand upward, away from his chest but toward his throat, all the while twisting the man's wrist with all his might. Slowly Running Turtle's arm weakened, and he watched in horror as Ta-na turned his hand around, the blade moving away from Ta-na and ever closer to Running Turtle's own neck.

"Traitor!" Ta-na raged, throwing all his strength

against the man's wrist. There was a sickening crack of splintered bone, and then Running Turtle's arm went limp. Ta-na wrenched it around cruelly and drew the blade across his throat. Running Turtle fell over onto his side, his arms flapping spasmodically as the blood spurted from his neck.

Ta-na-wun-da snatched up the knife and turned to help his father. To his relief he found Renno on the far side of the room, straddling the prone Victor Coughtry, hands wrapped tightly around Coughtry's neck. He hurried over, but it was clear that Renno needed no help. Coughtry's eyes were bulging, and his arms flailed about wildly, but he was unable to break Renno's hold. The struggle lasted only a few moments longer. Then Victor Coughtry's body went limp, and the color drained out of him.

"Father!" Ta-na exclaimed, dropping to the floor and throwing his arms around Renno.

"M-my son . . ." Renno gasped, fighting for air, his hands shaking as he pulled himself off the dead man's body and knelt on the floor.

"It's over!" Ta-na exclaimed with a smile of relief. "He's dead!" He nodded at Victor Coughtry, then glanced back across the room at the three dead Cherokee. "The sentence of the council has been carried out. It's over at last."

When Ta-na looked back at Renno, his father was shaking his head slowly, sorrowfully. "I . . . I'm s-sorry," he stammered, his head lowering.

The world seemed to slow as Ta-na-wun-da followed Renno's gaze down to the red stain spreading across his shirtfront just over the abdomen. He was clutching at a gaping gunshot wound, trying to keep the lifeblood from flowing out of him. He slumped to one side, into the arms of his son, his head lolling forward as he strained to speak.

"Rest now," Ta-na told him, his eyes flooding with tears as he eased his father onto his lap. In the distance, he heard glass shattering and footsteps pounding up the stairs. "Help is coming," he tried to reassure his father. "It's on the way."

"Ta-na . . ." Renno moaned. Reaching up, he gripped the front of his son's shirt. "It . . . it's finished."

"No . . ." Ta-na muttered, hugging his father to him. Across the room, the door flew open, and he glanced up to see Mist-on-the-Water standing there, rifle in hand, her eyes wide with terror as she took in the scene. "No!" he raged, burying his face against his father's cheek. *"No!"*

"Listen . . ." Renno whispered, pawing weakly at Ta-na's chest. "Not much—" He gagged several times, a thin stream of blood bubbling between his lips. He forced calm into his voice. "Not much time . . ."

"I won't let you!" Ta-na railed, shaking his head in fury.

"It's t-t-time," Renno sputtered.

He managed to reach up to his son's face, forcing Ta-na to look at him. Then Renno gazed beyond and saw Mist-on-the-Water kneeling beside them. He closed his eyes and smiled.

"Yes . . . I see you . . ." Renno whispered, cocking his head as if listening to someone. Then his eyes opened wide, and he stared up at Ta-na. "They're waiting . . . in the west. Ghonkaba . . . El-i-chi . . . Cornplanter . . ." He nodded. "I must go to them."

"I don't want you to go," Ta-na protested feebly.

Renno tried to speak but was overcome by a fit of coughing and gagging. Ta-na tried to comfort him, but his body stiffened with each racking spasm. Slowly he calmed, and when he spoke again, his voice was a faint whisper.

"It is for you now . . . the sachem's robe." His face tightened, as if he were straining to understand something. Then his features relaxed, and he smiled. "I see it clearly now."

Ta-na had to lean close to understand the words.

"I was wrong. . . . It's not my robe. It's a far different one you must wear. The medicine shield . . . it will help you find the sachem's robe . . . and the way."

His eyes fluttered open, and Ta-na saw in them a last shimmer of light.

"Tell them I love them. . . ."

He let out the gentlest of sighs, and the spirit of Renno Harper, the last in the line of men known as the white Indian, passed from this earth.

Twenty-three

Hawk Harper stood as patiently as possible while the sergeant patted him down, making sure he was carrying no hidden weapons. When the man was satisfied Hawk was unarmed, he snatched a ring of keys from the wall. "This way," he muttered, leading Hawk down the corridor. A pair of armed soldiers fell in behind them.

The guardhouse contained a half-dozen iron-barred cells, home to a motley group of drunkards and deserters—all the cells, that is, except for the last one on the left. It held someone quite unique, a man whose fate could not be entrusted to the rickety local jail. He was Nashville's most celebrated murderer, and the town officials feared an Indian war party might try to set him free, if a lynch mob didn't get him first.

"Ta-na-wun-da," Hawk called to his brother as he stepped up to the cell door.

Ta-na was sitting cross-legged on the cold stone floor. He looked up and nodded in recognition but did not otherwise react. Hawk was not surprised. During the previous two weeks, since Hawk's arrival from Washington, his younger brother's detached, almost impassive mood had remained unchanged—even when the jury had found him guilty of participating in the murder of Victor Coughtry and the judge had imposed sentence. In fact, the only real emotion he had shown had been when Mist-on-the-Water was found innocent of complicity in the murder.

It took the sergeant a minute of fumbling to choose the correct key and remove the lock. As he pulled open the door, the other soldiers lowered their rifle barrels, training them on the prisoner.

"I have to lock you in," the sergeant explained to Hawk.

"That's fine," he replied, stepping into the cell. He waited while the door was closed behind him and the padlock secured. As the soldiers retreated down the corridor, he joined his brother on the floor.

"Beth sends her love," Hawk began, forcing a smile. "She'll come by this evening."

"No." Ta-na looked up at Hawk. "Tell her not to come. Mist-on-the-Water, too."

"But they want to be with you, and the court has said that today we can spend as much time—"

"Not tonight," Ta-na said emphatically, his eyes narrowing with resolve.

The brothers left unspoken that this was the last night the women—or anyone, for that matter—could visit. At dawn the next day, Ta-na-wun-da would be led out to the parade ground, where a gallows had been constructed to carry out the sentence of the court.

"I . . . I've tried everything I can think of, but—"

"Don't apologize," Ta-na told him, and for an instant Hawk detected the trace of a smile. It was not a smile of joy but acceptance. "I am at peace. I'll be with Renno soon. And Gao."

"Perhaps if I'd been here . . ."

"Be grateful you weren't. Nothing would have changed, except that we'd both be facing the gallows. And there's Michael Soaring Hawk to consider. And Ma-ton-ga." He gazed up toward the ceiling. "I worry about Mist-on-the-Water. First her husband, and now . . ."

"She has her son. She will be all right."

"I hope so." He reached forward and took his brother's hand. "Hawk, I want you to promise you'll take care of her. You and Ma-ton-ga."

"I will," Hawk assured him, his eyes welling with tears. "We both will."

Ta-na nodded. "I can go to our father in peace knowing you're watching over her for me." His smile returned. "I used to worry that Gao might not approve if I took Mist-on-the-Water for my wife. I know now that he was always there beside us, bringing us together."

They sat in silence a long while. Hawk wanted to inquire about his final wishes. Did he want to be laid to rest at Huntington Castle or in Rusog's Town? Or perhaps Hawk should bring him north to lie beside his cousin and friend, Gao. He tried to speak, but he could not bear to give voice to the thought.

Ta-na looked up at him, and when their eyes met, he said, "I wish you to carry my body to the lake of our ancestors. Place me on the same hill where my cousin sleeps. I want to look out upon the water and hunt at Gao's side."

The tears flowed down Hawk's cheeks, and he nodded. He was about to speak when the sergeant appeared at the cell door and began to open the lock.

Hawk wiped his eyes and glowered up at the soldier. "I showed you the judge's order. We're to be allowed as long as we want today."

"You don't have to leave, but there's a courier to see you—just rode in from Knoxville." He pulled open the door. "He's waiting out in the yard."

"All right." Hawk rose and stepped into the corridor. "I'll be right back," he told Ta-na, who did not respond.

Hawk did not wait for the sergeant but instead strode quickly down the corridor, through the outer guard room, and out into the yard. He walked over to a corporal standing beside a gray gelding that was still wet from a long ride.

"Captain Harper?" the man asked, giving a brisk salute.

Hawk did not bother to point out he was no longer in the military but merely saluted and said, "You have something for me, Corporal?"

The man reached into his pouch and removed a sealed letter. "This came from Washington. I brought it as quickly as I could."

Hawk took the document and broke open the seal.

"I'll see to my horse, then be at the canteen if you need me," the soldier offered.

"Yes, thank you, Corporal," Hawk replied distractedly as he unfolded the papers and perused their contents. His hands were trembling, and he had to force them steady. When he had read enough, he turned, jerked open the guardhouse door, and hurried back inside.

Ta-na-wun-da sat alone in his cell, thinking of his cousin and his father and his father's father—all those who had gone before him and would greet him when he arrived. He was no longer so certain, however, that there was a world beyond this one or even a Master of Life, who gave them all breath only to snatch it away so cruelly. He thought, too, of Mist-on-the-Water, and his heart ached at the prospect of leaving her.

"It is finished," he muttered, lowering his eyes to the floor. "All is death."

As if in reply, his brother came rushing down the corridor. Looking wild with excitement, he gripped the bars of the door and waited impatiently for the sergeant to open the lock and let him in. This time he did not sit down but paced in front of the cell door, watching the corridor as the soldiers withdrew, waiting until they were gone. Finally he spun around and shook the papers he was holding.

"You're a free man!" he exclaimed. "You're not going to hang!"

Ta-na heard the words but was not sure he understood them. "What are you talking about?"

"This is what I'm talking about." Again he shook the papers. "It's from Washington. From the President."

"President Madison?" Ta-na said in disbelief.

"I didn't mention it before because I wasn't very hopeful about it. As soon as I got here and saw where the trial was heading, I sent a courier to Washington. I doubted it would come to anything—or even that a return message could get here before . . . well, before it was too late."

"What does it say?" Ta-na asked, trying to keep his voice calm, not allowing himself even a glimmer of hope.

"You've been given a presidential pardon. And that's not all. Apparently Madison received a full report of the land scheme—not just from me but from General Jackson and others. He's declared it illegal and issued an order prohibiting the sale. The land—all of it—is to remain in Cherokee hands!"

Ta-na felt as if a hand had reached into his chest and was gripping his heart. He fought for breath, his head light and dizzy. Above him, his brother was grinning boyishly, repeating again and again that he was to be set free.

Slowly Ta-na rose to his feet. He took a cautious step forward, then opened his arms wide and fell into his brother's embrace. They held each other tight for what seemed like long minutes, and then Ta-na pulled back and shook his head in wonder. "Is it really true?" he asked. "Am I going home?"

Hawk's smile froze, and he tried to speak.

"What is it?"

"There . . . there's something more."

"What do you mean?" Ta-na pressed, feeling a sudden pit of fear.

Hawk held forth the document. "I guess there were political realities to consider. The President knows he'll face criticism for letting so much land slip away, and for issuing a pardon to a—"

"A murderer?" Ta-na snapped, stepping back a few feet.

"No!" Hawk blurted. "But someone the public perceives as one."

"You mean a red man who dared kill a white—even one as low as Victor Coughtry."

"Ta-na, I did my best," Hawk apologized. "And perhaps given more time I can do more. But for now we're going to have to accept the terms of the President's pardon."

Ta-na's gaze was drawn to the papers in his brother's hand. "Which are?" he asked suspiciously.

"You will be freed only if you agree to leave Tennessee and Cherokee lands. You must cross the Mississippi River and never come back. If you do, the pardon will be rescinded and the death sentence carried out."

"Banished?" Ta-na muttered as the true import of what had happened sank in. "Banished from my own land? My own people?"

"This isn't the last word," Hawk insisted, holding up the document. "After some time passes—when things have quieted down—the President might reconsider. Perhaps—"

"No," Ta-na declared, nodding in acceptance. "You have done more than anyone could have hoped. It is enough. It is finished."

Hawk continued to talk about possibilities for the future, but Ta-na no longer heard what he was saying. Already he was heading west, far beyond the Father of Waters. He did not understand why, but he sensed that the President's pardon was only a temporary reprieve and that the journey on which he was about to embark would lead him not to a new home in the Sacred Hills or the Shining Mountains but to the world beyond this one, where his cousin and his father and his father's father were waiting.

As Ta-na surrendered to the will of the Master of Life, any last vestige of fear washed out of him, leaving only a deep, abiding peace.

After accepting the terms of the pardon, Ta-na-wun-da was turned over to the custody of his brother and released from the fort under the cover of darkness so as not to arouse the public, which was not yet aware of the presidential pardon. A group of Cherokee and Seneca warriors made the journey at his side, along with family and friends who had been in Nashville awaiting his execution.

Ta-na did not want to bring trouble on the community because of his presence, so he decided to stay only one night in Rusog's Town before going west. He publicly announced, however, that he intended to spend a few days. This would allow him the opportunity to slip away unnoticed. He knew that Mist-on-the-Water planned to accompany him, but he had no idea of his destination and did not want her and Little Gao risking so uncertain and dangerous a journey. He also felt that Wind Catcher would be better off here among the Cherokee and Seneca, where he would be properly raised and educated.

Upon reaching home, Ta-na had dinner with Beth and Hawk at Huntington Castle, then rode to Mist-on-the-Water's cabin in Rusog's Town. Ma-ton-ga must have realized her friend wanted to be alone with him, for she had taken Little Gao and Wind Catcher and gone to sleep at another home.

When Ta-na came to Mist-on-the-Water's bed that night, he found her completely undressed, waiting for him. He wanted her, too, more than he could bear. Removing his clothes, he climbed beneath the blankets and took her in his arms, feeling her body pressed tight against his.

"I . . . I can't—" he started to whisper, but she placed her hand upon his lips.

"I am your woman," she said, smiling through her

tears. She leaned closer and kissed his cheek, moving down to his neck and chest.

"No," he said, pulling her back up until she was looking at him.

She stared at him curiously, then nodded and rested her head in the crook of his arm. She wrapped one leg over his and lay close to him, their breath blending into one.

He wanted her so terribly. But he would not take the chance of leaving her without a husband and with yet another child to raise. He would not allow himself to finally know her love, only to lose it forever.

It took him a long time to drift to sleep, but when he did, it was deep and dreamless. When he awoke, he thought only a few hours had passed, but he saw through the bedroom window the faint blue of the predawn sky and knew he would have to hurry if he was going to get away without being seen. He slipped out from under the covers, found his clothes, and carried them out into the main room. Without lighting a lamp, he dressed and carried his bags outside.

Ta-na slung the bags over the back of his pinto and lashed them in place. He strapped the medicine shield and lance to them, then walked the pinto away from the cabin. He had gone only a short way when he caught sight of someone approaching on horseback through the woods. He tried to pay no attention but stopped abruptly when a voice called out, "Ta-na-wun-da!"

He peered at the rider, then exclaimed, "Hawk!" as his brother rode up. "What are you doing here?"

"I might ask you the same." Hawk gestured at the bags on the horse's back.

"I . . . well, I—"

"You're leaving, aren't you?"

Ta-na lowered his head and nodded.

"You didn't think I'd let you ride off without a proper good-bye?"

"How did you know I was going?"

"I know my brother well enough," Hawk explained, dismounting. "Now tell me why you're sneaking away like this."

"I thought it better this way." He glanced back toward the cabin. "I don't know where I'm going or what I'll find. I figured she'd be better off . . ." He hesitated, then continued, "Wind Catcher, too. He's better off here in the village with Michael and Little Gao and everyone."

"That's going to be pretty hard," Hawk replied.

"What do you mean?"

Hawk turned and gestured, as if signaling someone. "What I mean is that some of those people might not be here to take care of Wind Catcher. Or Mist-on-the-Water."

"What are you talking about?"

"Well, me, for one. I'm not staying here any longer. Or Michael."

"You're taking him back with you to Washington?"

Hawk shook his head. "I sent word I won't be accepting the President's job offer. I've something more important to do. We all have."

As the sky continued to brighten, Ta-na saw first one and then another person approaching from various points in the village, some on horseback, others on foot, leading packhorses loaded with supplies. There were about a dozen people, and as they drew nearer, Ta-na recognized Ma-ton-ga and Wind Catcher and the Seneca warrior Ho-ta-kwa among them. He heard a door close behind him, and he spun around to see Mist-on-the-Water standing in front of her cabin, dressed in winter buckskins.

"What . . . ?" Ta-na muttered, looking around him in wonderment.

"You wouldn't say good-bye, and neither will we."

"What's happening?"

"You won't be going alone across the Father of Waters," Hawk declared, reaching out and gripping his brother's forearm. "Some of us have decided to seek our destiny out there in the west, beyond the reach of land speculators and politicians. As for what the future may hold, we'll leave that in the hands of the Master of Life."

"You're coming with me?" Ta-na said incredulously.

"That's right—Mist-on-the-Water, Michael, Ma-ton-ga, Little Gao, and a half-dozen or so friends . . . all but Beth, who has her own journey to make."

"Beth?"

"Yes. With Renno gone, there's nothing left for her at Huntington Castle. She's moving to Washington to be with Renna and her family."

Ma-ton-ga and Wind Catcher came up to stand beside them. Mist-on-the-Water joined them, as well, and took Little Gao from Ma-ton-ga's arms.

Hawk drew Ma-ton-ga close and held her a moment. "Are you ready?" he asked.

"Yes, my husband," she replied, and the others nodded in agreement.

"Then we'd better get started." He took up the reins of his horse. "We've a long journey ahead of us."

Mist-on-the-Water slipped her arm through Ta-na's. "Come," she whispered. "Our sachem must lead us."

The small group of family and friends was gathered around Ta-na-wun-da, and he looked from one to the other, reading the expectation and love in their eyes. He sensed they were waiting for him to begin, and for a moment he wondered if he was up to the task. But then he heard a voice sounding deep within him. The voice of his father:

It is not my robe but a far different one you must wear. The medicine shield will help you find the sachem's robe . . . and the way.

Ta-na gazed into the eyes of the woman he loved and nodded. He walked over to his horse and touched the medicine shield, then lifted his fingers to his lips.

"Yes . . ." he breathed.

Leaping onto the back of his pinto, Ta-na-wun-da led his family west, to their future beyond the Father of Waters.

Acknowledgments

I would like to thank Elizabeth Tinsley for her creative advice and excellent work editing this manuscript, Pamela Lappies for her invaluable assistance in developing the story line and for her work on my previous novels, Harry Helm for his support and encouragement, and Tom Burke for all his assistance over the years. A special thanks to all my other friends at Bantam Books and Book Creations Inc., with whom it has been such a delight to work over the years.